The Seven-Year List

'You're getting married in a week's time, Julia. I'm not going to touch you,' said Steve. 'Why don't you touch yourself?'

His expression was a potent mix of nerves and excitement. Julia was already mad with frustration and Steve's whispered suggestion was the push she needed to abandon herself to the desires controlling her body. She would touch herself for him, show him the hidden delights of her body and drive him wild with lust. No man would be able to cling to his principles faced with a writhing, pleasure-seeking woman.

He *would* have to take her, whether it was right or not.

The Seven-Year List

ZOE LE VERDIER

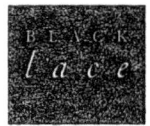

Black Lace novels contain sexual fantasies.
In real life, make sure you practise safe sex.

First published in 1998 by
Black Lace
Thames Wharf Studios,
Rainville Road, London W6 9HA

Copyright © Zoe le Verdier 1998

Reprinted 2001

The right of Zoe le Verdier to be identified as the
Author of this Work has been asserted by her in
accordance with the Copyright, Designs and Patents Act
1988.

Typeset by SetSystems Ltd, Saffron Walden, Essex

ISBN 9780352346667

*All characters in this publication are fictitious and any
resemblance to real persons, living or dead, is purely
coincidental.*

This book is sold subject to the condition that it shall
not, by way of trade or otherwise, be lent, resold, hired
out or otherwise circulated without the publisher's
prior written consent in any form of binding or cover
other than that in which it is published and without a
similar condition including this condition being
imposed on the subsequent purchaser.

Contents

1	Prologue	1
2	David	13
3	The Reunion	39
4	Lies	71
5	Strangers on a Train	84
6	A Very Different Reunion	97
7	The Challenge	125
8	Marianne	135
9	Nick	147
10	Steve	181
11	The Final Reunion	231

Prologue

'Come on, Julia. Your turn.'

Julia stretched out on the rug, her belly full of food, her mind hazy with sunshine and beer. She sighed and looked up at the clouds as they slowly made their way across the brown-stained sky of her sunglasses. She blinked sleepily. 'I don't want to, Steve. Count me out.'

He stood at her feet, blotting out the sunshine and casting a long shadow over her body. 'But everyone else is doing it. Don't be a party pooper.'

The fact that everyone else was doing it was usually good enough reason for Julia not to. But, realising Steve wasn't going to go away, she reluctantly sat up. Hugging her knees, she ignored the piece of paper Steve was threatening her with, and looked across the lawn. Nick was at the table, loading his arms with cans of lager.

'Come on, Jules.' Steve sat down beside her and pushed the paper and a pen into her lap. 'You're the only one left.'

Julia looked around. Strewn across the gentle landscape of the school grounds, the upper-sixth pupils were completing the forms Steve had eagerly handed out. Some had distanced themselves from their friends and sat in serious, solitary contemplation. Others giggled together in twos and threes, oblivious of Steve's watchful glare. Julia glanced down at her own form and laughed silently to herself.

'The Aims and Aspirations of Julia Sargent,' she read. The title was typed, but her name had been filled in in Steve's precise hand. 'I am now eighteen, about to leave school and embark upon life. By the time I am twenty-five I will achieve the following:'. Seven numbered spaces sat empty on the page, awaiting answers. At the bottom was a signed reminder from Steve that each participant would be called to a school reunion in seven years' time, in order to bask in success or admit to failure. The tone was typical of Steve: overly serious, businesslike, a little pompous.

'Steve, I can't.' She turned to look at him. As usual, the intense and constant hurt in his pale grey eyes almost made her flinch. 'I'm sorry –' she passed the paper and pen back '– but I don't believe in planning ahead. We can't possibly predict what's going to happen tomorrow, let alone in one year's time. Let alone *seven* years' time.'

'But you must know what you want.' Steve brushed her hand away, making her keep hold of the form. 'Everyone has plans, and ideals, and goals for the future.'

'You know what my ambition is.' Julia put the paper down decisively and leant back on her hands. She dropped her head back, arching her spine and enjoying the heat of the sun on her throat. 'I want to be a photographer. A good one. I want to travel the world, go to war zones, infiltrate places where women aren't allowed. I want to uncover corruption, and bigotry, and injustice. I want to show the truth.' She lifted her head. Turning back to Steve, she wasn't surprised to find his eyes flickering down her neck towards the slight mounds of her breasts, provocatively and purposely obvious beneath her flimsy green dress.

'Well then,' he blustered, annoyed to have been caught. 'Write all that down.'

'But it isn't that simple. Things can change so quickly. I mean, I desperately wanted to do well in my exams, but then I got distracted.' A wry smile crept across her face like the slow uncovering of a secret. 'And, all of a sudden, the difference between getting As and Ds didn't seem so important any more.'

'Hmmm,' Steve murmured. It was a sound of uncertain disapproval. He looked up at Nick as he approached, and Julia watched him for a moment before following his gaze.

What a distraction to have in A level year, she thought, self-satisfaction clasping warmly to the back of her neck. What a way to lose her virginity. Nick Trent was the most sought-after boy in the sixth form, and it wasn't hard to see why. Tall and athletic, pleasantly muscular, he was more of a man than the others. He had a confident swagger, an attractive arrogance and a knowing look in his dark-brown eyes. You want me, those eyes said. All the girls want me. And who can blame them?

Nick noticed Julia following his progress across the grass and a slow, gratified smile lifted one corner of his wide mouth. With a flick of his head, he got rid of the thick, sandy-coloured lock of hair flopping in front of his eyes. His hair settled back into its usual insouciant perfection: long at the front, shorter at the back, thick and shining. Beneath the weight of the barbecued food in her stomach, a faint gurgle pushed its way into Julia's guts.

'Will you please talk to your girlfriend, Nick?'

Nick settled down at Julia's feet and handed out the lagers. 'Why? What's she done now?'

'It's what she won't do. She won't fill in my list. It seems she's allergic to planning ahead.'

'I don't like the idea, that's all.' Julia was beginning to feel a little guilty. Steve had been organising this day since before their exams: not only the list, but the barbecue, the alcohol and the distinct lack of teachers were all down to his sensible, head boy's air of responsibility. 'I believe in living for the moment. *Carpe diem*. All this planning ahead ... it's so ... so grown up and tedious.'

'See what I mean?' Steve moaned.

Nick winked at Julia and wrapped his fingers around her ankle. 'I can't make her do anything she doesn't want to, Steve.' His golden eyebrows flickered suggestively. 'Believe me, I've tried.'

'Try harder,' Steve insisted.

Nick slid his hand upward along Julia's shin, beneath the hem of her dress. 'Go on, Jules. I've done mine. It's a laugh.'

'Only those who complete their lists get invited to the reunion,' Steve urged.

Nick squeezed her knee. His warm eyes drifted longingly. 'I wonder if your tits will be any bigger in seven years' time?'

Julia tutted and pushed his hand away. 'Is that all you ever think about? My breasts?'

'Pretty much.'

Despite herself, his lascivious smirk excited her, as it always did. She rolled her eyes and sighed heavily. 'Oh, all right.' She retrieved the paper and pen. 'Pass me something to lean on.'

Steve delved into his rucksack and passed her a book.

'What's this? A little light summer reading?' She weighed the thick volume in both hands. '*Marketing Strategies: A Study of the World's Corporate Giants*.' Her eyebrows furrowed as she turned to Steve.

'Preparation for university,' he explained.

'Steve,' she admonished, 'you've only just finished revising. Don't you think you should take a break from the books for the summer?'

Steve took his glasses off and polished them with his shirt tails. 'I want to get a head start on Nick.'

Bristling, Nick sat up a little straighter. 'You've no chance, mate.' Self-assurance radiated from his grin. 'I've got a photographic memory, remember?'

Steve huffed and put his glasses back on. 'How could I forget?' He gave each of them a reproachful look, as if it was their fault. 'It's so unfair. While you two were partying, I was slogging. I have to work so hard for everything.'

Nick shrugged. 'What can I say? Some of us are born to win.'

Steve nodded slowly. 'We'll see. You need more than a photographic memory to get a good degree.'

'And you need more than a degree to get on in business.' Nick took a long swig of beer. 'You need guts, instinct, and passion.'

'And I haven't got those?'

Nick let out a faint snort: faint, but loud enough for Steve to hear. 'We'll see.'

A fractious silence slowly expanded between them. From behind the shelter of her sunglasses, Julia watched them surreptitiously as they stared at each other, Nick attempting to deflect the indignation in Steve's eyes with an annoying smirk. She wondered at what age they would finally grow out of this childish rivalry.

'Do you think it's wise for you both to go to the same university?' she asked at last.

'Strathclyde's the best for business studies,' Nick said, still looking at Steve.

'You two won't have any time for studying. You'll be too busy worrying what the other one is up to.'

Nick pulled his attention back to Julia. His hand slid across the rug until his fingers laced with hers. 'You'll have to come up and visit us, Jules.'

'If I have time. I hope to have a job by the end of the summer.' She teased him with her eyes. 'I'll probably be far too busy photographing world leaders to consort with lowly students.'

Nick clasped her hand tighter. 'I'll miss you.' He raised an eyebrow and dropped his eyeline suggestively, to emphasise precisely what it was that he would miss.

Steve quietly cleared his throat. 'I'll miss you, too.'

Slowly, Julia turned to Steve. 'Will you?'

'I'll hate not having you to talk to.'

Time slowed. Suddenly oblivious of Nick's presence and his hand, still in hers, she suspended herself in the pale intelligence of Steve's wide-eyed, earnest gaze. There had been moments like these before, moments when she felt so close to Steve, and so far removed from Nick's easy confidence. And in those moments she selfishly wished that Steve was better looking. With his uncontrollable chestnut curls, his round baby face, his heavy, square glasses and the childish fat on his long limbs, he just wasn't her type. And yet he was precisely her type. She sometimes despised herself for being so shallow.

'I'll miss you too, Steve.'

Nick coughed, but the sound was distant and it did nothing to interrupt Julia and Steve's mutual appreciation. It wasn't until an envelope was dangled in between their eyes, that Julia blinked back into the real world.

Marianne giggled and dropped the envelope on to the rug. 'Done it, Steve. And no peeking. I think some of my goals are actually illegal.' Her giggle rose into a dry, rasping cackle. Julia looked up and smiled as Marianne flicked her long blonde hair over to one side. 'Coming to play footie, Nick?' she asked, fluttering her eyelashes.

'Yeah.' Nick scrambled to his feet. He glanced at Julia, then at Steve. A definite glance: a warning. 'Come on, Steve.'

Marianne was talking to her, but Julia wasn't listening.

She was sending telepathic messages to Steve, urging him to stay.

He must have picked up her thoughts, as he often did. 'You know I hate football, Nick,' he said.

Nick smirked cruelly. 'You could do with the exercise.'

'I want to talk to Jules.'

Nick shrugged and ran off with Marianne. One by one, the others delivered the sealed envelopes containing their seven-year plans to Steve, and then stumbled into the football match. Julia smiled as Marianne skilfully dribbled the ball up the lawn, only to be tackled by Nick. She dived dramatically to the floor. Nick collapsed beside her, and they rolled around in mock agony for a moment, laughing raucously, before rejoining the game. Watching them, they reminded Julia of young Olympians with their sculpted, athletic bodies, shining hair and tanned complexions. 'There's something very attractive about blondes,' she murmured.

Steve lay down beside Julia, propping himself up on one elbow. 'Is there?'

She looked down at him. 'Don't you think Marianne's pretty?'

'Very. But not as pretty as you.'

The grey of his eyes was enough to make her shiver. 'You're my best friend. You've got to say things like that.'

'But it's true. You're different.'

Julia knew she was different; that was the problem. She longed to swap her pale skin for a healthy tan, her dark-brown, straight hair with its deep auburn glow for Marianne's pale, wavy yellow. 'I'd love to be blonde.'

'No, you wouldn't. If you had blonde hair, you'd only dye it brown.'

He knew her too well. An internal smile glowed beneath her skin. 'I'd like a tan, at least. I hate being pale.'

'Pale and interesting.'

She huffed scornfully.

'Are women ever happy with anything they've got?' He shuffled closer to her, tentatively resting his fingers on the back of her hand. 'You're gorgeous, Julia, and you know it.'

Julia looked down. Beneath his touch, her skin prickled with cold. Unnerved, she pulled her hand away. 'I'd better get on with this.' She huddled over the blank paper, grateful that her thick hair, cut into a bob, swung forward and hid her blushing from Steve.

She stared at the paper for a long time. It stared back at her, taunting her with its empty spaces. But she couldn't concentrate. The atmosphere between her and Steve was so heavy and full, the tension almost visible as it crackled between them.

Julia felt him shuffling closer. Out of the corner of her eye, from behind the veil of her hair, she saw him raise his free hand. Slowly, as if he was moving something rare and delicate, he gently pushed her hair back and behind her ear. The intimacy of the gesture shocked her. She held her breath.

'You having trouble?'

Julia put the book she was leaning on to one side, and sat back on her hands again. 'I think I'll do it later. It's difficult. I find it scary.' She glanced at Steve. 'I suppose you've done yours?'

'I did mine at the beginning of term.' He winced. 'Does that make me very boring?'

She shook her head and smiled. 'You're not boring. You're just committed. In a way, I envy you, knowing precisely what you want. You'll get it all. I know you will.'

'I envy you. I wish I could be more impulsive. Live for the moment, instead of planning everything down to the last detail.'

'Do something impulsive. Now,' she challenged.

Looking up at her, Steve reached out for her wrist. He

held her for a moment, his thumb pressing gently over her pulse, then he pulled. Julia allowed herself to be eased backward until she lay on the rug. Rolling on to her side, she propped her head up on one hand. Her heartbeat began to quicken as Steve carefully took her sunglasses off.

'Julia, there's something I want to tell you.'

She blinked once, trying to steady herself. A kiss was brewing inside her, forcing its forbidden way up from her belly and into her brain – and not for the first time. Her mind jumbled with the ridiculousness of it. Steve was her best friend; he was Nick's best friend. She was going out with Nick; he was only yards away. It would be impossible and stupid. She didn't even fancy Steve; it would cause a fight.

'Yes?' she whispered.

He hesitated, glancing from her left eye to her right, left to right, as if he were searching for inconsistencies. Her lips parted. Steve's did, too, as his eyes dropped from hers, to her mouth, and back up again. Imperceptibly, inevitably, their faces moved closer together.

'Julia,' he breathed.

'Yes . . .'

His gaze flicked over her head, and he began to blink rapidly. 'Nick's coming.'

In a flash, Julia was sitting up. Grabbing her sunglasses, she put them back on, disguising her disappointment. She looked up guiltily as Nick ran, panting, towards her.

'My darling Jules,' he giggled, flinging himself down at her side. Roughly, he pulled her into his arms and squeezed her close. She could feel the sweat seeping through his T-shirt and on to her skin. He pushed his mouth to hers, dissolving her bewilderment with his forceful, hungry kisses. In an instant, she had forgotten about Steve, cringing on the rug beside them. Trapped in Nick's arms, his muscles hard against her soft body, Julia could think of only one thing.

'Let's go,' he urged.

She mumbled in agreement as Nick grabbed her hand and pulled her to her feet.

'Hang on.' She paused and turned. 'What did you want to tell me, Steve?'

His eyes had hardened with cold resentment. 'Doesn't matter,' he said, through gritted teeth. 'I'll tell you next time I see you.'

She could feel him watching as she ran away.

'I like this dress.'

Julia knew that. She'd chosen her outfit especially, aware that she wasn't going to see Nick over the summer. Aware that this could be their last time together. Julia put her hands behind her back and leant against the wide trunk of the old oak.

'It's a lovely colour.' Nick put one hand on the tree, beside her face. His other hand slid around her neck and into her hair. 'It matches your eyes.'

She knew that, too. The light emerald blended perfectly with the pale drama of her irises.

Nick lowered his head to kiss her. Julia arched her back slightly, pushing her breasts forward, wanting his big hands on their delicate shapes. 'There's only one thing I hate about this dress,' he admitted, when he pulled away from her lips.

'What's that?'

'These buttons.' His eyes drifted down her throat to the low neckline, then continued onward to the hem, halfway down her calves.

'What's wrong with them?'

He raised his hands to the top button, nestling at the beginning of the soft valley of her cleavage. 'Too many of them,' he complained. 'Too fiddly.'

Julia dropped her eyes to his thick fingers as he

struggled with the tiny mother-of-pearl fastenings. She brushed his hands away. 'Here. Let me help you.'

She basked in his impatient attention as she slowly revealed her pert, bare breasts. Grumbling softly, his eyes drooled; his fingers hovered. With her dress open to the waist, Nick slid his palms over her swelling mounds of flesh. His eyes fixed avidly on his fingers as they greedily squeezed. Pulling at her wide, pale-pink areolae, he teased them into stiff excitement. Julia's breathing grew shallow as the tender circles of skin crinkled and darkened.

'Nick?'

His head dipped, and his wide lips fastened over an areola. 'Hmmm?' he asked, his mouth full.

'Do you think Steve's all right? He seems a bit strange.'

He paused in his suckling to look up. 'Doesn't he always?'

Julia put her hand to the back of his head and pulled him down on to her other breast. 'He seems different today. On edge.'

'Mmmm.'

'Oh.' Her breath caught as his teeth grazed her nipple. Behind her, the bark scratched her bare shoulders as she pushed herself further into his mouth. 'Do you think there's something on his mind?'

'He's jealous.' He left her breasts and began to fumble with her buttons again. Julia helped him.

'Jealous of what?'

'Of you and me.' Watching eagerly as she bent forward, his hands cupped her dangling breasts while the last buttons were undone. 'The three of us do everything together – except this.' She straightened up and he moved his body very close to hers. His left hand clamped over her breast, while his right slid without hesitation over her belly and into her white knickers. 'Ooooh,' he moaned appreciatively, looking down into her eyes. 'You're all wet.'

Julia opened her legs a little wider as his finger slid between her damp labia. 'I feel sorry for him.'

'Do you mind if we don't talk about Steve while we're ... you know. It puts me off.'

A shudder ran along her inner thighs as his thick finger poked easily inside her. 'I'm sorry,' she whispered, her voice shaken by the familiar pleasure bubbling inside her. 'He's our best friend. I can't help worrying about him.'

Nick took his hands away. With a deft flick, his belt was undone and his baggy shorts crumpled at his ankles. Reaching inside the opening of his stripy boxer shorts, he unfurled his long, hard penis. Placing a hand either side of her face, he leant into her, trapping her in the dancing warmth of his eyes. Then, slowly, he looked down. 'I thought *he* was our best friend.'

Julia's gaze fell longingly down his broad, hairless chest. Giggling, she eased her back down the tree trunk, and got to her knees. 'Some best friend,' she smiled, stroking his velvet warmth, inhaling his muskiness. 'He kept me up all night. Stopped me from revising. It's his fault if I get bad grades.' She glanced up at his impatient face. 'That little fella will be my downfall, I'm sure of it.'

'Not so much of the little.' He grinned.

David

Julia's eyes roamed appreciatively over David's body as he got out of bed, rediscovering the details of his flesh after two weeks apart. Last night they had been drunk and desperate. It had been late, and they had collapsed gratefully into bed, into each other, rolling around and around in the dark. But now, in the morning sunshine, she had the chance to savour him all over again. His golden hair, thick and left quite long on top for the part he was playing. His dark-blue eyes, the angular strength of his chin. His torso, smooth, tanned and muscular without being muscle-bound. His long, strong arms, and broad shoulders. His wide chest, narrowing to a washboard stomach, the ridges of which were emphasised in the slanting light. His dark-brown, delicious nipples.

'Perfect,' she whispered to herself, her gaze straying downward. He turned his back on her, and the tight beauty of his backside made her wince. 'Come back to bed,' she pleaded, her fingers straying wistfully beneath the sheets.

'I can't.' He turned his back on the mirror and inspected his rear view over his shoulder. 'Got to get to the gym before I go and see my agent. I've been on location so long, my body's gone to pot.'

One of Julia's eyebrows arched in surprise. 'It has?'

'Hmmm.' He swayed and stooped in front of his reflection, tutting frustratedly as he discovered flaws that were as obvious to him as they were invisible to Julia. 'All that hanging about on set – it's fatal. If I'm not filming, I'm eating.' He pinched the nonexistent flab at his waist. 'I'm getting love handles.'

'Good.' Julia smiled, impatiently patting the space beside her. 'They'll be useful for holding on to.'

He turned side on to the mirror and ran his hand over his stomach. 'I'm serious, Julia. The camera can be cruel. I'm pushing thirty-five now. I've got to look after myself.'

Julia pulled back the covers to reveal her body, still warm with sleep, hoping to tempt him. 'Come on,' she purred. 'I'll give you a good work-out.'

In the mirror, his eyes caught hers. He stopped his self-appraisal and began to study her instead. As he slowly walked towards the bed, Julia smiled at the wonderful sight of his morning erection. He sat down beside her, and she curled around until her head was in his lap. Nuzzling into the dark-golden hair surrounding his glorious cock, she inhaled the memory of last night, salty and warm. David's cool hand ran over her buttock. Saliva began to flow as Julia stuck out her tongue.

'Damn!' He carefully extricated himself from beneath her head, and retrieved his mobile phone from his bag. Julia sighed resignedly and curled herself into a ball.

'Sorry, darling.' David finished his call and disappeared in the direction of the bathroom. 'Got a voice-over at one o'clock,' he shouted, above the sound of gushing water. 'I'll have to get a move on if I'm going to make it to the gym.'

Julia rolled out of bed and padded into the bathroom. 'Don't go.' Standing behind him, she folded her arms and watched as he filled the basin for a shave. 'Stay here, with me. I haven't seen you for so long, David.'

He squirted a palmful of foam and began to pat it on to his cheeks and chin. 'I know, darling, and I'm sorry. Believe me, I'd love to stay.'

Julia huffed loudly and looked up at the ceiling. It was peeling; she would have to get round to repainting it. One of these days. 'Your agent sees more of you than I do.'

'And your editor sees more of you.' He dipped his razor into the water. 'We're busy people, Julia, we knew it would be like this.'

She moved closer. Resting her hands on his shoulder blades, she delighted in their movements as he started shaving.

'It'll be different when we're married, I promise.'

'No it won't.' She kissed the back of his neck, closing her eyes and enjoying the smell of his skin. 'You'll still be away filming all the time. I'll still be working stupid hours.'

David stopped again. Shrugging her off his back, he turned to face her. His forehead was creased with concern. 'You're not having second thoughts, are you?'

Julia swallowed quickly. 'No,' she insisted, her eyes wide with what she hoped looked like sincerity. She turned away and went back across the hall to her bedroom. 'I'm just feeling a bit down, that's all. Work's getting on my nerves. And it doesn't help that I barely see you.' She scuffed up to the full-length mirror, and stared forlornly at her reflection.

She felt terrible, as if her body had been drained of energy and filled with weighty listlessness. But she looked good. The guys she worked with at the paper never stopped telling her how good, and she enjoyed their flirting. Apart from a couple of minor gripes, she was happy with her appearance. It was her inner self that wasn't so attractive.

She studied herself, as David had done. She wasn't as tall as she would have liked, but she was well-proportioned. Her neck was elegantly long, her shoulders gently sloping, her breasts lusciously full and high, and upturned attractively where her nipples formed gentle peaks. Raising her hands, she absent-mindedly traced the wide circles of her pinky-brown areolae, sighing as the tender flesh responded to her touch. Her fingers trailed downward, exploring the appealing form of her curves, confirming her tactile beauty. As if she was an attentive lover discovering her shape for the first time, she smoothed her touch over the inward arc of her waist and the generous flare of her hips. She felt the firm slopes of her buttocks, the slight muscularity of her upper legs, the delicate softness at the very tops of her inner thighs. Her fingers and eyes strayed to her groin, to the neat triangle of curls that hid her sex from view: a dark, wild contrast to the purity of her pale skin. She opened her legs and touched herself, feeling the warm wetness which was the remainder of her arousal. She looked up again, and took a step forward.

Her cheekbones gave subtle definition to her oval face. Her lips were small, her nose fine and straight. Her short bob suited her, skimming sexily along her jaw and glowing strongly auburn in the shaft of light coming through the window. Yes, she looked good. But there was something missing in her eyes, something infinitesimal, barely definable, but vital.

She had beautiful eyes. She knew they were her best feature; she had known it even before her boyfriends had told her. They were wide, and fringed with long, dark lashes. Their pale-green intensity was what attracted men like David to her in the first place. But if he'd met her today, he wouldn't have given her a second glance. Where there used to be sparkle, there was dull boredom. Where there used to be fire, there was frustration.

Out in the main hallway, the letterbox clattered faintly. Turning her back on what the mirror was telling her, Julia went to the front door of her flat, opened it slightly, and tentatively poked her head outside. Confirming that the rest of the house was completely silent, she made a naked dash for the doormat. Collecting what was hers, she darted across the cold tiled floor and back inside her flat.

Going into her tiny, messy kitchen, she flicked through the post. The first three envelopes were junk, the next two, bills, and the last, something rigid and official looking which had been forwarded from her old address. Intrigued, she was about to open it when she was distracted, and she abandoned the mail for the papers. Reverently, she laid the broadsheets out on the round kitchen table and bowed over them.

A bomb had exploded yesterday in a block of flats in Berlin. Right-wing fascists had been blamed for the carnage, which had killed several young immigrant families. The front page of *The Times* had a stunning shot of the building, showing the gaping hole in its façade. The *Telegraph* had a similar shot, together with a portrait of one of the children who had died in the blast. The *Guardian* had a huge, eerie picture of the mass demonstration that had taken place that evening. It was an evocative, deeply moving shot, telling more than words could have done. A young neo-Nazi with a shaven head, and a swastika tattooed on his neck, stood in the foreground with his fist raised. He was flanked by police in riot gear who were restraining him with their truncheons. Facing him, a young widow dressed in black held her hands out, pleading. Behind her, stretching far into the distance, thousands of people held hands, their tear-streaked faces held high, their expressions stoical in the face of incomprehensible tragedy. Julia shook her head slightly. She felt a tear looming in her eye as she took in the perfection of the shot: its composition, its emotion, the way it captured the moment. If she had been there, she told herself, that was the image she would have made.

But she hadn't been there. She picked up the *Daily Chronicle*, and flopped it down on to the table. Flicking through the tabloid's grimy pages, she stopped as she found her picture in the showbiz section. She felt her jaw harden with dismay as she looked at the shot.

'Poppy reveals her assets' the headline screeched. While the *Guardian* photographer had been in Berlin, Julia had been at the opening of a new nightclub. 'Poppy's' was owned by a young glamour model, who had imaginatively chosen to name her latest investment after herself. Since those in the know were heralding the club as the new place for the 'in' crowd, Julia's editor had insisted she be there for the official opening night. 'I don't want the usual celeb parade,' George had warned. 'Poppy's an exhibitionist. Get me something . . . spicy.'

'I'll bring you a curry,' she had replied.

Julia had dutifully waited outside and snapped the young and the beautiful – as well as the old and not so beautiful – as they had arrived. Along with the other photographers, she had accepted the proprietor's invitation to join the sparkling crowd inside. But, as the evening had been carried along on the multi-coloured tide of complimentary cocktails, Poppy's ageing rockstar boyfriend had shown more than a passing interest in Julia's career. The young peroxide blonde had spotted them from across the dance floor, her wide eyes homing in on the darkly tanned arm around Julia's waist, and she had stomped towards them. Struggling in her impossibly high heels, she had tripped. Barely contained within her dress to begin with, one of Poppy's pendulous breasts had fallen out of her scooping neckline as she had stumbled. The furious girl had hurled abuse at her man and raised her tiny hand to slap him; he'd caught her wrist, twirled her around beneath his arm as if they were dancing, and pulled her in close.

'Take the picture,' he'd said, his smile causing deep wrinkles to crease his face.

'Are you sure?' Julia had asked, watching Poppy and slowly raising her camera.

'It'll be good for publicity,' the slimy boyfriend had urged.

'OK.' Poppy had smiled, slipping effortlessly into modelling mode: arching her back, narrowing her eyes, pushing her collagen-inflated lips into a pout.

And so, the sordid instant had been caught on film. 'Fantastic!' Julia's picture editor had roared down the phone at her.

'Yeah, fantastic,' she muttered bitterly to herself.

'What is?' David's deck shoes squeaked on the wooden floor as he came into the kitchen.

'Oh, nothing.' Julia turned the page. Overleaf, the paper's 'political' section carried an in-depth study of the prime minister's wife's various hairstyles. Julia groaned.

'What's the matter?' David knocked about by the sink, attempting to tidy up the mess of last night's abandoned takeaway.

'I'm sick of doing what I do. I've got to get out.'

'Not this again, Jules.'

Julia leant right over the table, resting her elbows on the paper and her chin in her hands. 'Yes, David, this again. It's driving me insane. I didn't get into photography to plug other people's careers.'

'You provide a service, Julia. People want to see what celebrities get up to.'

'I don't.'

'It pays the bills.'

'It doesn't pay the intellectual bills.'

David laughed quietly. 'Lighten up, Jay-jay.'

Julia closed her eyes and gritted her teeth. She hated that nickname, and the patronising tone in his voice.

'You're good at what you do. It bought you this flat, didn't it? You said yourself it could take years to break into serious journalism. You've got an advantage, being the only woman on the paper. Your female subjects either like you or hate you and the men fancy you. You get good pictures.' His footsteps came out from behind the breakfast bar and moved closer to her. 'If you had told me at drama school that I'd end up being an adulterous vet in a soap opera, I'd have been devastated. But we can't all be Gielguds and Redgraves, and it's a living. A good one.' His footsteps stopped behind her, and his hands came to rest on her waist. 'Besides, if you hadn't been working on the *Chronicle*, we'd have never met.'

'Mmm,' Julia mumbled, as his fingers slid over her hips.

'And that would have been such a shame.'

'Mmmmm,' she moaned in agreement as he shuffled closer, and she felt the hardness beneath his trousers pressing against her sex.

'You've got such a gorgeous arse, Julia. God, I've missed your arse.'

Julia smiled. David's well-spoken voice was known to millions, not only as the TV vet but as the voice-over for a cereal, a supermarket and a brand of dog food. If only they could hear him now, extolling the virtues of her backside. She pushed back against him, rubbing herself from side to side like a cat wanting to be stroked.

'Oh, Julia, don't. I've got to go,' he protested.

But he didn't go. His hands slid up over her ribs and around on to her breasts. Cupping them gently as they dangled towards the table, he weighed them in his palms. 'I've missed these, as well.'

Her back arched languidly as he squeezed her flesh in his strong fingers. The tendons pulled at the backs of her thighs, and she moaned softly. 'Oh, David,' she whispered. 'That feels so good.'

His right hand drifted away, back down her body. There was a faint clink of metal, the muffled sound of buttons popping open, then his hard rod was nudging at her open sex. Her pelvis writhed, searching for the source of her pleasure, longing for relief. His hand clasped her waist, steadying her while the tip of his penis snaked towards her vagina. He brushed roughly against her tender clitoris on the way, making Julia shudder. She held her breath, aching with anticipation. Then he was inside her, slowly easing between her fleshy lips until he filled her completely with his thick cock. His fingers gripped her firmly as he began to slide in and out of her pliant flesh.

Gently, they bucked together, their hips moving in fluid harmony. David's right arm slid around her waist for leverage. The fingers of his left hand pulled at her nipple, pinching her into stiffness. Julia dropped her forearms on to the table and held on to its sides, desperately resisting the temptation to jerk her pelvis and spoil David's rhythm, letting him set his own slow pace. His thrusts deepened and he touched the neck of her womb, forcing a cold shiver to whirl like an icy cyclone beneath her warm skin. Her lower back arched sharply as his motion became increasingly urgent. Feeling as if she was turning inside out, she opened herself wider, spreading her legs further apart and lowering her face on to the newspaper. Her clitoris was rubbed with every push. Her legs began to tremble weakly. She moaned into the print, David joining in behind her, their desperation climbing in a crescendo of passion. Then, with a loud grunt and a final jerk of effort, he rammed himself into her body. Shuddering, he lowered his torso over hers and wrapped his arms around her.

'Julia,' he breathed into her hair. 'God, Julia, you're wonderful.'

After an eternity, their heartbeats slowed and, together, they unfolded themselves. David withdrew his penis from the clutches of her flesh and Julia turned to face him. Watching her fingers, she traced a path along his smooth jaw, down over his Adam's apple, and onward to the top button of his denim shirt. 'Come back to bed, David.'

He cupped her chin in his hand and kissed her. 'I can't, darling. I really have to go.' He smoothed her sweat-dampened hair away where it clung to her cheek. 'I wish I didn't. But I do.' He watched her for a moment, smiling at her disappointment. 'What are you up to today?'

She sighed, rolling her eyes. 'I'm shooting the Sparrow.'

The Sparrow didn't want to be shot, even if it was only with a Nikon. Even if it was to publicise the release of his long-awaited debut album. Julia had been warned about Leon Sparrow by a friend who'd photographed him the week before; still, she hadn't expected this. For a twenty-year-old who had only stumbled upon fame six months earlier, his lack of cooperation was remarkable.

Julia loaded another film into her camera and set it back on its tripod. She watched and waited as Leon was fawned over; floppy dark hair sprayed and fluffed, shiny nose powdered and yet another designer shirt minutely adjusted. And all the while he lapped it up, chest puffed, pale-grey eyes laughing along with the private jokes of his acolytes. Behind Julia, Leon's manager was making unnecessary calls on his mobile and gesticulating wildly at his protégé. Behind him, lurking in the unlit shadows at the back of the studio, was Leon's entourage: his minder, his brother, and his budding-actress girlfriend. Julia wondered how many people Leon took with him to the toilet.

There was a buzz on the studio's intercom. Glad of the distraction, Julia walked briskly to the door and picked up the phone.

'Sweetheart, it's George, your friend and editor.'

She buzzed him in and went out into the cool hallway to meet him. He took ages to come up the stairs, hindered by his beer belly and puffing on his usual cigar.

'I'm not your sweetheart, George. And you're not my friend.' Julia folded her arms and slumped against the wall as he finally appeared, his breath rasping loudly. 'I'm in a bad mood,' she added, unnecessarily. 'What do you want?'

'Just popped by on my way back to the office. Wanted to see how you're getting on with Leon. I heard the lad's quite a handful.' He winked conspiratorially. 'Think you can get him ready for Jimmy? He's interviewing him at two.'

Julia glanced towards the studio door, not bothering to lower her voice. 'I'd be surprised if Jimmy gets two spontaneous words out of him. The boy doesn't breathe without asking his manager first.' She flicked her fingers through her hair. 'And then there's the rest of the fan club. He brought seven people with him, George. Seven! I might as well not be here. They trooped in, en masse, and took over. They've ignored every single one of my suggestions.'

'Still, nothing you can't handle, hey Jules?'

She thought of her subject, proud and bright as a peacock amidst the attention. 'Don't hold your breath. I don't think we're going to get anything special today.'

She could almost hear George's mind working as he blew clouds of rancid smoke into the tiny hall. Leon Sparrow was big news: a bad boy done good, an obnoxious, loud-mouthed oik who lived the sex, drugs and rock 'n' roll cliché to the letter. Teenagers loved him as much as their parents hated him. His presence in the *Chronicle*'s Sunday supplement would boost sales, but only if they could promise a different view of the Sparrow. The paper's readers were interested in celebrities, but only if the celebrities had something to say.

'Look, Jules, I need some really strong images. Something different. I want you to find me the real Leon Sparrow.'

'Oh. And how do you propose I do that? He doesn't speak. He doesn't move without his manager's say so.'

George patted her cheek with a clammy hand. 'You can do it, Jules. You're the best.'

They both knew that wasn't true. 'I may not be the best, George, but I'm better than this,' she insisted, impatiently brushing his fingers away. 'I'm sick of actors and pop stars and models. This studio isn't big enough to accommodate their egos. Let me do something serious, like you promised.'

Using a well-choreographed move, as familiar to Julia as cleaning her teeth, George slid his heavy arm around her shoulders and walked her to the window. 'We can talk about that later.' His voice was as oily as his slicked-back grey hair. 'But I need you to get the Sparrow, first. And I need you to butter him up for Jimmy. I'm relying on you, Jules.' Suddenly, he lifted his chubby hands away, palms stretched tight as if she'd burnt him. 'Of course, if you don't think you're up to it ... if you're losing your touch ...' There was a knowing smile playing at the wrinkled corners of his eyes. George knew she couldn't resist a challenge.

'Three years,' she snapped, jabbing a long finger into his chest. 'Three years you've been promising me a chance to work on a proper story. I've got you every shot you've ever asked for, George. When do I get to prove myself on something *I* want to do?'

George looked down his rotund body to his badly scuffed shoes. This was another familiar move, an attempt to look forlorn, like an unwanted teddy bear. 'Julia, help me out here. Do whatever you have to do, but get me some dynamite shots of the Sparrow.' Slowly, he raised his head. 'Please, Julia.'

She blinked slowly in resignation. 'I'll see what I can do. But you've got to swear that, after this, you'll get me a decent assignment.'

George was already huffing, asthmatically, back down the stairs. 'Whatever you want, Jules.' He waved goodbye with his cigar. 'We'll talk.'

'Right.' Julia clapped her hands together. The sudden noise had no effect whatsoever on the chatter filling the studio's high-ceilinged space. She stomped into the centre of the room, her boots squeaking on the lino. 'Right!' she repeated, louder this time. Still no reaction. She put two fingers into the corners of her lips and let out a long, piercing whistle.

The bustle of movement around Leon stopped, and attention swung in her direction. She smiled sweetly. 'Thank you. Just thought I'd introduce myself. I'm the photographer.'

Leon's manager looked worriedly from his client to Julia. His mouth gaped, and he finally allowed his mobile phone to drift away from his ear. 'Er ... is there a problem here?'

Julia put her hands on her hips. 'Yes, there's a problem. I can't work like this.' Her eyes trailed around the studio. 'I want all of you out. Now.'

'No way.' The manager raised his hand defensively. 'Leon needs us here.'

Julia raised an eyebrow and fixed the Sparrow with her most disdainful glare. 'Is that right, Leon? You need all these people to hold your hand?'

The colour drained from his cheeks. 'Well –'

'It's important his image is right.'

Julia kept her eyes on the pop star. 'And it's important he gets the right sort of press coverage. And if you don't get out and let me get on with my job, he won't get any in the *Chronicle*.' Julia went back to the door and held it open. 'And the *Sunday Chronicle*, as you surely know, is the biggest selling paper in the country.' Nobody moved. 'His hair looks fine; he doesn't need make-up and his outfit is just lovely. There's a café on the corner. He'll meet you there in an hour.'

The hairdresser threw down his comb in disgust. The bodyguard got to his feet. All eyes were on the manager.

He smiled wanly. 'But ... but ...'

'What's the matter?' Julia challenged, motioning the brother and girlfriend towards the hall. 'Afraid he won't be able to stand up without you?'

'It's all right, Nigel.' Leon nodded at his manager before looking back at Julia. 'I'll see you later.' Behind the slight worry in his eyes, there was a faint and growing tinge of admiration.

'Thanks.' Leon accepted the beer Julia passed him. 'I enjoyed that. The look on his face ...' He chuckled wickedly, shaking his head. 'I don't think Nigel's ever been spoken to like that before.'

Julia bent over the fridge and got a beer for herself. As her jeans stretched tight over her buttocks, she felt Leon's eyes on her behind; sure enough, he blinked guiltily when she turned around.

Julia clinked bottles with him. 'I don't know how you put up with all that disgusting sycophancy.'

Leon's wide mouth opened and closed uncertainly. 'Erm, yeah.'

'Don't you get sick of it all? Being told where to go, what to wear, what to say?'

He shrugged. 'Sometimes. But Nigel is good at his job. Without him, I wouldn't be where I am today.'

'And where is that?'

His thick eyebrows twitched with confusion. 'Well, you know, two top-ten singles, a big record deal, merchandise, tours. I'm playing Wembley in November,' he added, his voice tight with the earnestness of a salesman about to lose an order.

'Are you happy?'

He took a long, thoughtful swig of his lager, eyeing Julia suspiciously. 'I'm rich, aren't I? I've got a posh car and a posh bit of skirt.'

Julia turned the corners of her mouth down and raised her eyebrows. 'That doesn't answer my question.' Slowly, she walked away from him. Putting her beer down, she pretended to be preoccupied with her camera, making tiny adjustments to the legs of the tripod. 'How did you get into the music business?'

'Nigel spotted me in a club.'

'What, singing?'

'No, just mucking about, causing trouble. He said he was looking for someone like me, said I was very "now". Told me how much money I could earn with the right management. Sounded better than being on the dole.'

'Enjoy it while it lasts,' Julia muttered, loudly enough for him to hear.

'What did you say?'

'This is your fifteen minutes of fame, Leon. Enjoy it.' She glanced up at him, her nonchalant smile a contrast to the furrow of concern crossing his forehead. He began to move towards her, faltered, then shrugged the cloak of bravado back on to his shoulders and strode purposefully to the camera. 'I intend to be around for a long time.'

Julia peered through the viewfinder, studying the empty backdrop. 'That's what they all say.'

'What do you mean?'

Without lifting her head, she pushed at him with her hand. 'Get back into position, will you? We haven't an awful lot of time.'

As he loped back into Julia's viewfinder, worry flickered across his face and dampened the fire in his eyes. 'What do you mean?'

Julia straightened up. 'I must have photographed a hundred minor pop stars. They all intended to be around for ever.' She shook her head sadly. 'It doesn't always work out like that. Look, you're an intelligent lad,' she lied, pausing while the flattery slowly wafted its way inside his mind. 'You don't need me to spell it out for you. Leon Sparrow is a product, with a limited shelf life. When the teenagers get sick of you...' Allowing her words to tail off meaningfully, she bent down to pick up her beer. Taking a sip, she watched as Leon drained his bottle and wiped his mouth with the back of his hand.

'You seem to know a lot about it.'

'Do you remember a group called The Time?'

Leon shook his head.

'Neither does anyone else. Six months ago they strutted in here with their manager, their stylists and their hangers-on. They were the next big thing. And where are they now?'

'I don't know,' Leon admitted.

'If you want to be around for a while, you've got to be clever. Very clever.'

'What should I do?' Panic was wavering at the edges of his deep voice.

Julia shrugged carelessly. 'Nothing you can do. Except, enjoy it while it lasts.' She ambled to her camera bag. Crouching down over its open mouth, she hummed softly as she rummaged inside. Suddenly she stopped. Tilting her head thoughtfully, she looked at Leon. 'Of course, there is something you could do. But it would take guts.'

He stammered soundlessly, his mouth opening and closing in search of the right words. With a huge effort he swallowed his discomfort and tried again. 'Tell me. Tell me what I should do.'

Julia stood up and moved towards Leon, her eyes narrowing as she looked him up and down, assessing his chances. 'You're a good-looking young man.' She nodded. Not her type, but striking beneath the fashionably unkempt haircut and the labelled clothes. 'You could appeal to an older market, my age group, for example.' Stepping closer, she lightly pushed his long fringe out of his eyes. 'But you'd have to do things differently.' She felt the strength of his gaze on her face, and the force of his attention urging her on. 'You'd have to stop looking to your manager for answers, and start speaking up for yourself. Women my age aren't so interested in image.' She fingered the soft collar of his shirt. 'Not this sort of image, anyway. This loud-mouthed bad boy isn't going to do anything for us.'

They stood in silence for a while, Julia allowing him to look at her, giving his thoughts a chance to catch up.

'So...,' he ventured at last. 'What would interest a woman like you?'

A quiver of excitement rippled down Julia's body, giving her goosebumps. It was so easy baiting young men like Leon, but that didn't make it any less satisfying. Moments like these almost made the job worthwhile; she felt empowered, invincible, incredibly aroused. Gradually, drawing out every ounce of tension in the air, she raised her eyes from his shirt to his face. She was taller than him, and he looked up at her eagerly, putty in her hands.

'All this –' she waved her hand dismissively over his outfit '– this isn't you.' Julia allowed a smile to creep into her eyes. 'A woman like me would want to see what's behind the image. I'd want to see the real Leon Sparrow.' She bit her bottom lip, stifling the beginnings of a giggle as she imagined George rubbing his sweaty hands together with glee. 'I'd want to know what makes you tick. What goes on in here.' She tapped her temples with her fingertips. 'Metaphorically speaking, I'd want you to bare all for me.'

The metaphor flew over his head and he unbuttoned his shirt and dropped it to the floor. He pushed off one trainer with his toes, then the other. As he unfastened his baggy jeans, dropped them to his ankles and stepped out of them, his eyes steadfastly watching Julia's, she imagined the screech of a million teenage girls.

'Is that better?'

Julia took her time inspecting his body: naked apart from his tight white shorts. She was surprised to find him lean beneath his baggy clothes; he looked boyish, small, vulnerable. 'Actually, I meant for you to bare your feelings, but never mind.'

'Oh.' His pale gaze fluttered over her neck and cleavage on its way to his toes. Julia savoured his discomfort as he shuffled from foot to foot. 'Shall I put my clothes back on, then?'

'No.' Turning her back on him, Julia returned to the camera. 'It's good. You look less sure of yourself. If it's OK, I'd like to take a few frames like this.'

He didn't reply. Fidgeting nervously, he watched as Julia bent her upper body behind the camera, keeping her back straight. Aware that Leon would have an uninterrupted view down the gaping V-neck of her T-shirt, Julia watched for his reaction. Reaching around, she brought him into focus, feeling her breasts move within her bra as she twisted the lens. Grateful for the predictability of young men, she saw his line of sight drift inside her top. His lips parted and his chest began to rise and fall as his breathing grew heavier. Julia lowered herself another inch and his nostrils flared. Ever so slowly, as if he was hoping she wouldn't notice, he moved his hands in front of his groin.

'Bingo,' she whispered, releasing the shutter and freezing the image for eternity. She pressed again and again, capturing his touching confusion. Standing amongst his discarded clothes, trying to hide the beginnings of an erection, he looked like a virgin, transfixed and yet petrified by the feminine form before him.

Julia emerged, smiling, from behind the camera. 'That was great.'

'Did you do that on purpose?'

Her brow creased. 'Do what?'

'Oh God.' He closed his eyes and pushed his fingers through his thick, dark hair. There was so much gel and hairspray there, that several locks stuck up in protest after he took his hands away. Julia went up to him, raised her hand to flatten his hairstyle, then changed her mind. It looked sweet, as if he'd just got out of bed.

She noticed beads of sweat on his upper lip. 'Are you all right?'

'Yeah.' Clasping his hands firmly over his growing excitement, he gazed up at her, silently begging her for mercy. Inside her chest, Julia's heart pounded rapidly. Excited as much by the sense of power as by Leon's arousal, she took a deep breath. She didn't want Leon but it warmed her to know that she could have him. As a tingle spread between her legs, she wondered whether he'd ever slept with a woman like her: a woman who was a little taller than him, a lot wiser, and completely unimpressed by his new-found celebrity.

'We'll carry on, then.'

She turned to go. He stopped her with a hand on her shoulder and pulled her round to face him again. 'But I'm not all right. I've never met anyone like you. You're so . . . very –'

He lunged into her. His kiss was clumsy, missing her lips. He tried again, his generous mouth pressing on to Julia's, his hands grabbing at her shoulders.

'Leon!' she laughed, pushing him away.

'Oh shit.' He almost tripped over himself in his haste to back off. 'I'm sorry. I'm really sorry.'

'It's all right. There's no need to apologise.'

He dropped his face into his hands. 'I feel so bloody stupid.' He huffed despairingly. 'Why on earth would a woman like you want anything to do with the likes of me?'

He isn't my type, Julia told herself as she drifted towards him. He's too young; his hair's too long, his mind too dull. And yet she was drawn by something powerful and urgent. She was flattered by his need, touched by his humiliation, enthralled by the situation.

'Leon.' She gently peeled his hands away from his face, and lowered her lips to his.

Shocked for a moment, he was motionless. Then he returned her kiss, his lips sweet and gentle, then urgent and forceful. As Julia closed her eyes, his damp fingers trembled over her neck, afraid to touch her. Their tongues entwined, and Julia tasted beer inside his mouth, warm and slightly bitter.

He moaned as she lowered herself to her knees, and gasped as she hooked her thumbs beneath the fabric and eased his shorts over his slender thighs. Springing forward, his thick penis pointed at Julia, accusing her of his lust. Feeding from his astonishment as he looked down on her, she reached around, grabbed his taut buttocks, and eased him closer.

With her strong tongue she traced the bulging vein that ran from the base of his cock to its purple tip with its tiny, weeping eye. Grasping his stem with one hand, she lowered her head and began to massage his lightly haired balls with her lips and tongue, hearing him gently sigh as she increased the pressure. When she had nuzzled him on to the first stage of ecstasy, she turned her attention to his prick, gently pulling the knob of his penis between her lips. Slowly she sucked and licked, lavishing such attention on the first two inches of his length that she heard his breath catch in the back of his throat, fluttering for escape like a trapped bird. Then, with her fingers gripping him tightly at the base, she drew him into her mouth, pulling half his length inside her.

She held him tightly, preventing him from taking the rhythm and control away from her as she began to move her mouth up and down his length. As he gasped and groaned above her, her sucking grew quicker and more forceful, drawing him closer to orgasm with every flick of her tongue. Each time she withdrew, her tongue lashed at the engorged tip of his prick, and every time she pushed down on to him, his manhood touched the back of her throat. As she thrust her head forwards and back, her fingers explored the cleft between his tight buttocks. Passing over his sensitive, secret hole she became more and more convinced that no one had ever touched him there, and with this realisation came the intense desire to be the first. Within her clutches, his moaning grew loud and irregular and his body shuddered. It was now or never.

Pausing only for a second, Julia poked a finger into her mouth, wetting it with her warm saliva. As her lips resumed their motion in front of him, her finger moved behind and circled his puckered anus. Her clitoris began to throb violently as she felt his muscles spasm at her touch, and she almost wished she could swap places with him as, without further ceremony, she pushed her finger inside him.

Immediately she entered him, his body went rigid and she tasted his salty pleasure on her tongue. He was impaled on a spear of agonising delight, caught between the joy of her lips, sliding wetly along his penis, and her finger, thrusting insistently behind him. Shocked by the mixture of delight and pain that was flooding his already overloaded senses, he came, his stomach muscles rippling as his orgasm rushed over him like a wave, threatening to drown him in foaming, roaring ecstasy.

Julia sat back on her heels and admired him as she tasted his slippery come in her throat. Spent, he fell to his knees and ran his shaking fingers over her face.

Between her legs, under pressure from the seam of her jeans, Julia's clitoris throbbed demandingly.

'Oh God,' Leon whimpered, struggling to catch his breath. 'You're amazing.' His fingers began to journey down her neck. 'Let me ... I want to do something for you.'

Grabbing his wrist, she shook her head. 'I never sleep with my subjects.'

He blinked slowly. 'Never?'

'Well, I did once. But now I'm marrying him.'

'Marry me instead.'

'You're a little young for me,' she laughed.

Leon searched her eyes. Whatever he was looking for wasn't there and, reluctantly, he let his hand fall out of Julia's fingers. 'I knew it. I knew you didn't really want me.'

Julia cupped his hot cheek in her fingers. 'I never thought I would say it, but I do want you, Leon. You're very sweet. But I'm getting married in a fortnight. I shouldn't have done what I did.'

Her knees ached from the hard floor as she stood up. Uncomfortably wet, she moved back to her Nikon. 'We'd better crack on – your manager will be waiting for you.'

'I don't care.'

'So will your girlfriend.'

Guilty, he dropped his eyes. When he looked up again a moment later, Julia froze. Her lips parted and her breathing faltered. She'd seen that pale-grey, intense, lovelorn expression before.

'What's the matter?'

'Nothing,' she insisted, hiding her face behind the camera. 'You just reminded me of someone, that's all. Someone I haven't seen for a long time.'

'Who?'

The image of Leon in the viewfinder clouded as her eyes glazed. 'No one special. Just a guy I used to know.'

* * *

'Marianne?' Julia flopped on to the sofa and put her feet up on the coffee table. 'Guess who was in my studio this afternoon. And guess what he was wearing.'

Marianne tutted loudly on the other end of the phone line. 'Do I have to?'

'Yes.'

'You only do this to make me jealous.'

'Humour me.'

She sighed. 'Oh, all right. Sean Connery, wearing a tux.'

'No. Guess again.'

'Brad Pitt. Wearing chocolate sauce.'

'Been there, done that.'

'The prime minister wearing nothing but his Calvin Kleins.'

'These are your warped fantasies, not mine.'

'Oh, I give up. Go on, make my eyes turn green.'

'Leon Sparrow.'

'Ooooh, nice. Wearing?'

Julia bit her lip, replying with silence.

'Julia? Julia?' Marianne's voice grew urgent with envy. 'Are you trying to tell me he was naked?'

'Not all the time.'

In the distance, the faint, buzzing interference on Marianne's line seemed to grow louder. 'What's he like?' she asked, anxiously.

'Nice.'

'Nice?' There was disgust in her raucous voice. 'Nice! Come on, you're not getting away with it that easily. How did you get his kit off? What did you talk about? Did he try it on with you?'

Julia divulged the wicked truth, struggling to speak through her excited giggling. On the other end of the line, the buzzing moved around and grew deeper until she'd finished her confession. Then, abruptly, the humming stopped.

Marianne sighed heavily with relief. 'Thanks, Jules. I needed that.'

'You did?'

'I'm in bed. With my little friend.'

'Your little friend?'

'My eight-inch, battery-operated, ever-ready pal. I was just settling down for a session, when you rudely interrupted me.'

Julia giggled; that explained the buzzing. 'Thought I was your best friend.'

'*It* never lets me down,' Marianne snapped. 'So. Are you racked with guilt?'

'No. Should I be?'

'Well, I wouldn't be. But then, I'm not engaged to all-round nice guy, David.'

Julia hesitated at the sound of his name, listening carefully for any traces of regret in her conscience. 'I don't feel the slightest bit guilty. It was a bit of fun, that's all. I could have slept with him, you know,' she added, in her defence. 'He wanted to, but I said no.'

Marianne choked on her laughter. 'So giving a guy a blow job doesn't count as infidelity? You'd better give me a copy of the set of rules you live by, Jules, they sound much more fun than mine.' Her amusement gradually faded. 'Hang on, you realise what this means, don't you? You're having second thoughts about getting married. Your subconscious is saying, "No! Don't do it! Look at all the fun you could have with adolescent pop stars!"'

'Rubbish.'

'You are having doubts though, aren't you?'

Julia winced. 'No.'

'You don't sound so sure. Listen, we'll have a good chat about it this weekend, OK?'

Julia felt her triumphant glow rapidly cooling. The coming weekend held a nonstop whirl of delights: finding the right shade of red nail varnish to match her wedding dress, getting her legs waxed, and Sunday lunch with David's parents. She'd rather have picked the flaky paint off the bathroom ceiling. With her teeth. 'What've you got in mind?'

'Same as you, I expect. Nicholas.'

'Huh?'

'Nick.'

Julia's eyebrows twitched. 'Nick who?'

'Oh, come on.' Marianne sounded exasperated. 'You can't have forgotten the adorable Nicholas Trent. I thought first love never died?'

Julia's innards twisted themselves into a knot – a loose one, but a knot nonetheless. 'You're seeing Nick this weekend?'

'Er ... Julia, hello? We'll be seeing everyone this weekend.'

'Will you stop talking in code? I've no idea what you're going on about.'

'Have you opened your post today?'

'No, but –'

'Well, go and do it now. I'll wait.'

Julia went to the kitchen table. Putting the cordless phone down, she retrieved the mail. Throwing the junk and the bills aside, she tore open the final envelope.

Picking up the phone, she read out loud: '"Time's up! Seven years ago, you set out your aims and aspirations. The time has come to bask in success or admit defeat."' She skipped to the bottom. There was a hand-written note in a familiar, neat hand. '"Please come, Steve."'

'I didn't get a "please come",' Marianne grumbled.

Julia's body froze. This was uncanny. She'd only been thinking of Steve that afternoon, when she recognised a look of him in Leon's pleading eyes. And now this. 'I can't go,' she said.

'Why not?'

'I've got lunch with David's parents. My future mother-in-law would not be impressed if I cried off.'

'Stuff your mother-in-law. You're getting married in a fortnight.'

'That's another reason not to go.'

'Afraid you'll still have the hots for Nick?'

The image of herself kneeling at Leon's feet flashed inside her head. 'You know how hard it is for me to resist temptation.'

'Then don't resist. You'll be hitched soon. You need a final fling.'

'Another one?'

'Sure. It's compulsory.'

In her mind's eye, images of Leon and Steve were pushed aside by one of Nick: the warmth of his brown eyes, the youthful athleticism of his body, the golden shine of his thick hair. The way he used to grab clumsily at her breasts. The times they spent in the school woods. 'No,' she decided. 'It's impossible. I can't go.'

The Reunion

Marianne was still giggling when she emerged from the bed and breakfast. She had giggled nonstop since their arrival in the village on Friday night, desperately amused by the suspicions of the hotel's aged proprietor. 'He thinks we're lesbians,' she had snorted, bouncing about on the double bed. 'He told me there was only one room left, and I told him we only needed one. You should have seen his face!'

She skipped across the narrow street to where Julia was waiting at the car. Slinging her heavy case into the boot, she almost squashed Julia's overnight bag. Bemused, Julia asked how long she was intending to stay in Scotland.

Walking around the side of Julia's copper-coloured VW Beetle, she stooped to check her make-up in the wing mirror. 'You never know, Jules. I like to be prepared. Nick may confess that it was me he wanted all along. He may want to whisk me off to some isolated island where we can hole ourselves up in a crofter's cottage and make up for lost time.'

Julia smiled. 'I wouldn't be surprised. You look great.' Sickeningly great. Marianne had barely changed since the age of eighteen. Her hair was still long, blonde and wavy. Her figure still as athletically toned. She wore more make-up than she used to, but the dark mascara and red lipstick suited her. Her ever-present tan was shown off with a pale-blue, floaty summer dress which matched her eyes.

'You don't look so bad, yourself,' she said, getting into the car.

Julia got into the driver's side and glanced at herself in the rear-view mirror. She hardly ever wore make-up, but she'd made an effort today. Mascara lengthened her already luscious eyelashes. There was a hint of blusher on her pale cheeks and a touch of glossy colour darkening her lips. She rarely wore dresses either, but again she'd made an exception. School reunions demanded a pulling-out of all the stops. The dress was simple but effective in the way it clung gently to her curves. It had a wide collar, a low V-neck which hinted at her cleavage, short sleeves and a skirt which flared slightly before finishing just above her knees. Its rich brown was dramatic against the pale green of her eyes and the faint auburn glow in her hair. On her feet, her favourite knee-length leather boots added two inches to her height. If only she felt as good as she looked.

'I'm really nervous,' she confessed, easing the engine awake. 'I don't think I've ever been so nervous in my life.'

'Nervous?' Marianne got the road map out, opening it at the page they'd marked the night before. 'What of?'

The Beetle chugged its way out of the village's miniature one-way system. 'Oh, all sorts of things. Looking like a failure, mainly.'

Marianne snorted derisively. 'A failure? You're a well-known photographer, Jules. I bet you've done better than anyone else in our year.'

The sun reflected off the road and into Julia's eyes. She fumbled for her sunglasses. 'Steve must have done all right for himself, to be able to hire this castle for the weekend.'

'Yeah, well. Steve was always going to be a success.'

'I bet he's achieved everything on his damned list. I can't remember exactly what I wrote on mine, but I'm pretty sure I've failed on all counts.'

'You wanted to be a photographer, and you are one. How much more successful could you be, for Christ's sake?'

'I wanted to be a photojournalist. I wanted to cover issues. My taking naked photos of Leon Sparrow may please my editor, but it doesn't exactly fill me with a sense of achievement. It's not exactly important work, is it?'

'It's important to me. I need my daily quota of naked men.'

Julia tutted. 'You know what I mean. I had ideals. They seem to have disappeared.'

'I think you're being a little hard on yourself, Jules. Not many people end up doing what they wanted to. I never wanted to work in advertising.'

'You've got a great job.'

'I wanted to be a singer.' Marianne wound the window down and stuck her hand out into the breeze. 'What else are you nervous about?'

'Seeing Nick again.'

'Ah, the gorgeous Nick.' Marianne sighed appreciatively. Her lustful thoughts were almost audible as they drove in silence for a moment.

'I'm nervous about seeing Steve again, too.'

'He was always such a nerd, wasn't he?' Marianne laughed. 'Take a left here.'

As she swung the car into the corner, Julia glanced at Marianne. A tiny knot of excitement gathered in her chest at the thought of revealing something she'd never told her friend. 'I used to have a bit of a thing for Steve, you know.'

Julia felt her cheeks glowing as Marianne turned to stare at her. 'Steve!' she hooted. 'Steve? What on earth did you ever see in him?'

The glow spread down the back of Julia's neck; partly the warmth of the sun pouring through the car windows, partly remembrance of hours spent sprawled on the school lawn, discussing life in a way they thought was so mature. 'He was my best friend, apart from you. I could talk to Steve about anything. He was different to the other boys.'

'He certainly was,' Marianne chuckled. 'Always had his nose in a book. Never played sport. Never came out with us, didn't drink, didn't smoke. Always dressed like he was about to go for an interview.'

'I liked him.' Julia was surprised by the defensive edge to her voice. 'There was something between us.'

Incredulity huffed from Marianne's mouth. 'What, exactly?'

Julia shrugged. 'I don't know. Some sort of bond, I suppose. We understood each other. It was strange – most of the other boys were so immature compared to the girls. But Steve . . .'

'Are you trying to tell me that if Steve had asked you out, instead of Nick, you'd have said yes?'

'Aren't we supposed to turn off somewhere here?'

Marianne consulted the map. 'Yes, go right here. And don't try and avoid the question.'

An indecisive smile flickered across Julia's mouth. 'I don't know. I'll never know. Steve never asked me out. Nick did.'

'Much to my annoyance,' Marianne snapped.

Silence descended again, apart from the wind rushing through the car. Julia could feel Marianne watching her. She could tell she was itching to say something.

'Well, well, well,' she muttered at last. 'All these years I've known you, and you suddenly come out with a bombshell like that. Julia Sargent, secret nerd-lover. I'll never be able to look you in the eye again.'

'He wasn't a nerd. He was very clever, and very determined. Admittedly, he wasn't a stunner. But intelligence can be a big turn-on.'

'Intelligent men are hopeless in bed.' Marianne waggled her little finger in Julia's face.

'How would you know?' she laughed, pushing her hand away. 'You only go out with bimbos. Or should I say himbos.'

'Talking of himbos, how is David?'

Julia gave her friend a reproachful look. 'I can never work out why it is you don't like him. Could it be,' she teased, 'that you're just a tiny bit jealous?'

'It's not that I don't like him, Jules.' The serious tone of her voice was unusual, and it made Julia look across at her. 'I just don't think he's right for you. And I can't understand why you're marrying him. You've only known him a month.'

'Six weeks,' she corrected, quietly.

'It's too soon, even for someone as impulsive as you.'

Marianne was right. Peel away her frivolous exterior and she had a thick layer of common sense beneath. With people she cared about, she didn't mince her words. And she was rarely wrong.

The road became a blur of white lines and tall trees as Julia's mind drifted. She'd never wanted to marry before, never considered it to be part of her grand plan. But when David had asked it had seemed right; or had she been carried away by the wonderful sex they'd been having, by the romance of it all? It was a big step, committing herself to a man she hadn't known two months ago. Perhaps what she'd done with Leon was a warning sign. Perhaps her desire to look her best for the reunion was another.

'Julia! Stop!'

She slammed on the brake. 'What's the matter?'

'You almost missed it.' Marianne crouched forward in her seat, pointing up at the sign. 'Braeburn Castle,' she announced. 'We're here.'

As they pulled up to the castle, Julia had to grip the steering wheel to stop her hands from shaking. The patch of gravel at the bottom of the path was already full of cars, some old and battered like hers, some new and spotlessly luxurious. Not wanting the shame of parking next to a slinky black BMW, Julia squashed the Beetle next to a Mini. In silence, she and Marianne stared up at the castle.

It perched on top of a small hill, a miniature medieval wonder. It was small in castle terms, but stunning nonetheless. In the centre of its four turrets, a flag bearing an ornate coat of arms fluttered in the breeze. Tall, arched windows were carved into the stone; once, no doubt, they had been open to the elements, but now they were glazed and reflected the dazzling blue of the sky whilst staring blankly at the wild landscape. Bathed in late summer sunshine, the weathered granite had a distinctive pink tinge which was echoed in the roses climbing up the walls. A heavy, black portcullis was raised invitingly.

'Are we going to sit here all day?'

'I'm having a panic attack,' Julia cringed. 'You go in, I think I'll go for a walk first.'

'You will not.' Marianne got out of the car and slammed the door decisively. Julia followed her out. 'You've nothing whatsoever to be worried about, Jules. We're successful, gorgeous young women with hefty pay packets and hordes of men slavering at our feet.' She raised her fine eyebrows, urging Julia to agree. 'We can be proud of who we are.'

'I suppose so,' Julia admitted grudgingly.

'Well, I am, anyway. I don't give a toss about you. Come on.'

Marianne grabbed her hand and they began the gentle climb to the castle's entrance. Halfway up, Julia stopped.

'Hang on. What if this turns out to be really boring?'

'It won't be.' Marianne's eyes were already sparkling in anticipation.

'But what if it does? Shouldn't we have an escape plan?'

Marianne rolled her eyes. 'If it's boring, we'll leave early in the morning. If it's dire, we'll go this evening. It's not far to Glasgow – we could hit the clubs.' She squeezed Julia's shoulder to reassure her. 'But it won't be boring, I promise. I've got a good feeling about this. I reckon we'll get some action.' She winked naughtily. 'This is your last chance, remember, if you are going to get hitched.'

Julia ignored the 'if'. She smiled uncertainly.

'Although,' Marianne added, patting her handbag, 'if things get too desperate, I could always lend you my little friend.'

'You brought it with you?'

'Never leave home without it.' Marianne opened her bag for Julia to see inside. At the bottom, nestling amongst a month's worth of receipts, a few tampons and a spilt bag of sweets, was Marianne's vibrator: shiny, black and very long.

Julia shook her head. 'Sometimes I don't believe you, Marianne.'

A wicked grin was accompanied by a flicker of her eyebrows. 'Sometimes, I don't believe myself.'

An immaculate butler showed them into a high-ceilinged drawing room. They stood at the door for a moment, speechless at the scene before them.

'It's incredible,' Marianne gasped.

Julia nodded incredulously. 'They haven't changed a bit.'

Some had a little more hair, some had less; weight had

also fluctuated, and fashions were very different to those of seven years earlier. But, apart from minor changes, no one had altered much since the sixth form. It could almost have been the final day at school.

'Marianne! Julia!'

Someone noticed them and a minute later they were surrounded by a crowd of familiar faces. Kisses and hugs were exchanged, and news of the years since school was rapidly filled in. Personal tragedies were sympathised with, successes were congratulated, wedding rings and photos of children were dutifully admired. Servants circulated amongst the guests, keeping their voices lubricated with whatever they desired; the castle, it seemed, could cater for any taste. Testing one of the waiters, Marianne asked for Möet and Chandon mixed with Blue Curaçao and freshly squeezed pineapple juice. Five minutes later, the odd-coloured cocktail was served on a silver tray.

'I'm impressed.' She smiled sweetly at the young man. 'Do you do room service?'

'Behave yourself.' Julia nudged her. 'Stop teasing.'

'I'm just curious.' She straightened the boy's bow tie, making him blush. 'Are you thrown in with the castle, then?'

'Sorry, madam?'

'Do you come free when you hire the castle?'

He looked anxiously to Julia for help. 'I don't understand, madam.'

'Ignore her.' Julia smiled.

But Marianne, already well oiled with alcohol, would not give up. 'I simply want to know whether the staff come free when you hire the castle, or whether you have to pay extra?'

'The castle isn't for hire, madam.'

Julia exchanged glances with Marianne. 'Who owns Braeburn?' she asked.

'Mr Roth.' The waiter smiled shyly, glad Marianne's pestering had finished. 'Steven Roth.'

He used the moment of amazed quiet to slip away. Marianne stared at Julia, mouth gaping. 'Steve owns this place? My God!' She waved her hands above her head. 'Everyone, listen! Steve owns this place! He *owns* it!'

A murmur of surprised excitement flowed across the room. Brian, a well-built man with short black hair and rich, dark skin, sidled up to the women. 'So, what's Steve doing now?'

Julia shrugged. 'I have no idea.'

'You two were good friends, weren't you?'

She nodded. 'I wrote to him for about six months, but he never replied to my letters. I gave up in the end.'

'He must earn a packet, to buy a place like this.'

Julia looked around the room at the gold picture frames and the pale blue, sumptuous furnishings. 'He always said he'd be rich by the age of twenty-five. Looks like he did it.'

Brian's attention was diverted by someone else, and Marianne poked Julia in the ribs. 'He's improved with age.'

Julia's brow furrowed. 'You always hated Brian.'

'Did I?' She looked wistfully at the way his buttocks filled his trousers. 'I can't think why.'

'He tried to kiss you once. You said he had bad breath.'

Marianne tutted ruefully. 'Teenagers can be so cruel.' She tipped her drink down in one gulp. 'I think he deserves another chance.'

Julia watched as, around the room, the sparks of adolescent flirtations were relit. Almost inevitably, the reunited men and women formed splinter groups, just as they had done at school. Desires which had lain festering and forgotten for so long were rekindled, as were ancient jealousies and childish rivalries. Slightly disappointed by how little things had changed, she found herself drifting apart from the others. It was more interesting to listen in on conversations, to observe. She remembered that her camera was in the car, and slipped out to get it.

She wondered what time Nick and Steve would arrive, and smiled at the thought that they would probably come together. Then she realised they had probably lost touch, too, as they had done with her. That was one teenage rivalry that must surely have died out with adulthood.

Standing at the bottom of the hill, she decided to take a photo of the castle. She set up her tripod and clicked the lens into place on her camera. The sun was above her and to the left, fingers of light slanting through the rapidly moving clouds and throwing dramatic shadows on to the granite walls. She bent her head to the viewfinder, waiting for the clouds to shift, waiting for the perfect moment.

'Beautiful, isn't it?'

Startled, she jumped, almost knocking her tripod over. Putting a hand to her chest, she tried to calm her heart. But as she turned to see who it was, her pulse began to race out of control.

'Steve?' Her lips parted. Involuntarily, her eyebrows twitched upward. 'Steve?'

He smiled at her confusion; he had been expecting it, no doubt, because, unlike the others, Steve had changed. Dramatically. The ungainly, weighty limbs had metamorphosed into firm muscle, obvious beneath his white T-shirt and dark jeans. His height was no longer cumbersome; now, he carried his tallness with proud confidence. His chestnut hair, so unruly at school, had been cut very short to emphasise the new angularity of his face. The slight chubbiness of his cheeks had gone, along with the heavy glasses; now, there was nothing to disguise the beautiful intensity of his grey eyes.

Julia swallowed hard, trying not to look too amazed,

and failing. She blinked quickly as she looked him up and down. 'Steve. You look . . .'

'Different?' he offered.

'You look amazing.'

Suddenly, there it was; the gentle smile that used to make her feel so warm inside. It still worked. 'Thank you,' he said. 'Let's face it, I needed a complete overhaul.'

She smiled back at him. 'You're a person, not a car.'

'I was a mess. No wonder I didn't get a girlfriend until I was twenty-one.'

Inexplicably embarrassed, Julia looked down at her feet.

'You look . . .'

She raised her head to find those eyes, trailing from her boots up to her face.

'Gorgeous. You look really gorgeous.'

'Thank you.' Unintentionally, her voice came out in a whisper.

'But then, you always did.'

Again, she felt the need to look away. She turned back to her camera. 'I was trying to get a shot of the castle. It'll look dramatic if I get it right, but it's quite amazing how quickly the light changes. I'm used to being able to set up my own lights. Mother Nature isn't quite as predictable –'

He interrupted her babbling. 'Are you coming in?'

'When I've done this.' She glanced round at him. 'You go. I'll be in, in a minute.'

'Don't be long. We've got a lot of catching up to do.' He set off up the path. Julia twisted her lens until she closed in on him, shaking her head slightly at the incredible changes to his appearance. Even his walk had altered, the clumsy, self-conscious shuffle replaced by long strides of confidence which reminded her of someone else.

'Steve!' she shouted, straightening up as he turned. 'Where's Nick?'

Even at that distance, Julia noticed Steve's expression hardening. Perhaps that rivalry was still going strong, after all.

'He can't come. He's working.'

'Oh.'

Steve began to walk back down the hill towards her. 'You sound disappointed.'

A few minutes earlier and she would have been. Now, she was almost sure that she didn't care. 'It would have been nice to see him again, but I'm not that bothered. What's he doing now, do you know?'

'Have you heard of Rothco Developments?'

'Should I have done?'

'Not unless you're interested in real estate. It's a property development company.' A broad, self-satisfied grin spread across Steve's mouth. 'It's my company. Nick works for me.'

Julia thought for a moment. 'And you couldn't give him a day off?'

'Something came up.' He shrugged. 'It was Nick's choice to work.'

'Oh, well.' She dipped to the camera again. He waited for a moment, then turned back up the path. 'I'm sure we'll manage to have fun without him,' she murmured, watching his backside as he walked away.

The dining table was long enough to seat all the guests, and still leave some empty seats. By the time the meal had finally been cleared away, the high room was full of drunken laughter. Everyone was having fun – not least Marianne and Brian – except for Julia. Sitting at one end of the long oak table, she was flanked by the class bores. The man and woman were twins and had an annoying habit of finishing each other's sentences. They had seemed middle-aged at eighteen; at the ripe old age of twenty-five, they were almost unbearably dull.

Julia watched Marianne, huddled conspiratorially with Brian. She wouldn't need her 'little friend' tonight. Her gaze drifted up the table to the head, where Steve was sitting. Deep in conversation, he supported his jaw with one hand. His other hand hovered over his wine glass, one finger making slow circles around the rim. Transfixed, Julia allowed the voices at her side to fade away as she followed the sensuous movement of his long fingers. His touch moved down over the side of the glass, stroking up and down, up and down, as if it was a woman's curve he was enjoying. To Julia, the room was silent now, save for the measured sound of her breathing. She squeezed her thighs together, trying to suppress the urge she had to run down the room and replace the curve of the glass with that of her breast. Her lips parted as she imagined those long, cool fingers on her skin, in her mouth, between her legs.

She looked up just as he did. Shocked by the sudden eye contact, they were both immoveable and emotionless for what seemed an eternity. The expanse of table that separated them seemed to vanish, and they were alone, communicating without words, as they used to do. Moving slowly through the heavy atmosphere between them, Steve picked up his glass and took a sip of red wine. He blinked slowly in appreciation, as if it was Julia he was tasting. It may have been due to the amount of alcohol she'd drunk, but Julia suddenly felt light-headed.

Steve's slight, shy smile broke the link as he looked back at the woman who was talking to him. He nodded slowly in agreement at what she was saying, while Julia begged for him to look at her again. He may have done, but she wouldn't have known; Marianne asked one of the twins to swap places with her, and she began to fill Julia in on her progress with Brian.

The tinkle of a bell interrupted them. All eyes turned

to Steve, who was smiling gleefully. 'If I can have everyone's attention.' He slapped his hands together and rubbed them. 'As I said on my invitation, time is up. It's almost unbelievable, but it's seven years to the day since we all left school. And we all remember what we did, on the last day of school?'

Julia was one of the ones who groaned.

'Yes, I'm afraid it's time to own up. If you'd all like to open your envelopes . . .'

The sound of tearing paper rustled around the table as each of the diners retrieved the envelopes Steve had presented them with at the start of dinner. Quiet laughter bubbled up as the promises of seven years ago were finally re-read. Marianne shrieked raucously as she discovered what had been on her mind at the age of eighteen.

'Do you want to go first, Julia?'

She looked up from her list to find Steve watching her. 'Do I have to?'

'Someone has to start.'

'I'll start,' Marianne butted in. 'This is hilarious.'

Her list *was* hilarious; unsurprisingly, Marianne's goals were mainly sexual. Unsurprisingly, she'd achieved most of them. Her quest to be a singer, though, had proved more elusive. Up and down the table, career disappointments were admitted unanimously.

If it hadn't been for Steve's avid attention, Julia wouldn't have been so embarrassed about acknowledging her own shortcomings along with everyone else. But, with him watching, the nervousness she'd felt before came rushing back like an icy draught.

'OK,' she sighed heavily. 'Here goes. Number one, get into university,' she read, her voice faltering. 'Well, I got in, but not at the uni I wanted, because my grades were so bad. So I decided not to go.' She glanced around the table. 'Two, spend a year travelling, taking photos.' Her nose wrinkled. 'I spent a year in a town called Cranbrook instead, working for the local rag, taking pictures of garden fêtes and dog shows.' She sighed before continuing. 'Three, move to London and work on the news desk of a top daily.' She sniffed with self-reproach. 'Well, I did move to London, and I did work on the news desk, but only on the *Wandsworth Guardian*. I got to do the really gritty, action stuff like the campaign to install dog loos on the high street.'

'Everyone has to start somewhere,' Marianne comforted.

'Oh, certainly. I seem to remember Eve Arnold began on the local rag, too.'

Her sarcasm was lost on Marianne. 'Cut the self-pity and get on with it,' she urged.

'Four, get a job on one of the broadsheets.' She paused, wondering what had been going on in her mind when she had written this list. 'I got a job as a trainee on the *Daily Chronicle* instead. Of course, that's when I hit the big time. No more village fêtes and dog loos for me. I worked on the women's section, taking those pictures of laughing models that they use to illustrate the latest beauty regime.' Sighing, she wished she could throw the list into the fire and forget about it. 'Five, get on to the paper's political section and cover a general election.' Julia felt her jaw hardening with regret. 'The *Chronicle* doesn't have a political section to speak of. I got on to the showbiz section instead. Six, get assigned to a war zone.' She smiled wryly. 'Well, I do get to go to nightclub openings. They can be pretty dangerous.' She bit her lip as she saw her final goal. She hadn't remembered writing this at all, and its simple naïveté was poignant. 'Seven, never give up in the fight for peace, justice, truth and love. Well,' she muttered, 'I gave up that fight long ago, when I started living in the real world.' Slumping back in her chair, Julia tore her list up into tiny pieces and scattered them over the table. 'So there you have it. Not a single goal accomplished.'

Marianne patted her hand. 'You are a photographer, though, like you always wanted to be.'

'A good one.' Julia looked up as Steve joined in. 'I read the *Chronicle*. I've seen your work.'

Murmurs of agreement were added by the others; most of them bought the *Chronicle*. The Sunday issue, with its celebrity-packed magazine, was the biggest selling paper in the country. But the fact that her peers had seen her work did little to compensate Julia, since she didn't like most of it.

'Your turn, Steve,' she said, changing the focus of attention to the opposite end of the table. 'You're the only one left.'

Blinking several times, he raised his list. 'All right. One, get a first at uni.' He glanced around the table, almost embarrassed. 'I did. Two, spend a year travelling. I did,' he said, quietly. 'Three, get a job with a property developer and learn the business from the inside. Did that, too. Four, lose weight. Five, lose my virginity.' His gaze flickered momentarily towards Julia. When he spoke again, his voice was less strident. 'I did that, too. Although the weight was easier to get rid of than my virginity.'

Under the table, Julia kicked Marianne to stop her from giggling.

'Six, set up my own business. Buy a plot of land, build a house on it, and use the profit to invest in more land.' He paused. 'Actually, I didn't build a house.'

'At last, Mr Perfect has a flaw,' Marianne shouted down the table.

'My father died and left me a lot of money. I bought a much bigger plot of land than I could have afforded otherwise, and I built twenty houses.' The laughter drifted away. 'Property boomed, I sold them all and bought a plot of undeveloped land in the middle of Glasgow. I built a multi-storey car park on it. I made so much profit I bought some more land and sold it to a hotel developer. And so on, and so on . . .'

'You make it sound so easy,' someone said. Julia agreed; it sounded like he was reading his shopping list.

'I was very lucky,' he admitted. 'Without my inheritance, it would have taken me a lot longer to achieve all this.' He folded up his list. 'Well, that's it.'

'But that's only six,' Marianne said. 'What happened to number seven?'

He looked up guiltily. Even in the dim light of the dining room, Julia could see shifty discomfort in his clear eyes. 'I can't read it out. I haven't done it yet.'

'Ah-hah!' Marianne exclaimed triumphantly. 'At last, a bit of failure in your perfect life! You still have to read it out, though.'

He continued to fold the piece of paper until it was so small he could hide it in his palm. Looking straight at Julia, he said, 'I can't.'

Marianne stood up and walked purposefully to the head of the table. Hands on her hips, she stood at Steve's side. 'Come on! All the rest of us have admitted to our failures.'

Worried, Steve looked down at his fingers as they gripped determinedly at his list. 'This is personal. I can't read it out.'

Marianne held out her hand. 'Give it to me, then. I'll read it.'

Steve shook his head. Marianne lunged for him but, before she could grab the paper, Steve caught her wrist. 'Leave it, Marianne.' His eyes were as strong as his grip. 'I am not going to read it, and that's final.'

Shocked by his reaction, Marianne wrestled herself out of his grasp. As she stalked back to her seat, Steve raised his eyes to Julia's again. But the tension she had felt earlier had gone; he seemed on edge, embarrassed. The mood around the table was the same, everyone fidgeting uncomfortably.

'Well,' Steve sighed. 'Looks like I've brought the party to a standstill.'

'Nothing new there, then.'

He glared at Marianne. 'Come on, then, party animal. What do you suggest?'

'Let's go for a swim in the lake.'

'We're in Scotland, Marianne. It's a loch.'

'Whatever. Let's go for a swim in it.'

It was still light outside. The sky was streaked with sunset colours which were reflected in the small loch: purples, pinks and oranges. Julia walked with Steve. Together, they followed the path at the back of the castle, down to the water. The others ran past them, shrieking as they lost control and stumbled on their way downhill. Neither spoke, and in the comfortable silence Julia became attuned to the rhythm of Steve's slow pace beside her. It felt so right being with him again. Just like old times, and yet so different. She looked up at him, his handsome features set in deep thought.

'Do you come here often?'

He stopped walking. Glancing back at the castle, he smiled in admiration. Then he looked down at Julia, and his smile deepened. 'Are you trying to chat me up?'

She wrapped herself in the warmth of his eyes. 'I certainly wouldn't use that old line, if I was.'

'I should think not. I'd expect better of you.'

'So? Do you come here often?'

'Not often enough. I'm so busy with the business, this is the first weekend I've had off in ... let me see ... five months.'

'Sounds to me like you're working too hard.'

Steve shrugged slightly. 'It is hard work. But it's what I always wanted, isn't it?' He dropped his head.

'You don't seem so sure.' Julia put her hand on his arm. She looked at his bowed head, at his averted eyes, and it struck her that although he'd changed outwardly, inside, he was still the same uncertain boy he'd been seven years ago. 'You're not happy, are you?'

He turned his face away. Down by the loch the guests were pairing off as if for a party game to be played out beneath the romance of the setting sun. Steve seemed to withdraw further into himself. Julia watched her fingers as they moved down his bare arm and into the palm of his hand. She looked up as Steve looked down. He seemed bemused by the sight of her fingers, lacing with his.

'Steve?'

'I'll be happy when I achieve the last goal on my list. The most important one. Without that, all the rest is pointless.' His voice was soft and full of longing.

'Will you tell me what it is?'

'Later.' His eyes met hers. 'When we're alone.'

Her eyelids did an involuntary double flutter. 'We'll be alone, later?'

He gently squeezed her hand. 'I hope so.'

Julia held her breath, caught in the moment. His words echoed endlessly in her mind. Her pussy clenched in anticipation.

'Julia! Julia! Get yourself down here!'

Marianne's shrill laughter shattered the stillness of the moment. Reluctantly, Julia wrenched her eyes away from Steve's and looked down the hill. Marianne and Brian were flinging their clothes on to the grass. Marianne waved urgently.

'Come on!'

Julia kept hold of Steve's hand as they continued down the path to join the others. Some were already in the loch, gasping breathlessly as the temperature shocked them. Others were dawdling, admiring the changes the last seven years had brought to each other's bodies. By the time Julia reached her friend, she had her greedy hands on Brian's smooth, dark buttocks as he bent over. Julia's eyes flickered over his naked body before smiling appreciatively at Marianne. He was just the way Marianne liked her men, thickly muscled – all over. Marianne smirked back, her expression full of wicked intent. 'Coming for a dip, Jules?'

Julia looked up at Steve. 'Are you coming in?'

He shook his head. 'I know how cold it is in there.'

'Oh, come on,' Marianne whined. 'Don't be such a spoilsport.'

Steve sat down decisively. Resting back on his hands, he ignored Marianne and gave Julia a faint smile that made her flutter inside. 'You go in. I'll watch you.'

Julia stood motionless for a moment, almost overwhelmed by excitement at what she was about to do. A loop of silent communication hummed in the air between her and Steve as he urged her on, and she teased him with another second's wait. Then, her eyes fixed on his, watching intently for his reaction, she began to undress.

Her dress was first, slowly pulled over her head and dropped to the ground. Next, her boots. Bending over to unzip each leg in turn, she watched as Steve's line of sight drifted downward, moving between sleepy blinks over the black, silken cage of her underwear. The grass was cool on her stockinged feet as she straightened up and stepped out of the soft leather boots. Her fingers deftly unfastened her suspenders and, slowly, she unrolled first one sheer stocking, then the other. She pushed her suspender belt down over her hips and nonchalantly threw it towards Steve. Without looking away from her, his hand stretched out along the grass towards the band of satin. Smoothing his touch over it, his head tilted and his lips slowly parted, like an art lover lost in rapture as the sculpture of Julia's body was revealed. Reaching behind herself, she unhooked her satin bra, arching her back slightly as she did so. Bringing her hands back round, she slid the straps from her shoulders, cupped her breasts, and slowly pulled the dark silk away from her pale skin. For an instant, Steve closed his eyes, as if it was too much for him to bear. Opening them again, his gaze alternated from one breast to the other, his eyebrows dipping as he seemed to struggle to comprehend the perfection of her shape. Julia felt an icy tingle between her legs as she lowered the skimpy triangle of her knickers. And then she was naked, every curve exposed to Steve's grateful gaze, her breathing as shallow as his as she stood, and he stared.

Marianne grabbed her hand and pulled her away from Steve's attention. Dazed, Julia was too weak to argue as she was dragged towards the water. Oblivious of Marianne's excited chatter, it was as if she was in a bubble, unaware of anything except Steve's eyes on her body. Like an actor in a nude scene, she suddenly became intensely aware of every movement. She reeled with sensations she had never noticed before: the feel of her buttocks moving as she walked, the slight bounce of her breasts, the contracting of her nipples as a cool breeze wafted by. The feeling of power, of commanding Steve's attention, uplifted her until she felt she hovered over the grass. The sense of arousal, the sharp, almost unbearable ache of anticipation, nearly drowned her.

The loch was cold but she waded right in, wanting every action of her body to be as fluid as the sun-streaked water. As if she were moving in slow motion, Julia dipped her body until the water took her weight, and she swam a few gentle strokes. Swimming towards the spot where a small crowd had gathered, she turned on to her back. The cool air hanging over the lake caressed her breasts as they emerged from the water. She could feel Steve's gaze on her nipples, could feel his desire burning between her legs.

Marianne splashed her and Julia laughed and stood up. Brian joined in the childish game, his eyes flicking hungrily between Marianne's delicate tanned breasts and Julia's pale, full ones. Despite the cold his erection was long, looming above the water like a mythical monster. Wondering what effect it would have on Steve, hoping it would drive him to distraction, she taunted Brian into a fight. They pushed each other down, hands grappling clumsily over wet skin, innocent, drunken laughter masking the sexual tension hiding just beneath the surface.

Marianne pushed Julia's head underwater. When she came up, gasping for air, Julia glanced to where Steve should have been, but he wasn't there. Empty with disappointment, she pushed Brian away and swam off, out into the still centre of the tiny loch.

Something soft brushed against her leg. Without stopping to think about what it might be, Julia turned round to swim ashore. Steve had returned and was doling out towels to the others as they ran from the cold water, while the young waiter was offering a tray of hot toddies to the guests, and clearly enjoying the view.

As Julia reached the shallows and stood up, Steve took a step towards the edge of the lake. Unfolding a huge, white towel, he held it out in welcome. Smiling, Julia strode the short distance towards him. Turning her back, she settled into his arms as he wrapped the blanket of warmth around her. He held her tight against his body until she stopped shivering.

'Julia,' he whispered longingly, his breath warm on her neck, his voice curling softly around her name. 'Julia, I've wanted you for so long.'

She sighed in agreement and leant her head back on his shoulder. Steve released his hold on her. Keeping the towel closed around her in his left hand, his right pushed down on to her breast. He pressed gently at the soft mound, making her ache inside as he slowly rubbed his broad palm all over her shape. The hard button of her nipple poked between his fingers as he discovered her beneath the thick, fluffy cotton. His breath was loud in her ear; his head tilted over her shoulder, looking down at his hand.

His touch slid further, down over her waist, over the delicate curve of her belly and onward. His fingers delved into the fire burning between her thighs, rubbing over her sex with soft, slow strokes. Julia moaned and turned to face him. Grasping the edges of her towel, she put her arms around his neck so that he was enclosed in the huge white sheet as well. Steve looked down, shaking his head as he took in her naked flesh, so close to his still-clothed body. His eyes came back up to meet hers, and she read the longing and gratitude in them before they dropped once again to her breasts. Watching avidly, he raised one hand and lovingly squeezed her ripe flesh. His other hand tentatively felt for her pussy.

Julia sighed and opened her legs as he found her wetness. One finger pressed between her labia, easing them apart and sliding along the infinite smoothness of her inner flesh. While the tip of his finger poked at the entrance to her vagina, his other hand trailed up her neck, a fingertip moving over her chin and between her open lips. Breathing hard, Julia wet his skin with her tongue. A second later, her pussy clenched as his finger pushed inside her.

She didn't hear the beeping at first; all she noticed was Steve's body freezing. Then his warm touch was gone, and he was reaching inside his jeans pocket.

He turned the pager off, read the message, and returned it to his pocket. 'It's the office.' His long sigh was pure regret. 'I'm afraid I've got to make a phone call.'

Julia blinked several times in disbelief. 'Do you have to? Right now?'

Steve eased his way out of Julia's tenacious grasp, unwrapping her hands from his neck. 'I'm sorry. This shouldn't take long.'

He pressed his palm to her cheek. Julia leant her head into his hand. 'Hurry back.'

The waiter appeared at her side as Steve turned and

strode back up the path. She accepted a glass of warm, golden whisky and swallowed it in one. Steve glanced back at her and, as the alcohol sank to her belly, she reached for the waiter's elbow to steady herself.

Two hours later, Steve had still not reappeared. Everyone else had gone up to their bedrooms, leaving Julia to try and work out how many teenage relationships had been rekindled and how many old enemies had dissolved their differences in favour of sharing a bed. Staring forlornly into the drawing-room fire that the butler had lit for her, she began to wonder whether Steve had changed his mind. He was handsome, rich and intelligent, and more than likely to already have a girlfriend. Perhaps that had been her on the phone. Perhaps guilt had cooled his desire. The thought reminded her of David, but the image of his face inside her mind did nothing to stop her wanting Steve. Since he'd gone, she hadn't been able to get warm, despite sitting practically in the fireplace; having her arousal brought to boiling point and then suddenly interrupted had left her chilled to the core.

'Madam?'

She looked up from the hypnotic dance of the flames. The butler was at the door. 'Mr Roth asked me to tell you he's finished on the phone. He suggested you go to your room.' A polite cough masked his embarrassment. 'Mr Roth will join you there shortly.'

Warmth immediately began to seep back into Julia's body. Her legs trembled slightly as she stood up. Leaving the butler to his discomfort, she climbed the stone staircase to her room. In the mirror above the mantelpiece, she checked her reflection. A flush of excitement coloured her cheekbones and the old sparkle was back in her eyes.

* * *

'Sorry that took so long.' Steve silently closed the door behind him.

'I was just about to give up on you,' Julia admitted.

'Well, I'm glad you didn't.' He moved to her side. 'It's so good to see you, Jules.' Raising his hand, he lightly stroked her cheek with the backs of his fingers. 'I've missed you so much.'

'I tried to keep in touch for a while, but you never replied to my letters.'

'There was a reason for that.' His fingers moved downward over her long neck.

Julia smiled wryly. 'What was her name?'

Steve's hand stopped in its progress as it reached the collar of her dress. He looked very serious. 'There's never been anyone special. I never stopped thinking about you, Julia.' He squeezed her shoulder, then dropped his hand into hers. 'There's something I need to tell you.'

'Oh?'

He pulled her towards the wide four-poster bed. They sat together on the edge, Julia's heart racing as she watched Steve glance up towards the pillows.

'What's this?' He leant across the mattress. Picking up the paper-covered cylinder, he stared in amazement as the paper unrolled to reveal Marianne's 'little friend'.

'That belongs to Marianne,' Julia giggled. 'She must have left it for me for a joke.'

Steve read out the note. '"I won't be needing this. Hope you won't either. Enjoy your final fling."' His eyes narrowed as he looked up. '"Final fling?" What does that mean?'

Sheepishly, Julia twirled her engagement ring around her finger. 'I ... er ... I'm getting married in a fortnight. But that doesn't mean we can't ...'

Steve got up, waving her quiet. Seemingly frozen, he stood with his back to her, hand raised, shoulders tensed. 'You're getting married?'

'Yes.'

'Who to?'

'You don't know him.'

'Who is he?' His voice was hard, insistent. 'Tell me.'

'David Tindall. He's an actor.'

'I know who he is. He plays a vet.'

'I didn't think you'd have time to watch television.'

'I don't. I read the papers. He's always in the *Chronicle*, isn't he? Is that where you met him?' Slowly, he turned to face Julia. 'Tall, blond, good-looking chap.'

Julia nodded.

'How long have you two been together?'

'Erm . . .' Much as she wanted to, she couldn't lie to Steve. 'Six weeks.'

His eyebrows shot up. A sigh followed, his whole body slumping. 'Six weeks,' he muttered bitterly, sitting back down on the bed, further away from Julia now. 'I've waited seven years to tell you, and I'm six weeks too late.'

An icy shiver gripped Julia's spine. 'What is it you want to tell me?'

'It doesn't matter now.' His eyes glazed. 'Thought I was so clever, planning everything out. I should have thought. I should have known you'd already have someone.'

'Steve.' Julia reached out for him, but he flinched away from her.

'Please, don't touch me.' His eyes were heavy with sorrow as he glanced up at her. 'Don't make this any more difficult for me.'

'Steve, we can still be together tonight.' She rested her fingers on his knee. 'I know you want to. I want it, too.' She dipped her head in front of his, retrieving his line of sight. 'Steve. Make love to me.'

He closed his eyes and bowed his head. He spent a moment alone in his thoughts. When he looked up again, his eyes were as hard as the granite of his castle walls. 'I think it's fairly obvious, Julia, that I would love to spend the night with you. I've been planning this day for ... well, for a very long time. But I didn't count on your being engaged. No matter how much I want you, I can't do it, Julia. It wouldn't be right. It wouldn't be fair on David. Or you.' He held up a hand to stop her as she tried to butt in. 'And it wouldn't be fair on me.'

'What do you mean?' she whispered.

'I don't want to simply be remembered as your final fling.'

'Steve?' Julia leant towards him, gripping his knee, pleading with every nerve and sinew of her quivering body.

He shook his head, avoiding her eyes as if she were a siren who would seduce him with eye contact if he wasn't careful. 'No, Julia.'

'Oh, God.' It was Julia's turn to stand up. Distractedly, she paced to the mantelpiece and back again. 'Oh God, oh God.' She ran both hands through her hair. 'I don't know what to say, don't know what to do. I've never been as turned on in my life as when you touched me, down by the lake. I've never wanted anyone as much as I want you, now.' She held up her hand, palm facing the floor. 'Look at me. I'm shaking.' Moving towards Steve, she ran her trembling fingers along the strong ridge of his cheekbone. 'Please, if you won't make love to me, just touch me like you did before.'

Gently, he brushed her hand away. 'Do you love David?' he asked, watching her face.

Her eyelids fluttered nervously. 'What a strange question. I'm marrying him, aren't I?'

'Then I'm not going to touch you.' He clasped his hands together in his lap, as if that was the final word. But as Julia sat back down beside him, sighing with despair, his eyes softened and caressed her, fluttering over her hair, her neck, her cleavage. 'Why don't you touch yourself?'

'Sorry?'

He hesitated, looking into each of her eyes in turn; his expression a potent mix of nerves and excitement. 'Touch yourself,' he suggested, almost under his breath.

Julia was already teetering on the edge of insanity. Steve's whispered suggestion was the push she needed to abandon herself to the desire controlling her body. She would touch herself for him, show him the hidden delights of her body, and drive him wild with lust. No man would be able to cling to his ethics, faced with a writhing, pleasure-seeking woman. He would make love to her, whether it was right, or not.

Julia smoothed her palms down over her swollen breasts, over her hips and down to the hem of her dress. Lifting her pelvis from the mattress, she peeled off the soft brown material and, for the second time that evening, dropped it to the floor. Lowering her head, she watched her fingers as they swirled over the black satin cups of her bra. Beneath the shiny fabric, her nipples were sensitive to her touch, and she circled them and lightly scratched with her fingernails. Squeezing her breasts together, she deepened the gentle curves of her cleavage into a dramatic plunge. She slipped her fingers beneath the gentle mould of her bra and folded the cups down beneath her bare breasts. Steve's faint gasp was gratifying as she slowly teased her wide nipples into dark stiffness, pulling at the tips until they pointed at him, the source of her desire.

Sitting up straight, her back arched with pleasure as one hand continued the downward journey. She edged her bottom forward on the mattress, and opened her legs as she delved inside her knickers. Moving through the soft, dark hair, she found the curling, clasping lips of her sex, wet and slightly open. Sleepily, she blinked as the tip of her middle finger entered her warm moistness. Moaning softly, using the wordless language of arousal, she told Steve that she was imagining his finger, there. His finger, easing its way inside her sex.

She looked up as Steve's breathing became heavy and laboured. He was transfixed by the narrow strip of satin covering her pussy, his eyes feasting on her creamy, pale inner thighs, on the wisps of dark-brown hair escaping from beneath the edges of her knickers. Julia could almost hear his mind whirling chaotically as he became hypnotised by the slight movement of her hand beneath the material. The inner muscles of her pussy clutched at her finger as Julia bathed in the surreal sensuality of the moment. While she imagined it was his touch that was pleasuring her, he sat only inches away, undoubtedly imagining the same thing, held back by a promise that he would soon have to break.

Julia eased her finger out of the hot tightness of her sex and rubbed her juices over the tiny bump of her clitoris. Immediately it began to grow beneath her circling fingertip, nerve endings springing to life and swelling with urgent arousal. Julia let out a soft gasp, as a quiver of sensation was released along her spine. Pressing more forcefully around her tender bud, the muscles in her thighs twitched with involuntary delight.

'Use this.'

Marianne's toy was pushed towards her. Carried away, desperate to show Steve the strength of her longing, she didn't hesitate for a second. Taking the thick black rod with her, she shuffled backward into the centre of the wide bed. Getting rid of her damp knickers, she knelt back on her heels, her knees apart.

Without turning the vibrator on, she pressed it to the pouting lips between her legs. Rubbing its cool length backward and forward in the opening of her wet labia, she sighed and gently rolled her neck. Beneath the shaft of ridged plastic, her sex swelled with readiness. With every touch, her clitoris throbbed for attention.

She swivelled the base and the vibrator struck up a

quiet hum. Raising herself up from her heels, Julia positioned the smooth, tapered tip beneath the triangle of her pubic hair. She saw her labia, heavy with dew, open and reaching for the toy. Slowly, she lowered herself on to it.

The hum reverberated deep within her body as her flesh encased its synthetic joy. Julia didn't own a vibrator, but now she realised why Marianne was so attached to her 'friend'. The pleasure was easy and mindlessly fulfilling. Julia settled back on her heels, turned the base to increase the vibrations, and began to slowly ease the rod in and out, in and out.

'This is incredible.'

Her heart missed a beat at the strangled sound of Steve's voice. He almost seemed in pain, unsure of where to look, overwhelmed by the situation being played out for him. As she resumed the movement between her legs, she watched his eyes dance uncertainly from her swollen nipples to her gaping pussy, to her hand and back up to her flushed face.

'You look so beautiful. How do you feel? Please ... please tell me,' he begged.

'I feel ... fantastic.' She pushed her knees further apart and arched the middle of her back, pushing her breasts towards him as she eased the vibrations deeper inside her. 'But I wish it was you. I wish it was your hand on my body.' To emphasise her point, she cupped her breast with her free hand, gently squeezing as she cradled its weight. 'I wish it was your body, inside mine.'

She pushed the rod, now lubricated with her juices, even deeper inside her yearning pussy. A deep, grumbling moan in her throat echoed the sound shuddering at her fingertips. Her head fell back, exposing the length of pale throat she longed to be covered with his kisses. Desperation overtook her and she increased the tempo of her wrist, thrusting harder and quicker, pushing more remorselessly, needing to come.

She pushed herself into a frenzy; fucked herself to the very brink of pleasure. Pulling the rod from inside her, she twisted the base until the hum turned into a scream of effort, and stood it up on the bed. She pressed its length up against her weeping sex, its smooth helmet hard against the deep ache of her clitoris. Almost immediately, her limbs began to jerk, muscles twitching in and out of spasm as pleasure raced around her body from the screaming centre of her clitoris. Julia resisted the urge to fling the vibrator away and escape the overwhelming rush; she forced herself to press its unyielding hardness further into her flesh, imprinting its ridges into her tender skin. As her climax took control of her senses, she was barely aware of Steve moving closer to her. And then, like so many times before, she was aware of only him, of his fingertips hesitantly closing over her trembling wrist, of his pale eyes wide with gratitude and awe at what he'd seen.

Gripped as much by his gaze as by the power of her orgasm, she was still for an eternity. They stared at each other, communicating soundlessly as they always used to, knowing each other's thoughts. Slowly, their eyes drifted, and they took in each other's bodies. Julia hadn't realised that Steve had been masturbating. He obviously hadn't finished, because his long, thick cock stood up proudly from his lap. Julia couldn't help herself; she gasped with admiration.

'What is it?' he asked, following her line of sight, his hand jumping away from her arm as if her skin had burnt him.

She turned the vibrator off. 'Nothing.' She smiled. 'It's just that ... well, Marianne has this theory about intelligent men ... that they're not very well equipped. You're obviously the exception.'

'You think I'm intelligent?' Steve fumbled with himself, struggling to hide his erection back inside his dark jeans. 'The truth is, I'm stupid,' he spat. 'Unbelievably stupid. I've never met anyone as stupid as I am.'

Julia laughed uncertainly. 'What on earth do you mean?'

Fidgeting uncomfortably, he stared down at his hands. 'I thought I had everything all worked out. I waited and waited for everything to be perfect.' He looked up. 'I waited so long, I missed my chance.' Tentatively, as if his body was aching from overexertion, he stood up.

'Where are you going?' Already, Julia's pleasure was fading and being replaced by panic. A vibrator was all very well, but now she wanted the real thing. She wanted her old friend, the intense, serious adolescent who had turned into an intense, serious and beautiful man.

But he was already at the door. 'Good night, Julia.'

'Don't go, Steve. Please.' He turned the door handle. 'You can't go. You haven't told me about the last goal on your list. You said you'd tell me what it was.'

'It doesn't matter any more,' he muttered, as he walked out.

Lies

'Marianne. Get up. Now.'

Julia flung the curtains open as Marianne groaned her way into consciousness. 'What time is it?'

'Time to go. Come on, get up.'

Marianne extricated herself from Brian's heavy arms and tried to sit up. She clutched her forehead, squinting as she retrieved her watch from the bedside table. 'Five o'clock.' She looked accusingly at Julia. 'Five o'clock. What the fuck are you doing, waking me up at five o'clock in the morning?' Her speech was slurred but she was definitely more awake than before.

Julia stalked across the room to the other window and flung those curtains open, too. 'I've got lunch with David's parents today. If we leave now I can still make it.'

'What?' Marianne's pretty face creased in sleepy confusion.

'Come on,' Julia urged. 'Let's go.'

Marianne jerked her blonde head towards her sleeping partner. 'And leave him? You must be joking.'

Brian was lovely. His thickset body was sprawled, stomach down, across the bed. His black skin shone in the morning sun. But Julia couldn't bear another moment in the castle, even for her friend's sake. It had taken enormous self-restraint, like a child on Christmas morning, to stop her from waking Marianne in the middle of the night. 'Look, I'm sorry. Get his phone number.'

Marianne raised an infuriated, finely plucked eyebrow. 'What's the hurry? What's going on?'

'Nothing. I just have to go. Please, Marianne. I have to get out of here. Now.'

For an hour, Marianne sat in a silence that was a third annoyance, a third hangover and a third tiredness. Julia had to navigate and drive, which was difficult, and she took a couple of wrong turnings which Marianne acknowledged with a tut or a grunt. When they eventually found the motorway, her passenger promptly fell asleep. Several hours later, still what Marianne would class early morning, Julia pulled into a service station for breakfast. Her friend woke as the engine went quiet.

'So,' Marianne snapped, after a plate of sausage, bacon and eggs and a mug of coffee had brought her back into the day. 'Are you going to tell me what's going on?'

Julia stared blankly at the crumbs on her plate, wondering where to begin. She wasn't quite sure what was going on, herself. Absent-mindedly, she twirled her engagement ring round and round on her finger and sighed heavily.

'Jules?'

She reached for her coffee but her hand was so unsteady she had to put the mug straight down again.

'Julia?' Marianne held on to Julia's wrist. 'You're shaking. What's the matter?' Her mouth, which had been set hard with resentment at being woken so early, began to soften with concern. 'God, you look awful. What's going on?'

'I don't know.' Julia lifted her shoulders, trying to ease her aching neck. 'I've no idea what's going on.'

Still holding on to Julia's hand, Marianne leant across the table. 'Why don't you start with why we had to run away in the middle of the night. I was really looking forward to a lie-in, you know. With Brian.'

Julia blinked guiltily. 'Yes . . . I'm sorry about that.'

'Don't be sorry. Just tell me there was a good reason.'

Julia's brow twitched with confusion. 'It's Steve. I really couldn't face seeing him this morning.'

Marianne's eyes widened as she drew conclusions. 'Why?' she breathed, enthralled. 'What did he do?'

'Nothing.' Julia looked around the café at the faceless travellers, pausing on their way to God knows where. She loved watching people; airports were her favourite. Thousands of strangers passing each other on their way to different destinations, sharing fleeting moments of each other's lives.

'What do you mean, nothing?' Marianne squeezed Julia's fingers in her own. There was a familiar glint in her eye. 'You two seemed to be getting on pretty well down at the lake. I saw you.' She winked. 'Shocking – what was going on underneath that towel.'

Julia smiled fondly at the remembrance. 'If only he hadn't been called to the phone.'

'Didn't you see him later?'

'Oh, yes. He came to my room. Said he had something to tell me.' She slid her fingers out of Marianne's. Using both hands, she took a sip of her coffee. 'I think he was going to tell me what the last goal on his list was.'

'The one he got in a temper about at dinner?'

Julia nodded.

'And? What was the big secret?'

'I still don't know.' Julia sniffed. 'The conversation got side-tracked.' Her eyes glazed and she shook her head in disbelief. 'It was the most bizarre evening.'

'Oh, get on with it,' Marianne huffed, making the table wobble as she bounced back in her seat. 'What happened?'

Julia told her. Some of the details were hazy, blurred by the wine she had drunk that night and the incredible intensity of the situation. But she managed to convey her sense of desperation, the way Steve had aroused her and then abandoned her, the way he'd looked at her, the things he'd said. When she'd finished sharing every second, the way that only best friends do, she sat back and waited for the verdict.

Marianne nodded sagely. 'So that's why he got so angry with me. It all makes sense now.'

'It does?'

'Don't you see? His final goal was something to do with you. When he found out you were getting married, it ruined his plan to have his wicked way with you.' Marianne pressed her palms to her cheeks. 'Oh, shit. I'm so sorry. This is all my fault, isn't it?'

'Huh?'

'If I hadn't left that note for you, he'd have never known about David. You could have had a final fling to remember.'

'I don't think I'll ever forget it, even though I did end up sleeping with your "little friend". Who isn't so little. And who I'm keeping, by the way.'

'What?' Marianne's mouth gaped in mock horror.

'I think it's the least you can do, after spoiling my chances with Steve.'

'He must have the willpower of a saint,' Marianne tutted. 'I've never known impending nuptials to get in the way of lust before.'

'I told you Steve was different.'

'He's different, all right.' She stared off into the distance for a moment, a sly smile playing at her lips. Julia could tell she approved of the way Steve had altered since the sixth form. Suddenly, she blinked herself back to reality. 'And what about David?'

'What about him?'

'First Leon Sparrow, then Steve. You're frighteningly

willing to be unfaithful, considering you're two weeks away from swapping wedding rings.' She leant right forward, staring deep into Julia's eyes. 'You can't tell me now that you're not having doubts.'

'I love David,' Julia murmured, averting her eyes. 'He's everything I ever wanted in a man. I'm just having the usual nerves, like everyone else. I just want to be sure I'm doing the right thing.' She slapped her hands down on to the coffee-stained table. 'And this weekend has convinced me. That's why I had to get out of the castle. I can't wait to see David again. He'll be so pleased if I make it to lunch.'

Marianne gave Julia a look that said she didn't believe a word of it.

Julia was exhausted by the time she arrived in Oxford. The Beetle sounded tired too, chugging noisily in protest at too many miles done in too few days. Julia wound the window right down as she followed the path through suburbia to the house where David had grown up, on the outskirts of the city. The breeze woke her slightly, but not enough. It would be more of a struggle than usual to make polite lunchtime conversation over the Sunday roast.

She pulled in to the wide gravel driveway and looked up at the mock-Tudor semi. The Tudors certainly would have mocked, had they seen the symmetrical rows of houses on the quiet, middle-class estate, with their neatly manicured gardens and their precisely trimmed hedges. So this is it, Julia thought, plastering a sweet smile on her face. This is what Sunday lunches are going to be like with David. Lucky he was worth it.

As she stood on the doorstep, she took a deep breath. Putting her shoulders back, she raised her chin, adjusted her smile, and prayed that David hadn't changed his plans and stayed at home.

'Julia! How lovely to see you! We weren't expecting you, but what a splendid surprise...'

Julia dutifully kissed her future mother-in-law on her perfectly powdered cheeks, holding her breath to avoid being swamped by her floral perfume. 'Hope you don't mind my just turning up, Yvonne.'

'Not at all, dear. We were very sad when David said you couldn't come. Look, James, look who it is.'

James emerged from the living room, a caricature of late middle-age, upper-middle-class man with his Pringle sweater, slippers and pipe. 'Julia! So pleased you could make it.'

'Julia?' David followed his father out into the hall, a look of sweet incredulity on his face. 'I thought you weren't coming back until tonight?'

'I wasn't.' Julia smiled. She reached up for him and kissed him on the lips. 'But I missed you too much.'

The in-laws cooed appreciatively and shuffled off into the kitchen, mumbling about 'leaving the lovebirds in peace'.

'How was the reunion?'

Julia curled her lip. 'Oh, terribly boring. You know what these things are like. I couldn't wait to get away.'

David shook his head with pleased disbelief. 'I'm so glad you made it.' He kissed her forehead. 'Mum will be impressed,' he whispered gratefully. Pulling away, his eyes dropped over her body. 'You look wonderful. I haven't seen that dress before.'

The dress she'd bought for the reunion. The dress she'd taken off for Steve. The dress she'd had to put back on that morning, since she'd never got round to bringing her overnight bag in from the car. 'No.' She smiled. 'I've only just bought it.'

'You look amazing.'

'I'm glad you like it.'

James poked his head tentatively into the hall, like a

tortoise checking whether spring had arrived. 'Dinner is served.'

The meal was tasty but predictable: tender chicken, crispy roast potatoes, slightly overdone sprouts and carrots and restrained conversation. Yvonne fawned over David, asking whether he was eating properly, since she'd seen him on television the night before and he'd looked ever so slim. James concentrated on his meal, occasionally mumbling in agreement when prompted by his wife. Julia joined in as much as she could, the dutiful daughter-in-law, a model of polite deference. But beneath the muted exterior she simmered violently. There was a private slide show going on inside her head. Steve's arms around her. His finger in her mouth. Between her labia. His eyes on her naked breasts. All of a sudden, realising that they'd never kissed, she boiled over.

'Isn't that your phone, David?'

The clinking of cutlery stopped as everyone paused to listen. 'I can't hear anything,' David said.

'I'm sure I can hear your phone. Where is it?'

'In my jacket. In the hall.'

'I'll go and check.' Heart pounding furiously, Julia got up from the table. 'Excuse me.'

Out in the cool hallway, she glanced at herself in the long mirror. In the light streaming from the frosted glass window, her hair seemed to be on fire, glowing red. She ran her hands over her breasts, squeezing them together until a deep cleavage formed in the low V-neck. One hand eased downward to her pussy, bare beneath her dress, and as she ached for contact a flush spread across her pale neck.

'David!' she called. 'It's your agent on the phone.'

He stumbled into the hall, anxiety on his face. 'Is it about the commercial? Did I get it?'

'Shh.' She pressed a finger to his lips. Delving into the

pocket of his jacket, she pulled out his mobile phone. She unflipped the mouthpiece and put it to his ear.

His majestic brow furrowed with bewilderment. 'What's going on?' he whispered, his lips moving against her fingers.

'You'll get a better reception outside,' she said loudly. 'Go out into the garden,' she added in a whisper. 'Act like you're on the phone,' she urged, turning his shoulders and giving him a push towards the living room. She followed him, a hand on his back, guiding him through the archway to the dining room and out of the French windows. 'Bit crackly indoors,' Julia said sweetly in explanation as they passed David's parents. 'Carry on eating,' she insisted. 'It's his agent. He could be quite a while.'

Outside, the sudden heat of the sun brought goose-bumps rippling over Julia's skin. Pulling David by the elbow, she walked him down to the bottom of the garden and behind the small shed. Out of sight of the house, she took the phone away from his ear.

'You can stop acting now. Although, you weren't doing it very well.'

'What's going on, Julia?'

'I want you.'

'Sorry?'

'I want you, now.' She grabbed his sculpted chin and pressed her lips to his. 'On your knees,' she commanded.

'What?'

'You heard.' She pressed her hands to his shoulders and pushed him to the ground. Crouching, she put the phone down on the grass and hooked her fingers beneath the waistband of David's trousers.

'Julia? What are you doing?'

She smiled sadistically, delighting in the confusion flickering across David's face. 'Wait and see.'

'Julia?'

She flicked at his belt. Pulling the strip of leather from

the loops of his trousers, she moved around behind David's back. Kneeling, she pulled his hands together behind him, wrapped the belt around his wrists several times and buckled it tight. David didn't protest. He just kept repeating her name, over and over again, with a question mark in his voice.

'David,' she soothed, 'shut up.' She admired his hands, his fingers long and thick and resolutely masculine; it was exciting to see his strength bound up. She lightly tickled his short, strong neck, delighting in the velvety feel of the close-cropped golden hairs at his nape. With gentle strokes of her fingertips, she lulled him into a false sense of security before nipping his skin between her teeth, leaving a vicious crimson patch on his tanned neck. He flinched and sharply drew in his breath as Julia stood up. Moving in front of him, she quickly unbuttoned his shirt, lifting it from his broad shoulders and pushing it down his arms where it perched on his back like the white rumple of a broken sail. As she bent over him she saw him look down the front of her dress, and his smooth pectoral muscles twitched as his arms involuntarily reached out for her, forgetting he was restrained. He let out a huff of disappointment; like a wisp of smoke curling in the warm air, the noise twisted until it became something different, a gurgled sound of disbelief.

Julia had lifted the skirt of her dress, exposing the tops of her stockings and her suspenders: a taut frame around her naked sex. Delighted by his obvious shock at finding her knickerless, she gathered the material up higher, holding it in one hand while the other dropped into his line of sight. Parting her legs, she rubbed her middle finger between her throbbing, swollen labia, making David gasp.

Watching desire flicker in his lips and eyes, she slowly pushed her finger inside herself. Gently, relishing his agony, she moved in and out of her wet vagina. Another finger joined the first, probing the succulence of flesh beneath the hairs clasping damply at her hand. Her thumb began to tease her emerging clitoris and she moaned quietly.

David's head rolled as if he was intoxicated by the scent of sex wafting towards him on the early autumn breeze. He sighed in anguish as he watched her fingers sliding in and out of her pussy, and he tried to shuffle on his knees towards her, desperate for contact with her. Sensing his urgency, she stopped him, grabbing his shoulder and pushed her wet fingers into his open mouth. He rolled his tongue around them, murmuring approval at the taste of her arousal, whimpering as she took her hand away and slid it around the back of his neck. With a firm, demanding push, she brought his face towards her.

He breathed deeply, inhaling her musk, if as she was the drug that fed his craving. He pressed his mouth to the lips of her sex and lapped in her warm cleft with his strong tongue. His neck muscles strained beneath Julia's hand as he poked inside her, pushing as far as he could into her body, trying, it seemed, to lick at her soul. Her thighs began to quiver as his nose pressed against her clitoris, but her voice never faltered as she told him what to do.

She knew exactly what she wanted and she commanded him precisely. Following her instructions, he swirled and pressed with his tongue, teasing all over the bundle of raw nerve endings. He nipped at her delicately and sucked her between his wide lips, making her struggle for air. Her clitoris radiated waves of intense pleasure throughout her body. As her orgasm approached, the images of Steve replayed in her mind, and she began to silently mouth his name. Suddenly, it was him kneeling at her feet, his mouth sucking, his tongue lapping, his teeth nibbling. It was Steve pleasuring her, and she wanted more. More intensity. More pleasure. She wanted Steve to fill the chasm he'd left in her.

She pushed David away and he fell back on his heels. Falling on to one hip, he unfolded his feet from underneath him and shuffled backward on his buttocks until he leant against the shed. Julia could see from the shuddering in his biceps that he was struggling to free himself from his bindings. Before he could do so she pounced, unzipped his erection and straddled his cock. Sheathing his hard flesh within her soft flesh, she lowered her hips on to his.

Closing her eyes, she concentrated on Steve. Conjuring up the memory of his features, she filled her mind with him until she felt dizzy and had to press her palms against the rough wood of the shed to steady herself. As she fucked David, she felt Steve beneath her, and the sensation of her sex, stretched tightly around his erection, mingled with the delight of her clitoris rubbing on his hardness. Desperate for release from the frustration of last night, she pounded David with violent thrusts of her hips. Her breasts bounced; she threw back her head and pulled his mouth on to her throat. His breath was hot on her neck as he kissed her. His penis was hot as he throbbed, deep, deep inside her. With a series of rapid, juddering thrusts, she jerked to climax. David's body twitched beneath hers, and his unintelligible words of agreement grumbled into her shoulder as his head fell with relief. Opening her eyes, Julia shrugged him away.

'Julia? David?' A shrill voice sang out from the house.

Julia stood up and hurriedly smoothed her dress down. Her pussy clenched with sudden emptiness. She retrieved her fake, sickly smile and peered around the corner of the shed. 'We'll be in in a minute, Yvonne.'

Yvonne waved her napkin. 'Jolly good. Only I don't want the apple crumble to burn.' She stepped out of the French windows, craning her neck towards Julia. 'Is David still on the phone? Is everything all right?'

'Everything's fine,' Julia said, silently urging her back inside the house. 'David's just coming.'

Ignoring David's snort of amusement at her double entendre, Julia waited until Yvonne had gone back inside before she untied him. Kneeling by his side with her face close to his, she felt him watching her.

'What was that all about?' David flexed his wrists as they were freed. He draped an arm across her waist, preventing her from standing up. 'Julia?'

She glanced guiltily at him. 'I missed you.'

'We've only been apart a couple of days.'

'So? Can't a girl miss her fiancé?'

'We're apart almost every week, Julia. You've never missed me quite so . . . forcefully, before.'

'Didn't you like it?'

Lifting his hand, he smoothed her tousled hair back into its sleek bob. 'I loved it. You just shocked me, that's all. First, you turn up here when I wasn't expecting you, then . . . this, behind my father's shed. But I'm not complaining.'

'Should hope not.' She smiled weakly.

'It's ever so flattering when the woman you love wants you so desperately. Perhaps you should go to school reunions more often, if this is the effect they have.' Julia dropped her head; David gently lifted her chin again. 'I hardly know you, do I?'

She shrank away from his touch. 'What do you mean?'

'I'm still finding out who you are. You're still surprising me.'

Julia scrambled to her feet, her cheeks heating up. 'I often surprise myself.'

'That's what I love about you – your spontaneity. Never knowing what you're going to do next.' David stood up, refastening his shirt and hiding his fading erection. 'I just hope you carry on surprising me when we're married.'

'Oh, I think you can count on that.' Wincing, she bent

down to pick up the mobile phone. As she handed it to David, she looked into his eyes for a moment. They were bright and clear, and completely oblivious of the turmoil raging in her guts. She wanted to be spontaneous then, to tell him that she'd been wishing he was someone else, to try and unravel her confusion. But he held her close and stroked her hair, then gently broke the news that he was going to be filming on location in Yorkshire for the next week.

She smiled, and said she would miss him.

Strangers on a Train

Monday morning, five o'clock, and Julia was setting off again on another long journey. David had left even earlier to get to Yorkshire for his nine o'clock call. He would be tired today; they had hardly slept at all: David aroused by Julia's forcefulness behind the garden shed; Julia restless for other, private reasons.

When David left her flat that morning, she was relieved. She needed space and time to think. There would be plenty of both on the train, she thought, as the taxi chugged throatily towards Euston through streets that were never empty, even at that hour. The morning train got into Glasgow at one; by then, she vowed, she would have her mind in order.

In the station concourse, she deliberately avoided the newsagent's and headed straight for the platform after buying her ticket. No matter what was happening in the outside world today, she didn't have time for it. She would use every moment of the long hours ahead to sort out her life. For once she would think things through. For once she wouldn't act on impulse.

Although it was impulse that had got her on this train, she admitted to herself, as she strode down the platform.

It was impulse that had made her leave a message on George's answerphone at the *Chronicle*, a message in a voice hoarse with imaginary illness. Her performance would have made David proud, but it had left Julia feeling decidedly uneasy. It was the first time she had ever rung in sick.

Still, George would cope. He could get another photographer to deal with whatever actor, model or musician she was due to shoot today. She had more important things to handle. Like her marriage and whether she still wanted it.

Julia found an unreserved window seat and threw her light bag up into the rack above. Settling down, she spread her fingers out on the table in front of her and stared at her ring. There would be another ring there, in less than two weeks' time. A bond that would link her for ever to David. Like strands of yarn, their lives would twist together until they formed a whole, a rope that would bind them inextricably.

The carriage began to fill up. Turning away from the bustle, attempting to look undisturbable in the hope that it would deter anyone from filling the other empty seats around the table, Julia stared vacantly out of the window.

Marriage. Marriage. Marriage. A strange word, if you said it often enough. A strange concept, promising yourself to one man. She had never considered it before David but somehow, with him, it seemed to make sense. He was all the best bits of her previous boyfriends, neatly assembled in one package. Like a multi-vitamin, he had the right amounts of everything she needed. He was good-looking, bright, successful, kind, gentle and caring. The sex was good too, varying between loving and lustful. She trusted David and he adored her. So why did she feel a fist of dread, clenching in her guts?

She put her cold hands over her face and closed her eyes. In the darkness Steve appeared, controlling her thoughts as he had done since the moment she'd seen him on Saturday. Since before then, if she was honest. His hand-written note on her reunion invitation had sent shivers scrambling across her scalp, because fragments of Steve had been filtering into her fantasies for years. There were moments she had shared with him, back when they had been in the sixth form together, that had haunted her adult life. Nothing sexual had ever happened between them then, and yet, years later, she would catch her breath as she recognised a detail of him in another man. On the brink of adulthood, on the brink of life in the real world, they had spent endless hours talking. Julia had felt so close to Steve and her unanswered letters had kept her interest far keener than if she'd seen him every week. She had never forgotten their last day together, lying on the school lawn, when he'd nearly kissed her. Like the one that got away, Steve had ingrained himself in her memory, teasing her with what might have been.

Julia sighed and pressed her eyebrows with her fingertips until she felt an ache of tension. Would she have been so confused if Steve hadn't metamorphosed into such a handsome man? Why was she heading off to Scotland to see him? What would she say to him? Would he be pleased to see her? Would he even be there? She screwed up her eyes, wincing at the noise of too many questions colliding in her brain.

'Is anyone sitting here?'

Another question. Looking up, she gave the long-haired student a disdainful glare. 'What does it look like?'

'Just being polite.' He struggled to squeeze his bulging rucksack into the luggage rack before sitting down opposite Julia. Desperate to return to her thoughts, she hid her face back in her fingers.

'Are you all right?'

She opened her hands again, just enough to enable her

to peer out at him. 'I'm fine. I just want a bit of peace and quiet.' She turned around, searching the carriage for an alternative empty seat, but there wasn't one. She sighed heavily, and a little too loudly.

'Well, I think you're out of luck on the peace and quiet front.' He smirked, jerking his head towards the sound of whining children in the row behind them. 'Summer holidays,' he explained, rolling his eyes. 'Hell, aren't they?'

Julia slumped in her chair. She'd been on trains a hundred times before and no one had ever spoken to her. Why now? Why today? She wished she'd gone first class.

'My name's Richard.' He held out his hand. Julia folded her arms. Richard lifted his faded blue T-shirt to his nose. 'Do I smell? I had a shower last week. Or was it the week before?' He grinned cheekily.

Julia clenched her teeth and gave him a withering stare. She wasn't in the mood for this. 'Look, I really don't want to talk.'

'Why not?'

Amazed at his persistence, her mouth gaped. 'I beg your pardon?'

'Why won't you talk to me?' He ran his fingers through his shoulder-length, wavy black hair. 'I'm friendly, I'm highly intelligent, and we've a long journey ahead of us.' He tutted sadly, shaking his head. 'Honestly, we British are so repressed. If only we could talk to each other more, we could learn so much about each other. Instead, we wrap ourselves up in our own selfish lives, never daring to look up in case someone catches our eye, never daring to speak up or speak out. We don't want to know; we can't be bothered. No wonder our nation's full of narrow-minded intolerants. No one cares about anyone else. Everyone's so bloody anally retentive.'

Julia sat motionless for a minute, blinking with shock

at his diatribe. A typical university student, she thought, convinced he had the world all sussed out, offended by the constraints of a society he would soon have to live in. She clasped her hands on the table and leant towards him. She spoke slowly. 'Look, I'm neither narrow-minded nor intolerant. And my anus is no more retentive than yours. But I have no interest in you, or anything you might have to say. You'll grow up, one day soon, and you'll get a job, and you'll realise that you can't go around talking to strangers. If you want a debate on the shortfalls of modern society, I suggest you go and find another student to sit with – someone who isn't going to find you unbearably irritating. I make no apology for the fact that I'm wrapped up in my own life. My life's a mess. I need to think. So if you'll kindly keep your half-baked, immature opinions to yourself . . .'

Julia ran out of steam. Sitting back, she looked determinedly out of the window at the changing view. Her heart raced with exhilaration and she had to bite her lip to stop herself from smiling.

He didn't speak again, but he kept looking at her, which was almost as infuriating. Throwing surreptitious glances at her every few seconds over the top of his folded newspaper, he continued to interrupt her thoughts. Julia left it for as long as she could but it was driving her mad. She waited until she felt his attention on her again. Preparing herself for another confrontation, she glanced up to meet his eyes.

He held her gaze for a split second before guiltily returning to his newspaper. Almost immediately, he looked up again, and then it was Julia's turn to flinch away. But not before she had recognised the slight smile in his dark-brown eyes, understood the hint of nervous excitement in his wide mouth. She had aroused him with her outburst and now, like an itch he had been told not to scratch, he couldn't resist another look, and then another.

Usually, Julia would have been flattered as he stole fleeting glimpses of her from behind the shield of his paper. In different circumstances, she would have applauded her choice of outfit: a silky, pale-green T-shirt that matched her eyes and clung to her curves; a rich, dark-brown A-line skirt that rode halfway up her thighs when she sat down; and her favourite, calf-length brown boots. After all, he was attractive, with his olive skin and youthful arrogance. But today his admiration was just another distraction she didn't need. She had to concentrate and it was impossible with him ogling her.

She caught him at it again. 'Will you please stop it?' she hissed.

'Stop what?' His dark eyebrows lifted innocently. As Julia glared at him, he slowly closed his newspaper and put it down. There was laughter in his eyes as his attention dropped down her neck, lingering over her breasts before lifting again. He folded his arms, his lips expanding into a smirk. 'Stop what, exactly?'

Julia gasped at his audacity.

'Coffee, tea. Coffee, tea.'

She looked up thankfully as the waiter approached. 'Mineral water, please.' Her voice was unsteady.

The waiter handed her a plastic cup. Twisting the cap off the bottle, he leant over to pass it to Julia. At that moment the train juddered clumsily and a stream of icy water gushed over Julia's top. She grasped the edge of the table as the coldness seeped through to her skin.

'Oh, madam, I'm so sorry,' he flustered, grabbing a handful of napkins.

'It's all right,' Julia grumbled. She looked up at the sound of snorting. 'What are you laughing at?' she snapped at Richard. 'What's so funny?'

'Oh, nothing.' Struggling to control his sniggering, his eyes flickered suggestively.

Julia followed his line of sight. Her T-shirt was soaked. The silky fabric was stuck to her breasts, outlining her shape and clinging to her erect nipples, and Richard wasn't bothering to disguise his delight.

Julia felt her cheeks heating in humiliation. Avoiding his unashamed leering, she dabbed at the spill with a serviette.

'Here.' He reached over and took a napkin from the pile. 'Let me help.'

Jumping to her feet, Julia grabbed the bottle, threw the remaining water into his lap, and flounced off down the carriage.

She slammed the toilet door and looked aghast at her reflection in the mirror. Her face and neck were flushed and her chest was heaving with anger beneath her clinging top.

'The little creep,' she muttered, furious that Richard's staring had been rewarded with his own personal wet T-shirt competition. What incredible confidence, she thought, for someone so young. Would he really have touched her, if she hadn't stood up? Despite herself, the idea excited her. Wondering how she would have reacted, she raised her hand and stroked the outline of her areola beneath the wetness. Her sex suddenly clenched.

There was a knock at the door which made her jump. Covering her wet chest with her forearm, she tentatively opened it. It was Richard, grinning sheepishly.

'You again,' she hissed. 'Come to snigger?'

He rested one hand on the door frame. 'Don't think I'm in much of a position to snigger, do you?'

She looked down at the damp patch across the groin of his baggy chinos. 'Are you expecting an apology? You deserved that, the way you were behaving.'

'You were enjoying it.'

'Sorry?'

'Go on, admit it. It turned you on, me leering at you.'

Julia slowly shook her head, praying her eyes didn't betray her rapidly mounting arousal. 'I deal with arseholes every day, but I have never met anyone with an ego like yours.'

'Thank you.'

'Believe me, it wasn't a compliment. You're obnoxious, cocky, rude –'

'But you want me.' Richard's eyes were glinting knowingly. 'Go on, admit it.'

His arrogance was smothering and it made Julia catch her breath. Her lips parted wordlessly. She hung motionless in the darkness of his eyes.

'You want me.' He took a step towards her. 'You're wondering what it would feel like to have my hands on your body.' Moving closer, he shut the toilet door behind him and relocked it. Julia tried to edge away from him but there was only room for one pace backward before she reached the wall. 'You're wondering whether I'm a good fuck.'

Bewildered, Julia blinked several times. 'How . . . how old are you?'

'Twenty-one today. It's my birthday.'

Julia took a long, slow deep breath and allowed him a faint smile. 'Congratulations.'

Richard put a hand on the wall, just by her head. 'Would you like to help me make this a birthday to remember?'

She raised her chin defiantly. 'No,' she lied, taking a gamble that he would play along with her.

He did. With his other hand he pushed her shoulder, stopping her as she made a half-hearted move to the door. 'I don't believe you.' His fingers slid quickly down to her breast. As if he was trying to wring the water from her T-shirt, he squeezed her, hard. 'If you don't want me, tell me to stop.'

He was exactly the same height as Julia. She stared into his eyes, meeting his challenge. 'Stop.' Her whisper was barely audible.

'That wasn't very convincing.'

Julia arched her back slightly, pushing her breast further into his grasp. Her eyelids half closed as he mauled at her flesh. 'Stop it, please.'

He shook his head. 'Still don't believe you.'

'Stop.' She grabbed his wrist tightly. For a second, the first hint of uncertainty flickered in his eyes. Julia waited, teasing him. Then, watching his expression change back to pure, confident lust, she pushed his hand downward.

A strangulated groan got stuck in the back of his throat. His breathing grew louder as his warm hand slid up her bare thigh beneath her skirt. Julia opened her legs at the urgent pressing of his fingertips. And then he was there, all four fingers moulded to her softly throbbing pussy.

'Stop,' she gasped, her eyes smiling. Ignoring her, he stroked backward and forward over her sex, stimulating her beneath the white cotton of her underwear. 'Don't,' she sighed breathlessly. 'I don't want you.'

'Of course you don't.' He eased a finger beneath the elastic of her knickers. 'That's why you're so wet.'

Julia shuddered as his long finger slipped easily inside her. 'I was thinking about my boyfriend, not you,' she insisted.

'Liar.' Pulling his finger out from the warmth of her sex, he grabbed the hem of her T-shirt. 'We'd better get this off, before you catch a chill.' He peeled off her damp top and threw it to the floor. His T-shirt was next.

Julia ran her hands over his dark, hairless chest, eyeing his young body appreciatively. Roughly, he lifted her chin, bringing her eyes back up to his. 'Still thinking about your boyfriend?'

'Yes.'

'Still don't want me?'

'No.'

'Don't want me to do this?' He flicked at the catch of her bra nestling in her cleavage. Pushing the lacy white cups away, he pinched her engorged nipples between his fingertips.

'Stop it.' Her voice was as shaky as her legs. This game was making her delirious.

One hand slid behind her back, over her buttock, and hooked beneath her thigh. He lifted her leg up until she could hook her foot over the ledge surrounding the washbasin. Delving between her open thighs, he pulled her knickers aside. With his other hand he unzipped his flies. Shuffling closer, he bent his knees and brought the head of his penis against her open labia. 'Push me away,' he invited. 'Push me away, now, and I'll go back to my seat and not look or talk to you again.' His breath was quick and hot on her face. 'Admit you want me, and I'll fill you up.' His voice dropped to a low, evil whisper. 'I'll fill your tight, wet pussy with my cock.'

Julia reached around to his tiny, taut buttocks. Over his shoulder in the mirror, she could see his body. He was bent slightly in worship of her open legs, shoulders tensed, hips poised to thrust inside her. Spreading her fingers over his arse, she urged him closer. 'Shut up and fuck me.'

He didn't hesitate. They both groaned loudly as he plunged inside her, stretching her inner flesh with his length. Julia slid the heel of her boot along the washbasin ledge, spreading her legs wider for him as he jerked. The train was travelling at speed, and they had to strain every muscle to stop themselves from falling. Julia clenched him tightly within her pussy and held on with an arm around his narrow waist. He leant his body into hers, his hot chest rubbing over her bare breasts, his head dipping into the curve of her shoulder, his mouth attaching itself to her skin like a suction pad. As he pumped in and out, rubbing the hot, ridged walls of her sex, Julia eased a hand between their bodies. Watching her own face in the mirror, she felt his penis entering her for a moment before she searched out her aching clitoris.

Her eyelids drooped involuntarily as she stimulated the stiff little knob of pleasure, adding her deep sighs of delight to the violent sound of his fucking. Rubbing over its swollen, sensitive tip brought her climax looming and, as ecstasy took over her mind and body, it seemed like the narrow toilet walls were closing in on her. She shut her eyes to escape the claustrophobia and focused on the separate sensations linking up to form her orgasm. His fingers cruelly closed over her breast. His cock was pumping further and further inside her soft flesh. His teeth were on her neck. Her inner thighs were pulling as she spread them ever wider. Her fingers were rapidly teasing her clitoris into release.

Moaning desperately, he beat her to it, as David often did. But, unlike David, he didn't abandon her once he had sated his own lust. Keeping his throbbing penis inside her, he pushed her hand away and took over manipulating her pleasure. As Julia held on to his shoulder, he pinched, rubbed and circled her clitoris until she quickly joined him with a trembling orgasm. Legs jerking, she let out a satisfied sigh.

He lifted his eyes away from her sex, along with his hand, and put the finger he had used inside her open mouth. Stroking her tongue with his fingertip, allowing her to taste her musk, he smiled knowingly. 'Still thinking about your boyfriend?'

She closed her lips around his finger, and her hand around his wrist. Sucking on his skin as she pulled his hand away, she smiled back. 'I was, actually.'

'Feeling guilty? Wondering how you're going to tell him?'

'Why should I feel guilty?' She ran her fingers through his long, dark hair. 'You're just a meaningless fuck. There's no need to tell him anything.'

He carefully withdrew his penis. Without bothering to wipe himself – as David would have done – he zipped himself back inside his trousers. 'Well, I'm going to tell everyone I know about you.'

Her skin glowed in the heat of his lascivious smile. 'Oh? What will you say?'

Sliding his hand along the underside of her raised thigh, he moved closer again. 'I'll say that I met my dream woman on the train. And that I got a hard-on, just looking at her fantastic tits.' To emphasise his point, he cupped a breast in one hand. 'And I'll say that she was in a bad mood, and didn't want to talk, which made me more determined to have her. So I stared at her until she noticed. She pretended she was angry, but really she was getting wet.' Dipping his head, he paused to bite her lower lip. 'I followed her to the toilet and fucked her senseless.' His fingers trailed down her neck, hovering over the slope where her shoulder began. 'I'll never forget her. And I gave her a love bite, so she wouldn't forget me.'

'Oh, you didn't.' Julia looked beyond him to the mirror. Sure enough, there was a wide crimson mark on her pale skin.

'What's your boyfriend going to say when he sees that?'

'I don't know,' she muttered to herself. And, with a shudder that struck her cold, she realised she didn't care.

They sat side by side for the rest of the journey. Richard kept his hand on her thigh, and his eyes on the low V-neck of the deep-orange T-shirt she had changed into. Julia let him; it was his reward for clearing her mind. She had lied when she had called him a 'meaningless fuck'. His flirting, or rather the way she had welcomed it, had swayed her decision on David. She hadn't needed hours of deep, analytical thinking, after all; her body had provided her with the answer she was searching for. If she was so easily drawn astray after only weeks with David, what would she be like after they were married?

It wouldn't be fair on David and it wouldn't be right for her to go through with it. Feeling only a faint pang of remorse, she found herself working through the arrangements. Thank God they had opted for a simple, registry office affair, since it left little to cancel. David's sister was doing the catering and wouldn't have bought the food yet, so there wouldn't be any waste there. The guests would have to be told, but that was easy enough since there were only twenty of them. Their busy schedules didn't allow time for a honeymoon and, since her wedding dress was dark red, it would come in handy for parties. The only difficult part would be telling David. She didn't want to have to wait until Sunday, but he wasn't back from Yorkshire until then. Much as she would have liked to call him on his mobile and get it out of the way, she owed him a face-to-face explanation.

Relieved and exhausted from two nights without sleep, she dozed off on Richard's shoulder. At lunchtime, he woke her with a hungry squeeze of her breast. In the tradition of students, he was penniless, so Julia bought him a sandwich and they talked about their lives, revealing details they would have kept secret had they not been certain they would never see each other again. Richard told her about the girl he was in love with, who didn't want him; Julia told him about Steve. The early autumn sunshine poured generously through the train windows and Julia basked in its warmth and in the newfound freedom she felt. The repetitive sound of the train on its tracks echoed inside her like her own personal mantra, clearing her soul of confusion. By the time they arrived in Glasgow, there was only one thing on her mind. Steve.

A Very Different Reunion

*R*othco Developments was one of several businesses housed in the glass-fronted office block. Not exactly qualifying as a skyscraper, it nonetheless towered ostentatiously above the red brick buildings on either side. Going through the revolving doors into the marble hallway, Julia followed the stream of water gushing upward from the fountain and gazed up at the ceiling, five storeys above her. Beneath the clouds floating silently over the transparent roof, each floor was set out in a square around the central space, balconies overlooking the fountain below. If this had been a department store, which it could easily have been, there would have been Muzak; instead, there was a hush of concentration, the faint lap of water cascading over the marble fountain and the muffled tap-tap of keyboards. The sound of money being made.

Julia walked towards the lifts. These were glass too, and rose quietly and efficiently in one corner of the square. Looking at the list of companies, she found Rothco at the top. She got into the glass capsule behind a couple of immaculate young women and a pinstripe-suited man and, feeling decidedly underdressed, she pressed the button for the fifth floor.

At the second floor, the women got out. Left alone with the man, Julia looked steadfastly out at the sumptuous hallway below, avoiding his eyes. He was staring at her, she was sure. When he took a step towards her, she coughed with discomfort.

'Julia?'

She looked up.

'Oh my God! It is you!' He went to hug her then stopped, his hands hovering with shock. 'I can't believe it! I thought, as I got in the lift, I recognise that hair, but then I thought it couldn't be ... but it is! This is incredible!'

'Nick? Nick!'

'What the hell are you doing here?'

'I ... er ...' All of a sudden, she wasn't so sure. 'I came to see Steve.'

'Oh.' His brow furrowed slightly. 'Well, he isn't here. He's gone to Edinburgh for a meeting. Won't be back till later. Have you had lunch?'

'Yes.'

'Me too. You'll let me buy you a drink, though?'

'Of course!' She smiled.

The doors opened as they arrived at the fifth floor. Keeping one foot inside the lift, Nick leant his head out. 'I'm going out for a while,' he said to the perfect, blonde receptionist.

'What if Mr Roth calls?' she chirped worriedly.

'If Steve rings, tell him I had to go out. He can reach me on my mobile if it's urgent.' He stepped back in and the lift doors closed on the receptionist's confusion. As they began their descent, Nick and Julia looked at each other, silly grins on their faces.

Julia settled into a dark corner seat and watched Nick as he got the drinks. He had changed a lot. Not the dramatic metamorphosis that Steve had gone through: these were superficial changes. His hair, which had been so glossy and golden, was dull and needed cutting. The perfection of his jaw was covered with a growth of stubble. He had always looked so good in clothes, as if it was their privilege to be shown off on his athletic body; now, his suit seemed to be wearing him. He was uncomfortable in its smartness, his collar unbuttoned and his tie loosened as if he was trying to escape. The boy who used to have effortless good looks and limitless energy seemed dishevelled and tired. If she had passed him on the street, Julia would have barely recognised him, and as he sat down at the table she told him so.

'I'm shattered,' he admitted, taking a sip of his pint. 'I haven't had a day off in months.'

'Steve said you were busy. It's such a shame you couldn't come on Saturday.'

'Saturday?' he asked, his lips pausing on their way back to his glass. 'What was on Saturday?'

'The reunion,' Julia laughed. Nick looked blank. 'You know, the reunion at Steve's castle. Seven years to the day since we made those bloody plans at school.'

Nick's eyes narrowed. 'That was on Saturday?'

Julia nodded. 'Did you forget?'

'I was never invited.' Sitting back, he thoughtfully rubbed the back of his neck with his hand. 'I should have known there was something going on.'

Julia was puzzled. 'What do you mean?'

His eyes were so hard, they went straight through her. Scowling, he took his mobile phone out of his inside pocket and turned it off with a flourish. 'I hope he tries to call. I hope he needs some vital piece of information that only I would know.' The old, wicked grin began to lighten up his features. 'That would teach the sneaky bastard.'

'What's going on, Nick?'

He took a long swig of lager. 'Steve's up to his usual

tricks – that's what's going on. He sent me out to Spain on Saturday, to check out a hotel he's thinking of buying. Told me it was imperative I went this weekend. I couldn't understand why, but it's obvious now. He wanted me out of the way.'

Julia took a tentative sip of her beer. 'So ... you didn't know about the reunion?'

'Do you think I'd have missed it, if I had?'

'Well, I did think it strange you weren't there, to be honest. I was really disappointed when Steve said you'd volunteered to work.'

'You were?'

'Of course.' A slow, unstoppable smile lifted the corners of her mouth. 'I was looking forward to seeing you again.'

Nick returned her admiration. A suggestion of his old confidence glinted in his brown eyes. 'We used to be good together, didn't we?'

She laughed softly. 'That was a long time ago, Nick.'

'It still bothers Steve that we were an item. Drives him insane with jealousy, always did.'

'What, you and me? But we were so young.' Julia shook her head, bewildered by the thought that their teenage affair could still arouse envy in Steve.

'What is it they say – first love never dies? Steve had a terrible crush on you when we were in the sixth form. We'd all been best mates since primary school, then all of a sudden you decided to grow breasts and everything changed. He's never got over the thought that you and I lost our virginity together.' One half of his wide mouth smiled fondly. 'Remember it, Jules? My parents were away, you came over ...'

Julia did remember it, but her mind had already moved on from that night of fumbled passion. 'Are you trying to tell me that Steve didn't invite you on Saturday, because of your being my boyfriend while we were at school?' She huffed with disbelief. 'That's ridiculous. It was over seven years ago. I haven't seen either of you since.'

'I'm telling you, he's never forgiven me for going out with you. How else would you explain the way he works me like a dog? Or the way he made sure I wasn't around at the weekend? What other reason could he possibly have for not inviting me to the reunion? It was all a wicked ploy. With me in Spain, he could finally fulfil his adolescent fantasies and get one-up on me at the same time.'

Julia slowly shook her head. That didn't sound like the sensitive, intense, deep-thinking Steve she knew. Certainly, the rivalry between he and Nick had been obvious at school, but it was inconceivable that someone as successful as Steve could carry a burning flame of envy into adulthood. 'I don't know, Nick. Steve might have been jealous of you at eighteen but we're all older now. Steve's a good-looking guy with his own company. He must have women falling at his feet.' She took a thoughtful sip of lager. 'Besides, if he was so fond of me, how come he never replied to any of my letters? I never expected you to keep in touch, but Steve and I were very close.'

Nick shrugged. 'All I know is, whenever he has too much to drink, he gets morose and talks about how wonderful you were. Every time he meets a woman, he splits up with her because she doesn't measure up to you. There's no doubt in my mind: he wanted me out of the way so he could complete his precious list.' Nick leant across the table conspiratorially. 'That's another thing he goes on about when he's drunk. Do you know what the last goal on his list is?'

'No. He wouldn't tell me.' Julia raised her eyebrows, urging him on.

'It's you.'

Julia's eyebrows twitched. Her lips parted as a blush of heat crept over her body. 'Me? What do you mean?'

'He wants you. That's his final goal – to get you into bed.'

As if there was an emotional vacuum cleaner in the pub, the heat was sucked away and Julia went cold. 'Bastard,' she whispered. 'How dare he put me on his shopping list.' She suddenly felt out of breath.

'I take it he didn't succeed.'

'Not quite.'

'I thought he was in a worse mood than usual, this morning. He hates failure.'

Nick left her for a moment while he went to get some more drinks. Julia glowered at her empty glass, fury seeping inside her. To think she had been so desperate to sleep with Steve. To think she had come so close to betraying David – kind, loyal David – with a man who counted her body like one of his business assets. Thank God she had bumped into Nick in time.

He returned with two more beers. Julia took an angry swig straight from the bottle, draining half the golden liquid. Smacking her lips, she glared at Nick. 'I can't believe Steve's behaviour. He's despicable. No wonder he got uptight when Marianne tried to read his list out.'

Nick sighed wistfully. 'Marianne was there, too? I used to like her. Has she changed?'

'Not at all. I see her all the time, you know. She's just the same.'

'You've hardly changed. Your hair's a little shorter. It suits you. And you're more womanly.'

She laughed. 'You mean I've put on weight.'

'I mean your curves are curvier. It's nice, sexy.' His eyes twinkled appreciatively. 'Your tits have grown.'

Julia giggled. 'Still breast-fixated, then?'

Nick's eyes hovered longingly down the low front of her T-shirt. 'Your breasts were fantastic. I was always obsessed with them, spent many a sleepless night wondering whether they would get any bigger.'

'I was a late developer.' Julia watched him wanting

her. As his brown eyes flickered over her face and body, his old self-assurance slowly returned. When he looked up he no longer seemed tired and stressed out; he seemed to shine.

'I'm sure you have better things to do at night than think about me.'

'Believe me, I don't.'

'Oh, come on,' she scoffed. 'Don't tell me you haven't got a girlfriend.'

'Not at the moment. I've had a few, but they never stick around for very long. It's hard to keep the impetus going in a relationship when you work every hour God sends.'

'Do you have to work so hard?'

'I owe Steve. I started up my own business but made a few bad decisions. Steve bailed me out and gave me a job as his right-hand man. No one else would have given a failed entrepreneur such a good position.' He smiled resignedly. 'It's a young company, an exciting place to work. I get to make decisions. Unfortunately, I don't get much of a social life but, then, you can't have everything.'

'Can't you?' Julia arched a defiant eyebrow. 'Who says?'

'It's the unwritten rule. Didn't you know?'

Julia gave a derisory laugh. 'No one ever told me. Besides, I don't like playing by the rules. As far as I can remember, you didn't, either.'

He looked at her in silence for a long time, his confidence slowly inflating. Holding her gaze in his, he rested his hand on her knee. Eyes smiling, waiting for her reaction, he gradually slid his fingers beneath her skirt. Sliding over the top of her leg, he pressed his hand between her thighs, grinning uncontrollably as they parted slightly for him.

'It's good to see you, Jules.'

* * *

It was four o'clock by the time they left the pub. They had settled into the dim corner with their drinks and slid easily back into their flirtation as if their seven years apart had been seven minutes. Talking nonstop about not very much, they giggled as they had caught up on each other's lives – Nick's hand between her legs as if that was where it belonged. He'd said he could stay there all day, but conscientiousness had won out in the end. He had things to do. He suggested Julia wait with him until Steve returned, then they could all three have dinner together, just like old times. Julia agreed; she wanted a word with Steve.

There was a small crowd going up in the lift and Nick squeezed in behind Julia. Two young men were laughing at something. Usually, Julia would have been curious to know what but, as she stood directly in front of Nick and his eyes bored into the back of her neck, she had the sense they were alone.

Someone got out at the first floor and Julia felt him moving closer. At the second, more space was created and she felt his breath, warm on her neck. Then he touched her.

She held her breath as his hands came to rest on her waist. One of the young men coughed uneasily as Nick's outstretched fingers eased over the flare of her hips and then backward. Julia bit her lip as he discovered the soft crease where her buttocks became thighs. The third floor came and went and he continued his invited exploration, ignoring the two remaining passengers in the lift, whose attention Julia could now feel as strongly as Nick's. His palms slid decisively upward, following her spine to her shoulders. The lift doors opened and closed again and they were alone. The two men got out but didn't walk away; transfixed, they watched through the lift's glass doors as Julia and Nick continued upward.

Nick pressed his face into the curve of her neck. She

felt his lips and nose on her skin, his hands grasping her upper arms. She closed her eyes as he inhaled greedily.

'You smell fantastic,' he murmured, the desperate edge to his deep voice making Julia shudder.

The lift whirred to a standstill and she realised with dismay that they had reached the fifth floor. The receptionist glanced up as the doors swished open, along with the motorbike courier who was leaning over her desk, no doubt trying to chat her up.

'We're here,' Julia whispered reluctantly.

'I know,' Nick mumbled into her shoulder. 'But I daren't move.'

'Why not?'

Nick pressed his body into hers. 'I've got an erection.'

She could feel it, hard against the cleft of her buttocks. In front of them, the receptionist and courier waited expectantly; beneath them, still staring up through the lift wall, the two young men watched with lopsided grins on their faces. 'Take your jacket off,' she giggled. 'Hold it in front of you.'

He followed her instructions. Smiling foolishly, his jacket draped strategically over his arm, he motioned Julia along the corridor past the reception desk.

'Any calls?' he asked, trying to appear nonchalant but struggling to contain his laughter.

'Mr Roth's been trying to reach you. He says it's urgent.'

'Good.' Ignoring the bundle of messages she was waving, he put his free arm around Julia's waist and guided her through the open-plan office. In the corner of the building were two adjacent offices; he ushered her inside the one on the left.

In keeping with the rest of the building, Nick's domain was predominantly glass. No good for vertigo sufferers, Julia thought, looking out of the back wall and down to the street below. And no good for those with secrets; the wide glass desk, and even the wall into the adjoining office, were completely transparent.

'Who works in there?'

'Steve.' Nick sat down in the huge leather chair behind his desk, fidgeting uncomfortably with his crotch.

'Doesn't it annoy you, being on show like this?'

Nick shrugged, shuffling through a pile of papers. 'You get used to it, I suppose. Although I sometimes wish it was one-way glass. You can't do anything naughty in here, there's always someone watching.'

'Can't you pull the blinds?'

'Blinds are only lowered in times of crisis, or when Steve and I are having a row.'

Julia sat down in the chair opposite Nick. 'So you can't pull them now, even though you've got a hard-on and you want me desperately?'

He swallowed nervously. 'I couldn't. The staff would know something was going on.'

'Shame.' She smiled wickedly and opened her legs, drawing Nick's eyes to the white triangle of her knickers.

'Oh God. Don't,' he pleaded.

'Don't what?' She ran her tongue slowly around her upper lip, a ridiculous cliché which made Nick laugh.

'You're incorrigible. I knew it was a bad idea bringing you back here. I knew I wouldn't be able to concentrate. You're a corrupting influence.'

'You're the one who got frisky in the lift. You're the one who had your hand up my skirt in the pub.'

He smiled wryly. 'You bring out the worst in me.'

Their eyes locked. Tension crackled in the air-conditioned atmosphere as they shared the same thought. Slumping down in her seat, sure that no one could see what she was doing behind the arms of the wide leather chair, she reminded Nick of where his hand had been. He gasped as she rubbed one finger over her cotton-clad vulva. Beneath her touch, Julia felt her sex swelling in readiness.

The phone rang shrilly. Pressing the speaker button, Nick closed his eyes, shutting out the vision laid before him. 'Yes?'

'It's Steve. Where the hell have you been? I've been trying to reach you for hours.'

When Nick's eyes opened again, they were smiling. 'I've been sat in the pub, talking to an old friend.'

'What's wrong with your mobile?'

'Nothing. I had it turned off. I didn't want to be disturbed.'

'For Christ's sake, Nick, what are you playing at?'

Nick drummed his fingers on the table, sneering down at the speaker as if Steve was in there. 'I was taking time off, in lieu of Saturday.'

'What?' Steve's voice sounded tinny and slightly crackly, as if he was on a car phone; still, his exasperation was clear. 'We always work on Saturdays.'

'Not when there's a school reunion to go to.' Nick winked at Julia.

'How . . . how did you find out?'

'I bumped into Jules.'

'Julia?' There was a long silence. When Steve spoke again, his voice was tight with worry. 'How is she? Did she say anything . . . about me?'

'Oh, we had a long chat about you. We'd both like a word, when you get back.'

'She's there, now?'

'Sitting in my office.' His eyes drifted. 'Looking as sexy as ever.'

'I'll be back in an hour.'

Julia parted her thighs further and slid her palm inside her panties. Nick grumbled, his eyes smouldering with lust.

'Nick?' Steve's voice snapped urgently. 'Nick? Are you still there?'

'Yeah.'

'I need you to do something. It's important.'

Nick sighed, withdrawing his eyes from Julia and picking up a pen. 'Go on.'

Julia watched as he and Steve discussed the intricacies of a deal. Nick was just as flighty as he had been, years ago. A moment earlier, his attention had been rapt as she'd teased him; now, his mind had shut her out and he was fully immersed in business talk.

'Nick,' she soothed, as the conversation ended and he stood up.

'Don't say a word.' He held up a hand to stop her, his eyes fixed on some distant point above her head. 'Please, don't make me look at you. I've got to get this done before Steve gets back.'

'Why can't you look at me?'

'Because if I do, I'll want to rip your clothes off, for old time's sake, and I haven't got time, now.'

'All right.' Julia removed her hand and curled her legs up into the spacious seat. 'I'll wait.'

An hour later, having rushed around the various departments of the business collating the facts and figures he needed, his mission was complete. One of the secretaries brought him a sheaf of papers to sign before she faxed them off, and then, apparently, he could relax. He poured himself a brandy from the decanter and one for Julia. Perching on the edge of his desk, he waved at the staff as they passed by his office on their way out.

'That's it,' he sighed. 'Alone at last. Now I can look at you.' His voice was as rich and smooth as her drink, mixing with the cognac, warm in her belly, and seeping over her skin until it prickled. He savoured the view, slowly taking in the details as if it was the first time he'd really looked at her. 'Stand up, Julia.'

Her legs trembled slightly as she obeyed.

'Come here.' He pulled her closer with a cursory flick of his hand. Reaching out, he raised his fingers to her neck. Slipping his touch down over her throat then over her collarbone, he curled his hand over a breast. His brandy was in his other hand. Swirling the dark liquid, he tipped it into his mouth and put the glass down. Then this hand was free to mirror the journey of the first, until both her breasts were within his eager grasp. Julia put her shoulders back and raised her chin proudly while his greedy eyes appraised her body. She was gratified to see a twitch reappearing in his trousers.

'You're not wearing a bra.' His voice had lost its smooth timbre and faltered at the edges.

Julia smiled to herself. She had packed a change of underwear but, after her bra had got wet on the train, Richard had persuaded her not to put another one on, insisting that he deserved a second birthday treat. According to him, bra-less women were the eighth wonder of the world. Nick certainly seemed to be in agreement.

'Does it turn you on, not wearing one?' His fingers and thumbs pinched her nipples, drawing them into stiffness beneath the deep orange of her T-shirt. 'Does it excite you to know that men are looking at you; on the street, on the train, salivating over your breasts, watching them bounce slightly as you walk and wanting to put their hands all over you?'

'Mmmm,' was all she could manage in reply.

'Does it excite you to wear short skirts? To feel men's eyes on your legs as you sit down?' He moved closer until Julia smelled his aftershave, faint and spicy. 'Does it make you wet?'

'You make me wet,' she murmured into her brandy. She sipped the dark amber warmth and felt her breathing deepen as Nick circled her. 'You always did.'

'You make me hard.' Standing behind her, he clasped the back of her neck in his fingers. Her short bob skimmed his hand as she turned to look at him. 'You always did,' he added, softly pressing his lips against her cheek. He brought his body nearer until Julia felt his erection, long and hard against her buttock.

She put her glass down. 'Screw me,' she whispered. 'For old time's sake.'

Groaning, he grabbed her shoulders and manoeuvred her towards the transparent wall that separated the adjoining offices. Julia allowed herself to be pushed up against the glass and for each hand to be planted on the cold surface. Watching Nick's reflection as he stood behind her, she arched her lower back ready for him. With quick, eager hands, he pushed her short skirt up over her hips and pulled her knickers down over her boots. Julia leant forwards into her hands until she was bent right over, wantonly displaying her sex for Nick. Throbbing deep inside, her heart pounding in her ears, she waited impatiently for his touch.

'Oh God. What a fantastic arse,' he breathed, as if she wasn't there. He placed a hand low down on each buttock, his thumbs teasing her swollen labia apart. Julia's back arched sharply until it hurt. Nick hooked a foot around her ankle, spreading her legs wider until she felt her knickers stretched to tearing point across her ankles. A delicious flame of anticipation licked up her thighs and across her pelvis as her sex opened and she imagined Nick, looking at her fleshy, crimson labia and their soft curtain of hair.

A moment later, without any warning, he plunged his long penis inside her. Julia's head rolled and every hair on her body stood to attention as Nick thrust his cock into her willing, soft flesh. Her arms could barely support her weight as he grunted behind her, and she had to summon all her strength to push back against him and stop her forehead from hitting the glass. His fingers gripped her firmly under the ribs as he fucked her, seeming to touch the neck of her womb with his length. Then his hands moved, one grappling upward underneath her T-shirt to cradle the weight of a dangling breast, pinching and pulling her large, stiff areola. The other moved behind her, lingering for a moment where his cock was plunging in and out, wetting his fingers with her juices. Slowly he began to circle Julia's anus, rubbing the lubrication of her body into its taut resistance. Pressing gently, gradually persuading entry, he continued until the tight hole gave way and sucked his forefinger inside her. Then he took up a new rhythm. Each time his long phallus slid out of her, almost to withdrawal, his finger pushed. The pleasure of having both holes filled at once was so intense it was almost painful, making Julia moan in anguish. Calling up reserves of strength, she concentrated on holding her body firm for his plundering. But it was difficult; like someone who was asked to sit still because they were about to be tortured, she flinched and writhed, seeking escape.

On the verge of orgasm she cried out and, as if it was a signal, Nick's finger left her and both arms wrapped around her ribs. Squeezing her tightly, he began to pump frantically between her legs. Her fingers outstretched on the smooth glass, her body helpless within his hold, Julia watched their reflections. She nearly laughed as she thought of how different this urgent, forceful coupling was, compared to their inexperienced fumblings of years ago.

And then, as if to complete her reminiscing, Steve appeared in the next-door room. He didn't bother to turn the light on but moved through the darkness until the light from Nick's office illuminated his face. Transfixed, he stared at them through the glass, his image mingling eerily with their reflections. His glare was as intense as a sniper's as he watched Nick's hands moving frantically over Julia's body. Looking over her head he watched Nick as, without a pause, he pushed her further towards climax. Slowly, his eyes drifted downward until they met Julia's, his expression changing from disgust to devastation. He nodded slowly as if this, too, was written on his list. A part of his grand plan.

'Do you think he's jealous?' Nick asked, his wicked smirk reflecting in the window over her shoulder.

'I hope so,' Julia replied, her eyes hardening as they locked with Steve's. 'It would serve him right.'

As Steve turned and strode out of sight, Nick shuddered and came. Julia's pleasure was deadened though, muffled by a thick layer of anger that made her breath quicken and her cheeks heat up. Watching Steve slouch off down the corridor towards the lift, head hanging and shoulders slumped under the weight of his despair, her fury boiled over. Wriggling out of Nick's arms, she pushed his hips away from hers, pulled up her knickers and smoothed down her skirt. Leaving Nick breathlessly asking where she was going, she ran after Steve.

'I want a word with you,' she shouted, as she strode towards him. At the lift he looked up, hurt in his pale eyes. 'You've got some explaining to do.' He averted his gaze as she approached, staring down at his feet. Julia stood in front of him, her hands on her hips, spitting fire. 'How dare you put me on your list, Steve. How dare you treat me like an object. I can't believe you! You lied to Nick, got him out of the way so you could get me into bed and tick off number seven on your precious plan.'

'I had to get Nick out of the way.' Guiltily, he looked up, barely daring to meet her venomous glare. 'I know it was wrong but, if he'd been there on Saturday, I wouldn't have stood a chance with you. Just like at school. You two could never keep your hands off each other. Still can't, obviously.' His mouth was set hard and his eyes were swimming with hurt.

Julia gasped. 'I can't believe how cold you are. You planned it all. Just like one of your property deals. You can't treat people like commodities, Steve.'

'Did I treat you so badly? You're the one who ran off without saying goodbye.'

Julia blinked slowly, struggling to make sense of his calmness. 'You don't understand, do you? You've no idea why I'm so angry.'

He shook his head. 'I know I deceived Nick, but –'

'I'm not talking about Nick.' Her eyes narrowed. Her face was burning. 'I wanted you, Steve. I wanted you so badly, I was prepared to cheat on my fiancé. I've thought about you every second since the weekend. And now . . . now . . .,' she faltered, her breath short with exasperation. 'Now, I find out that your ultimate goal was to . . . to fuck me!' Incensed, she raised her hand.

Steve grabbed her wrist, stopping her slap on its way to his cheek. 'Is that what you think? Do you really think I'd plan all that, just so I could fuck you? And do you think I'd have been able to stop myself after I found out you were engaged? I was the one who said no, if you remember.'

Her mouth opened and closed nervously, her hand suspended in his like an unfinished sentence. A moment earlier she had been trapped in Nick's arms; now, she was helpless in the pale grey of Steve's eyes. 'I don't understand. Nick told me –'

'Nick's never seen my list. Nobody has. Your name is on it but it's not what you think.'

'So . . . you didn't want to have sex with me?'

He let her wrist go, his face melting into a sad smile. He sighed and, as the air left his body, he seemed to visibly shrink. 'I desperately wanted to spend the night with you, Julia. I've thought about it so many times. But I couldn't, not with you about to get married. It wouldn't have been fair on anyone.' He held her cheek in his gentle fingers. 'I admit, the reunion was all planned out, just like my whole life. Everything I've done since the age of eighteen has been part of a strategy. You told me once that you knew I'd achieve everything I wanted. So I had to become successful, make some money, change my appearance, to prove myself to you. The reunion was supposed to be the culmination of all my years of hard work. I was going to impress you with my achievements. I was going to make you want me.'

Julia shared the sorrow in his eyes. 'I did want you.'

The lift quietly arrived behind him, and he stepped backward between the glass doors. 'And then I found out you were in love with someone else and I remembered another thing you once told me – that planning is pointless.' The doors began to close on his desolate smile.

'I'm calling off the wedding. I can't marry David.'

He slammed his hand on the button, opening the doors again and holding them wide. 'Why not?'

'Because I can't stop thinking about you.' She took a step towards him. 'That night, at the castle . . . I've never been so turned on in my life.'

His gaze switched suspiciously from one eye to the other, as if he couldn't quite believe what he was hearing. 'What are you saying?'

'That I came back to Scotland today to see you.' Watching his face, she stroked the dark grey of his jacket. As his mouth gradually dipped to hers, his hand left the button and fell to her shoulder. The lift doors began to close.

'Oi.' They looked round to find Nick's foot jammed in the door. 'I've a bone to pick with you.' He wagged his finger at Steve as he pushed his way between them.

Steve winced. 'Can we talk about it later?'

'We can talk about it over dinner. I'm cooking.' He raised a hand to silence Steve's protest. 'No arguments. You had Julia all to yourself at the weekend. You'll have to share her, tonight.'

Dinner was difficult. Steve was on edge, uncomfortable in the stark modernity of Nick's trendy bachelor flat. Nick was showing off. He was flirting outrageously and baiting Steve in retribution for the deception of the weekend. Julia, already tipsy from her afternoon in the pub, was caught between giggling at Nick's inane jokes and talking seriously with Steve. The wine flowed but Steve couldn't catch up and, as the other two sank further into silly drunkenness, he became increasingly withdrawn. The tension was tangible. Like a child with a wound, Nick wouldn't leave it alone, incessantly picking and digging at the frayed edges of their triangular relationship. Sooner or later, something had to give.

Julia stood up. Picking up a third bottle of red wine, she circled the round table to pour Steve another glassful. Her legs were slightly unsteady as she continued around to Nick's place. Standing by his side, she topped up his glass, spilling a drop on the table as his fingers slipped under her skirt and closed over her buttock. As she turned to look down at him, he tipped his chair back, watching her behind and grinning evilly.

'Her arse is still as gorgeous as it ever was,' he leered, ignoring her tutting and looking across the table. 'Her tits are even more fantastic than they used to be though, don't you think so, Steve? Have you noticed how she's grown?'

Julia looked up; Steve's eyes were glittering with cold resentment. Nick had been right about his jealousy. He seethed in silence.

'She's still an excellent lay, isn't she? Oh, sorry, I forgot. You've never had her.'

Steve flinched visibly. 'Do you have to be so coarse?'

'She enjoys it,' Nick sneered. 'It turns her on.'

'She's standing right next to you,' Steve snapped. 'Don't talk about Julia as if she isn't here.'

Keeping his hand on her bottom, Nick brought the front legs of his chair back to the wooden floor and leant forward on the table. 'Julia likes the way I talk. She likes the way I screw, too.'

'Nick!' Julia pushed his hand away.

'You're disgusting,' Steve hissed.

Pushing his hands on the table, Nick went to get up. 'At least I don't lie to my friends.'

In reply, Steve got to his feet.

Julia rolled her eyes. 'Sit down, both of you.' Caught up in their macho posturing, they crouched like animals, glaring at each other. Neither wanted to be the first to give in. 'Steve, please.' Keeping his eyes fixed on Nick, as if he feared a sudden strike, Steve lowered himself back down into his seat. 'Nick!' Julia leant over and gave his shoulder a push. He muttered incomprehensibly under his breath. 'Shut up,' Julia snapped, looking from one side of the table to the other. They were like a couple of naughty children, pouting sullenly. 'Honestly, I thought you two would have grown out of all this nonsense by now, but you're worse than ever. You're ruining this meal.' They continued their silent sulking. 'I haven't seen either of you for seven years. If you're going to carry on behaving like this, I'll walk out right now and you won't see me ever again.'

'Sorry, Jules,' Nick mumbled.

'Sorry.' Steve looked worriedly at Julia. 'I just don't like him talking about you like that.'

'Forget it. Shake hands with him.'

'What?' Steve looked horrified.

'You can't blame Nick for being angry with you. He should have been there, on Saturday. But you . . .' She turned to Nick, shaking her head with disappointment. 'You're behaving like a spoilt brat. Stop winding him up. Shake hands.' Grumpily, they stretched across the table and made their reluctant truce. 'Now, eat your pudding,' she insisted.

All three looked gladly away from the tension and down into their dessert bowls. The tiramisu Nick had made earlier was a masterpiece: rich and creamy and smelling strongly of brandy. Julia had sat with Steve on the balcony while Nick had cooked, laughing at the incongruity of his being in the kitchen. A good cook was the last thing she would have expected him to become. She giggled again, at the thought of him in his apron.

'What's so funny?'

'Just thinking about you in your pinny,' she laughed.

'Oh, that's nice. That's gratitude for you. I make you a lovely dinner and all you can do is take the mickey.' He flicked a blob of cream in her direction, landing it expertly on her cheek.

Julia wiped it off and sucked her fingertip. Biting her lip to stifle her foolish excitement, she scooped her spoon into her bowl and flicked the coffee-coloured goo at him.

He looked down as it squelched on to his shirt. 'Right.' He put his spoon down. 'That does it.' Getting up from the table, he moved behind Julia's chair. Leaning over her shoulder, he dipped his fingers into the huge serving dish and grabbed a handful of tiramisu. With a sadistic smile he smeared the cream across Julia's mouth.

She stood up and did the same to him. They looked at each other for a moment, their eyes dancing with devilish delight, then he grabbed the back of her neck and pulled her mouth to his. He licked her face clean, lapping at her skin with hungry strokes. When he finished he pulled away and looked down, grinning wickedly like a child searching for further mischief. He then gripped either side of the low V-neck of her T-shirt and ripped the fine material apart. Stunned, Julia looked down at the tear, her breath catching dramatically at the shock of cold whipped cream being rubbed over her breasts. Nick roughly pushed at her waist until she had her back to the table. Gripping on to its edge either side of her hips, he bent down to suck the sweetness from her skin, teasing her nipples with rapid flickers of his searching tongue. Throwing her head back, Julia sighed with pleasure.

Nick knelt down and Julia turned to Steve. Steve's pale eyes were full of anguish and uncertainty, just as they had been seven years earlier. Then, he'd had to endure the torture of Nick and Julia, rolling around on the grass, lost in their own private world. Now, there was no need for him to feel left out. She held out her hand, inviting him closer, urging him to join in. Shakily, he stood and moved to her side.

Almost imperceptibly, he shook his head. 'This isn't how I imagined our first time together,' he confessed in a whisper. He glanced down at Nick. His features were drawn as he looked back at Julia. 'This doesn't feel right. I don't know what to do.'

'Kiss me,' she urged, raising her lips to his. 'Just kiss me.'

In slow motion, his mouth descended. Softly, delicately, he kissed her, tenderly making love to her mouth. As his tongue eased its tentative way between her open lips, he moved into her. Holding her face in his hands as if he had found something sacred, his legs moved either side of one of Julia's. His thighs pressed to her thigh, and she felt his cock stiffening against her hip. Clutching his shoulder, she watched while he paused and pulled away. Blinking in amazement, his gaze flowed over her pale throat to her naked breasts. Sliding her hand over his strong neck, Julia combed her fingers through his short hair, urging his mouth back down. He kissed her again, more forcefully now as his passion grew strong enough to block out the thought of Nick.

Julia couldn't forget him, though. Kneeling at her feet, he had her knickers down again and was breathing heavily as his touch eased into her soft pubic hair. Julia moved her legs a little wider apart to accommodate him as one finger, then another, slid effortlessly into her sex. Her nails dug into Steve's arm as Nick probed deep inside her, stimulating her pussy into a spasm of ecstasy. She tensed as he slid his fingers out and up to the aching hardness of her clitoris, spreading her juices on to the tender bud. He began to tease her, and she moaned into Steve's mouth.

'What's the matter?' he asked.

'Nothing.' Her eyes fluttered uncertainly between the two men as Nick stood up.

'What do you want?' Nick asked.

She didn't know. She had to have something, someone, but how on earth could she make a choice? Nick was hovering expectantly, carrying his confidence on his broad shoulders. His brusqueness was incredibly sexy. He knew what he wanted and pursued it without hesitation. He had always been the same, even as an adolescent just stepping into manhood: dominant, arrogant, his sensuality almost brutish. Nick aroused everything base and primitive in Julia. She wanted him in the dirtiest ways; wanted his cock in her mouth; wanted her sex spread wide for him. She wanted to be on all fours with him humping her like an animal, to taste his sweat on her tongue, to have him hiss obscenities as she came. Sex with Nick would be faceless and frantic, and about one thing only – sex.

But, desperate as she was for quick relief, there was Steve to think about. Sex with him, she suspected, would be about more than just sex. The night at his castle, when he had touched her wrist as she had touched herself, was the most erotic of her life. Julia wanted Steve just as urgently as she wanted Nick, but in a different way. She wanted her breasts gently squashed against his torso. Their thighs locked together in an exquisite embrace. His eyes burning into hers.

She looked up at him and her lips quivered as the words faltered on their way from her brain to her tongue.

'I can't,' Steve whispered. Reading her mind, he ran the tip of one finger over her lower lip. He might as well have touched her sex; as if a raw nerve ran directly from her mouth to her pussy, she throbbed with longing. 'When I sleep with you, I want it to be perfect. I can't do it with him here.'

'Doesn't bother me.' Looming nearer, Nick grabbed her hand and pulled her away.

If her senses hadn't been dulled by so much alcohol, if her sex hadn't been pulsing so demandingly, Julia might have been put off by his boorishness. But there was a wicked twinkle in his eyes, one that she had never been able to resist. And it occurred to her, through a daze of desire and wine, that she could have both men – and everything she needed. Anxiously, she turned to Steve.

'I'll say goodnight.' There was resignation in his handsome features. Turning his back on them, he went to collect his jacket.

'Don't go,' Julia pleaded.

He spun round, his expression one of frozen confusion.

'Stay with me. Please.' She begged with her eyes as Nick took off what remained of her top, unzipped her skirt, and then her boots. He bustled around behind her, getting something from the table while Steve looked with desperation at her naked body. He was still watching when Nick pulled her down on to the cool wooden floor. Arranging her on to her hands and knees, he started up a commentary.

'She's got the horniest arse, the most beautiful, tight little arsehole I've ever seen. I'm going to fuck her up there, in that tight little hole.' His hot palms rubbed over her buttocks. 'I've never taken a woman up the arse before. I read somewhere that it's very sensitive in there, that it gives the woman the most incredible orgasm . . .'

'Come here,' Julia breathed to Steve, raising her head. Mesmerised, he took a step towards her and crouched down on his haunches. 'Lie down underneath me,' she urged. Horror widened his eyes. 'Please, Steve, just do it. I want to look at you.'

Carefully, he stretched his long legs between her arms and pushed his body down along the floor until his face was under hers. He looked terrified, but Julia knew it would be worse for him if he left now. He would be awake all night, trying to picture her with Nick, wondering just how incredible her orgasm was. This way was better; he could touch her, hold her, share in her pleasure.

'Have you done this before?' he whispered, his eyes echoing the fear Julia had felt, the first time a lover had suggested sex in that forbidden place.

Julia nodded.

'Is it painful?'

'That depends on the man.' Twisting her head round, she instructed Nick. 'You need lots of lubrication.' He raised a bottle of olive oil in reply, toasting her backside. 'Be patient,' she urged, 'and gentle.'

As a warm stream of oil trickled down into her cleft, she returned to Steve. He replied to her smile with a pained grimace. 'What should I do?'

'Touch my breasts.'

Gently, he cradled her dangling breasts in his hands, his eyes alternating between his fingers and her face. Behind her, Nick slid his oily thumb inside her anus and, as Julia held her breath, so did Steve. Waiting anxiously, he tried to read her expression as she gasped and shuddered, two of Nick's fingers now poking in and out of her. Gradually, her unconscious desire to expel his fingers from her most secret, sensitive hole subsided. Her muscles began to relax and accept him, and soon she wanted more.

Sensing her readiness, Nick shuffled closer and put the head of his penis against her anus. Julia's crack was prepared with so much grease that he slid off her at first. Then, grabbing her hips, he pushed with determination until her body swallowed up his full length.

Julia's mouth opened wide, but she had lost the power of speech and her cry never came out. The pleasure was agonising, complex and insane, wrenching her guts and scrambling her brains. Steve took his hands from her breasts and laid them, palms upward, on the floor.

Gratefully, Julia clasped his fingers. She needed something to cling on to, to stop her from falling out of control.

'Christ, you're so tight,' Nick groaned. With both hands now on her hips, he began to slide his phallus in and out, creating a friction which was almost unbearable. Her anus stretched; his passage eased. He lost all thoughts of gentleness or patience and slammed himself hard between Julia's quivering cheeks. The shock freed her voice, and a deep grumble of anguish flew up from her belly. Looking up at her, Steve watched intently as Julia's expression flickered disbelievingly between pleasure and pain. Spurred on by her loud, rhythmic moaning, Nick rammed again, harder still. The momentum made Julia's pelvis fall out of his grasp and her body lowered on to Steve's. Her bottom was still arched upward, but her breasts were cushioned on Steve's chest and she could feel the strength of his erection between her legs. With her mouth poised an inch over his, she gasped even louder as Nick's urgent pushing brought her sex rubbing over Steve's penis. He was still fully clothed and the heat of his trousers burnt her clit as she was pushed down hard upon him.

Nick began to jerk violently and, as he did, Julia felt as if her senses were shutting down. She was alone in a silent, black vortex of pleasure, every pore of her body open and screaming for release. Her orgasm raged over her, an incredible, indistinguishable blend of searing joy and glorious torture, a climax without a source. Clitoris, anus and mind were joined in an unending loop without start or finish. It was ecstasy in its purest form, manifesting itself in her used body and making her tremble uncontrollably. Tears welled up in her eyes and overflowed on to Steve's face.

Nick withdrew and Julia collapsed with relief. Falling into Steve's arms, she buried her head in his shoulder and sobbed quietly, wetting his shirt with her tears. He stroked her hair, soothing her, his other hand resting on her waist. His gentleness was such a contrast to the frenzy of before, and she could happily have slept there.

'You're amazing,' he whispered.

With a tremendous effort, Julia raised her head. Steve's eyes were brimming with emotion. 'I'm glad you stayed.' She smiled.

'So am I.' He pushed back the lock of hair that had fallen into her face. 'I've never seen anything so beautiful in my life.' He eased her head back down into his shoulder. 'I want you to myself, tomorrow night. I want to make you come like that.'

'I'm working tomorrow night.' She rolled on to the floor as he shrugged her off his body. 'I have to get the first train back in the morning,' she explained, in response to the question in his eyes. 'I'm covering a film première tomorrow.'

'You can't go back.'

Lying on the floor on the other side of her, Nick grunted in agreement.

'I have to. I've got work to do.'

'Ring in sick.'

'I did that, today.'

Steve snatched at her shoulder. 'What am I supposed to do?'

'You'll have to come down to London to see me.'

His mouth gaped. 'I can't ... I'm in the middle of a deal ... it's impossible, I have to be here.'

Julia shrugged. She suddenly felt very tired. 'It's up to you.'

'But ... I was planning to take you out to dinner, and then –'

She put a finger to his lips. 'Always planning. You can't stop yourself, can you?'

Nick flung his arm over Julia's hip, pulling her on to her back. He leered over her, grinning stupidly. 'Don't go, Jules, don't leave me. I need you.'

'You don't need me, Nick. You need a sex object. I could be anyone.'

'Not true,' he protested, his words slurred with exhaustion and alcohol. 'You're still the horniest woman I've ever known.' He pressed his lips to her ear, tickling her with his breath. 'That was the best damn fuck I've ever had.' He bent his head to her breast, kissing her nipple in thanks. 'Screw your job, stay here with us.'

Julia got to her feet, holding her head to stop it from spinning. 'Much as I'd like to, I can't. We've all got work to do tomorrow. You've got your deals; I've got my première. I'm sure we'll find time to meet up again, soon.' Nick tutted grumpily; Steve sighed in dismay. 'I need some sleep. Who's coming to bed?'

Disappointment momentarily forgotten, they both sat up.

The Challenge

The usual motley crew was already assembled outside the Odeon, Leicester Square, by the time Julia arrived. She showed her press pass to the policeman by the barrier and pushed her way into the photographers' enclosure adjacent to the cinema's entrance. She was late and everyone had claimed themselves good spots by now. But that didn't deter Julia. She was usually late for these things and yet she always managed to end up on the front row. It was a simple strategy, but it worked: a flirtatious smile here, a quick word there, and the almost exclusively male huddle would part to let her through. The *Chronicle* had clout, but that didn't count here, amongst her contemporaries. It was her breasts that won her favours in this game.

Breasts equal power, she thought, taking up a prime position right at the front of the press pack. She put her equipment bag down and crouched over to fix her long lens on to her camera. She smiled as she felt attention falling down the front of her top. Breasts could get you in the papers, into the music business, on to the silver screen. Behind the camera, far away from public slavering, Julia's breasts were still invaluable. She frequently had to compete for good positions on nights like these. If she had been a man, she would still have been relegated to the back row, having to balance on a stepladder to get the shots she needed. But the other photographers had taken her under their wing, easing her progress, allowing her to get to the front and smiling with pride when she did. Their protectiveness was amusing. Their sexism was quiet, gentle, inoffensive and easy to manipulate. Julia abused them so ruthlessly, she almost felt sorry for them – after all, they couldn't help themselves. They were men, and men were obsessed with breasts.

She smiled wryly as she was reminded of Nick. A quiver of excitement darted through her at the memory of yesterday. The quiver became a tremor as she thought of how Marianne would react to the news that she and Nick had finally been reunited. And what a reunion. By the time he had seen her off at the station that morning, Nick had been back on his old form. The stressed-out manager had woken up invigorated, rejuvenated and sparkling with energy. She'd brought him back his youth, he'd said, making her laugh. He was only twenty-five.

Steve, on the other hand, had seemed tired and down as he'd waved from the platform. He had moaned that he hadn't slept a wink in Nick's king-size bed. He'd found the situation too bizarre.

It had been bizarre: Julia flanked by the two men she'd grown up with. But, if the last two days had been strange, the last two months had been almost surreal. She had done things she'd sworn she'd avoid: gone out with an actor, of all people, accepted his marriage proposal, given one of her subjects a blow job in the studio. And she'd done things which had shocked her deeply: masturbated in front of Steve, forced herself on her fiancé, rushed straight back to Glasgow and had sex with a complete stranger en route. She had thought, at the end of that journey, that her mind was clear. But then she'd seen Nick, and now the confusion had started all over again.

As the first limousine drew up to the cinema, Julia raised her camera. She watched as the glossy young couple got out, waving to the crowd. She was an actress; he a footballer – they'd recently married, and they glittered with love as they held on to each other. Julia caught them perfectly as they posed for the cameras, the young man beaming with pride as his wife rested her head on his shoulder. Guilt speared through Julia's heart at the realisation that David didn't yet know that it was over between them. Immediately, that remorse was washed away and replaced with sorrow for Steve. She'd told him that she wanted him, that she'd come back to Scotland to see him, and yet it had been Nick who'd enjoyed her body that night. How must Steve have felt, lying beneath her while his old rival buggered her until she cried with pleasure? All the frustrations and jealousies of the years gone by must have tasted very bitter in his mouth. No wonder he hadn't slept; it must have been the ultimate torment for him, listening to Nick and Julia as they drifted off beside him, their bodies heavy with sex. To Steve, it must have been the torture of their last weeks at school together, magnified a million times.

Her eyes glazed and the image in her viewfinder lost its focus. She shuddered slightly as she realised just how little things had changed since those days. She still felt closer to Steve than Nick, and longed to talk to him – or even just to sit in silence together, Steve reading her thoughts as he always used to. But Nick's presence was an undeniably exciting distraction. He was pure, selfish lust. Nick didn't communicate with words; he didn't need to. His body was his voice and it was a very persuasive one. Together, Nick and Steve provided almost everything that had been missing from her life for so long.

She looked up as she heard her name being called. Celebrities were arriving in a steady stream now but she ignored them and scanned the crowd. She recognised that voice.

'Julia! Jules! Over here!'

Smiling incredulously, she waved at Nick. He was in a silver limo, leaning out of one of the mirrored windows and beckoning her urgently.

'I can't,' she mouthed, her pussy twitching as she wondered what he was doing there. 'I'm working.'

He opened the door and got out of the car. Grinning naughtily, he waved for her to join him. He looked like a star, himself – he'd had his hair cut, and was resplendent in a black tuxedo. 'Come on!'

Julia glanced around her. The other photographers had barely noticed as their lenses were pointing intently at a model and her boyfriend as they posed their way into the cinema. Julia was supposed to deliver her pictures to the *Chronicle* that evening. George would be waiting. He would be furious if she didn't turn up. He had spaces ready for these shots.

'Come on!' Nick shouted above the noise. 'What are you waiting for?'

She grabbed her bag and fled. Ignoring the protests of those she jolted on her way out of the madness, she ran to Nick. 'What are you doing here?' she panted. 'I'll be in serious trouble for this.' With a hand between her shoulders, he urged her inside the car. 'Steve! What's going on?' Nick got in beside her and closed the door on the screams and applause. The limo glided off through the crowds.

Pushing its way out of the throng, it turned southward to Trafalgar Square. Julia glanced from Steve, to Nick, to the chauffeur, who nodded at her in his rear-view mirror.

'What the hell are you two up to? You've really landed me in it, you know, turning up like this. I expect I'll get the sack.'

'So why did you come? You didn't have to. We could have driven around a bit, waited for you to finish.'

She grinned at Nick. 'You knew I wouldn't be able to resist. It's time I moved on from the *Chronicle*, anyway. Screw the job – I'll go freelance. I need a new challenge.'

'Talking of which...' Nick moved into the seat opposite Julia. The black leather upholstery squeaked luxuriously as he sat down.

'That's why we're here,' Steve added.

'I thought you were busy.' Julia teased. He looked stunning in his tux. 'Thought you had deals to do.'

'I have. They can wait.'

'We want to make a deal with you.'

Intrigued, Julia turned back to Nick. 'Oh? Go on.'

A secretive smirk twitched at the edges of his mouth. He shifted in his seat, fidgeting with excitement. 'We both want you.'

Julia arched an eyebrow. 'That's nice. But ... I sort of guessed that, already.'

'We want you to choose between us.'

Steve put his hand on her thigh. Beneath the fine cotton jersey of her black skirt, her skin went cold. 'Nick and I have talked about you nonstop since you left this morning. We've never met anyone like you, Julia. We both want to see you again – but not both at the same time.' He shook his head sadly. 'I don't think I could stand another night like last night.'

'Neither one of us is prepared to let you go. So it has to be up to you.'

Speechless, Julia looked from one to the other.

'I'll spend Thursday with you.' Nick nodded to his opponent. 'Steve's made arrangements to have the umbilical cord cut on Friday. You should consider yourself honoured – I don't think he's ever taken a day off from the business since he started it.'

Julia was honoured and flattered, and highly amused. 'You two have got this all worked out, haven't you?'

Nick shrugged nonchalantly, as if this sort of thing was a daily occurrence. 'We had to do something. I didn't want it to be another seven years before I saw you again.'

'And I didn't want to see you again, wondering whether you would really prefer to be with Nick,' Steve added.

Julia took a deep breath. 'So, let me get this straight. I spend a day with each of you, during which time you do your best to win my affections, and then I make my decision.'

Both murmured in affirmation.

'And whatever happens, you'll agree to abide by my choice?'

Nick nodded. 'Your decision is final. The loser will step aside graciously.'

Julia snorted derisively. 'I'll believe that when I see it.'

Steve gently squeezed her knee. 'There isn't any other way, Julia. It has to be like this, unless you already know who you want.'

'Unless I don't want either of you.' That silenced them. She looked away from both of them, out of the side window. Trafalgar Square was packed with tourists. The limo drew a lot of interest as it made slow progress around the bottom edge towards Haymarket. She tried to look calm and thoughtful, but it was difficult. She was close to screaming with the nervous thrill of it all. Outside, London carried on with its business, oblivious to the fact that Julia's mind was about to burst.

Quelling her excitement for a moment, she thought through the possible consequences but, with David away for a week, she told herself there was no chance of being found out. 'OK,' she said at last. 'But there's one condition.'

Nick leant forward eagerly. 'Whatever you want.'

'After this is over, you two have got to promise to remain friends.'

The two men glanced at each other. 'That won't be easy,' Steve muttered.

'That's my condition. If you can't agree to it, the deal's off.'

'All right,' Nick said quickly.

Steve nodded.

'Well, now that's settled, what shall we do tonight? Have you two had dinner?'

Nick opened up a small drinks cabinet beside his seat. He pulled out an ice bucket holding a bottle of champagne, and began to pick at its gold-foil collar. 'I'm afraid we haven't time for dinner, Jules. We've got a breakfast meeting tomorrow. We'll drop you off at home, then we've got to head back.'

She blinked the amazement from her eyes. 'You mean to tell me you've driven all this way and pulled me off a photo shoot for a quick chat? Couldn't you have phoned?'

'You didn't leave us your number.' The cork popped, and Nick poured three glasses of fizz. 'Besides, we wanted to surprise you.'

'Mission accomplished, I'd say.' She accepted a glass and drained it, feeling vaguely dizzy as the bubbles hit her brain. Taking the empty glass from her hand and replacing it with his, Nick got to his knees on the carpeted floor. Sliding his hands beneath her skirt, he parted her thighs. 'What are you doing?' Julia whispered. She caught the chauffeur's eyes in his mirror. 'He can see us.'

'Don't worry about him.' Steve put his fingers to her neck as she turned towards him, smoothing out her tension.

'But he's looking,' she hissed. Between her legs, Nick was rumpling her skirt up into her lap. Muttering his approval of the tiny, black scrap of lace covering her mound, he scrabbled at her hips, tugging her knickers down. Julia gasped, her eyes switching worriedly between the chauffeur and Steve. Both were watching her intently. 'Shouldn't he keep his eyes on the road?'

'He's an excellent driver.' Nick pulled insistently until she relented and lifted her hips from the seat, allowing him to remove her panties. Closing his eyes, he held them to his face for a moment while he drank in her scent. Then, resting his hands on her naked inner thighs, he pressed his face to her sex.

Julia tensed as his tongue swirled over her labia, prising them open. The chauffeur's dark eyes were leering appreciatively. Julia watched, dumbstruck, as he adjusted his mirror for a better view. Turning to Steve, her protest was caught in her throat. Outside, two young Japanese tourists had their faces pressed to the window and were peering in.

Her eyes widened. She gripped Steve's knee. 'Can they see anything?'

'I'm not sure. Shall I open the window and ask them?' He smiled. 'Does it bother you? I didn't think it would. You seemed to enjoy being watched, yesterday.'

Aghast, Julia dropped her head back on to the headrest. Steve was mocking her, which wasn't like him at all. The thrill of the situation must have warped his mind. 'Stop him,' she breathed, the heat of humiliation burning beneath Nick's tongue. 'Make him stop.'

Steve obliged, pushing Nick out of the way and back into his seat. Glaring at the chauffeur, Julia pulled her skirt back down. But a minute later his eyes glittered in the mirror once again. Steve had replaced Nick; her skirt was up around her hips again, his mouth descending to the wet lips of her gaping sex.

'Oh,' she cried, overwhelmed with helplessness. With the car stuck in the early-evening traffic, the driver was free to drink in her discomfort while the tourists tapped persistently on the glass. Nick watched, too, smirking as he slid his hand inside his trousers. She felt like a caged animal, trapped and on show, degraded – and yet aroused beyond belief.

'You smell wonderful.' Steve kissed her sex, just as he'd kissed her mouth the night before, slowly, tenderly. 'You taste wonderful, too.' His tongue poked inside her. Julia's buttocks tensed and she lifted her pelvis up into his face. Meeting the driver's gaze through her half-closed eyelids, she flinched. But her body abandoned all self-consciousness, betraying her with her own lust. Moaning quietly, she opened her legs as wide as they would go, until she felt the tendons pulling across her inner thighs.

Steve licked deep inside her, sucking out every drop of arousal. Julia's head rolled as she watched him, fastidious in his work, focused on pleasuring every inner inch of her. As ecstasy flowed on to his hot tongue, her body sank into a state of deep relaxation. Then he fastened his lips around her throbbing clitoris, and every muscle jerked. Hooking her knees over his shoulders as he leant into her, she squeezed his neck between her thighs and dug the heels of her shoes into his back. She rested her hands on his head, delighting almost as much in the feel of him moving beneath her fingers, as in the sensation of his lips around her pleasure.

She shuddered quietly: not the roaring orgasm of the night before, but something equally satisfying. A warm glow crept over her body as if she'd stepped into the sunshine. Blinking sleepily, she waited for Steve to return to his place beside her, then gratefully licked and kissed her musk from his shining lips.

'That was amazing,' she said when she'd finished.

'It was for me, too.' Putting his arm around her shoulder, he stroked her neck beneath her hair. 'It feels incredible to make a woman come. Especially when she's such a beautiful woman.' He kissed her reverently on the lips. 'You taste like heaven.'

She smiled, a smile that warmed her inside. He said the nicest things.

At the front of the limo, the driver coughed politely: a ridiculous gesture, considering what he'd just witnessed. 'Excuse me, miss, but where are we driving you this evening?'

'I suspect these two want to drive me insane.' She smiled as she felt Nick's hands on her knees once again. 'But you can drop me off in Clapham.'

Marianne

'You got my message, then?'

Julia took her hands off the edge of the desk and sat on them, to hide the fact that they were shaking. 'Yes, George, I got your message. Why else do you think I'd be here at the crack of dawn?'

He slammed his office door and the rattling of the blinds caused a draught to lift some of the papers off his desk. 'Don't you get stroppy with me, young lady.' He shuffled around the desk, heaving his body into his chair. 'You've a lot of explaining to do, Ms Sargent.' He emphasised the Ms, as he always did when he was livid, spitting it out like a flake of tobacco on his tongue.

Unfortunately for Julia, her mind was furry with sleep. She still hadn't thought of a good excuse, since getting home to find George's wrath recorded on her answerphone, and now time was running out. It was important, if she was going to leave the *Chronicle*, to leave on good terms. George had given her a big hand-up in her career, and she had repaid him by abandoning a plum job. She had delivered results for him, time and time again, but all the brownie points she'd earnt over the last three years would have been wiped out by last night. Somehow, she suspected, a plea of temporary insanity was not going to appease him.

'So.' He tilted back in his chair and took a puff on his fat cigar. 'I'm all ears. Tell me you had a good reason.'

Julia fluttered her eyelids, feigning innocence. She wanted to stall him while she kick started her brain. 'A good reason for what, George?'

'You winding me up?' He jabbed a stubby finger at her accusingly. 'What's the story here, Julia? First, you ring in sick with some bullshit about the flu. I mean to say, couldn't you have come up with something more original? Then, you walk off a job.' He raised his bushy eyebrows, waiting expectantly. 'Now, I know you. Despite all your moaning, you love this job. Why on earth would you let me down like this?'

Julia stood up. She walked to the narrow window and peered down at the street below. As far as she could see, there was only one way to play this situation. She had to be as honest as possible. 'I was bored.'

George choked on his cigar. 'I beg your pardon?'

'I was bored.' She turned her back on the window. 'I flipped. I know it was unprofessional, irresponsible, blah, blah, blah. But I just couldn't take it any more. Don't you ever feel like that, George?'

George's face was turning puce. 'Feel like what?'

'Like you've had enough. I looked at all those airhead celebrities; I looked at myself, pushing to get the shots, and I thought, what the hell am I doing here? Who cares?'

'I'll tell you who cares.' Wishing, no doubt, that he could use Julia's hand as an ashtray, he viciously stubbed out his cigar. 'I care, when I'm sitting here at eight o'clock in the evening, wondering where the hell you've got to. The editor cares, when I have to tell him we've got a hole in the paper because our showbiz photographer's gone AWOL. The financial directors care, when we have to pay for pictures from an agency when we've already paid a staff photographer.' He struggled to his feet, wheezing with anger. 'And the readers care. That's why they buy the bloody paper!'

Julia winced as a stream of spittle showered his desk. 'I'm sorry, George.'

'Sorry? Sorry! Ha!'

So far, this wasn't going very well. A bombshell was needed – but would it silence him, or send him over the edge? Julia took a deep breath. 'I've decided to go freelance.'

For a moment she thought he was going to keel over. His mouth fell open, his eyes bulged, and he grabbed the edge of the desk to steady himself. Slowly, he squashed himself back down into his seat and began to breathe again. 'Freelance.' He nodded, his voice worryingly calm in contrast to his expression. 'You want to become a freelance. Well, that's charming. After all I've done for you. I nurtured you, Julia. I'll be honest, you weren't the best of the trainees but I could see you had talent. I fought for your promotion and this is how you reward me.' His piggy eyes were black with anger. 'I take it you've put a lot of thought into this. You're not just basing your decision on the fact that you're "bored"?'

'Er . . . no,' she faltered. 'There are lots of reasons –'

'So you're fully aware of how many freelancers there are, out there? And you know they'd all give their right arm to be on staff? To have a salary, holidays, a pension?'

'I need a new challenge, George.'

For a long moment he stared at her, squinting through narrowed eyes, trying to make sense of what she was saying. 'Fine,' he snapped at last. 'But I can't give you a good reference, Julia, not after last night. And I can't let you go without a warning that going solo won't be easy. Word will get round that you walked off a job. No editor's going to trust you.'

Julia felt her cheeks going red. She hadn't thought of

that. Suddenly, the next mortgage repayment loomed like a creature from the deep. Shakily, she resumed her seat opposite George. 'I just want a chance to do something serious, something worthwhile.'

Leaning forward, he held her cold hands in his thick, clammy fingers. 'Julia, sweetheart, you're good at what you do. Your work may not be political, or important, but people like looking at celebrities. If you take my advice, you'll stick with what you know. There are hundreds of photographers out there who'd kill for your job. The grass isn't always greener on the other side.'

Perhaps he was right. She smiled uncertainly.

'You're used to having your subjects handed to you on a plate. Studio photography is a skill, Julia – one that you're good at. Politicians don't pose. News doesn't happen in the studio, under the lights. Photojournalism is a different world.'

She felt her jaw hardening. 'You don't think I could handle it?'

He gave her a patronising smile. 'I just think you should know all the facts before you make any rash decisions. You're just starting to make a name for yourself. It's going to be very hard to make the leap into news photography now . . .'

Despite herself, Julia found her attention drifting. He was talking sense but it wasn't what she wanted to hear. Escaping his lecture, she wrapped herself in thoughts of Nick and Steve, and nervous excitement began to bubble in her stomach.

'. . . and you haven't listened to a word I've been saying, have you?'

She jumped back to the present. 'What? Oh, I'm sorry, George. I've got a lot on my mind.'

Letting go of her, he sat back and lit another cigar. He used the pause to study her. Suddenly, he threw his hands up. 'Christ, I should've known. It's the wedding, isn't it? Women always go off the rails before they get married. Your mind's on other things, eh?'

'Er . . . you could say that.'

Swivelling round in his chair, he looked up at the huge wall planner behind his desk. On it were scribbled notes, incomprehensible to anyone but George. Swivelling round again, he slapped his palm down decisively. 'Here's what I'm going to do, babe. I'm going to give you the rest of the week off to sort yourself out. If I know you, you've probably got a thousand things you haven't done yet. So do them, and get some sleep while you're at it. You look exhausted.'

She bit her lip. With any luck, she wouldn't have much time for sleep. 'Thanks, George. You don't know what this means to me.' Standing up, she leant over and planted a kiss on his wrinkled forehead.

'Get out of here.' Blushing like a boy, he waved her away. 'You can thank me by forgetting all about this freelance bullshit. By Monday, I want the old Julia back.'

'Well, this is a nice surprise. To what do I owe the honour?'

Another desk, another office. In contrast to George's, Marianne's was spacious, plush, and frighteningly sparse. Ignoring her friend's invitation to sit down, Julia fidgeted at the window. 'Just thought I'd call in – see if you wanted to go for lunch.'

Marianne perched her Prada-skirted bottom on the corner of her desk. 'It's ten o'clock, Julia.'

'Brunch, then.'

'Aren't you working today?'

'I've got the rest of the week off.'

'Lucky cow. How did you wangle that?'

'George seems to think I'm freaking out with the pressure of the wedding.'

'You!' A shriek of laughter flew from her perfect red lips. 'Whatever gave him that impression?'

'I was supposed to be at the film première last night –'

'Did you see Pierce Brosnan? God, that man is gorgeous.'

'I didn't see anyone. I walked off. I went for a drive with some friends instead.'

Marianne was intrigued. Her eyes glittered. 'You've got a very silly smirk on your face, Jules. Now, spill the beans.'

'There aren't any beans to spill.' She waited, cruelly drawing out Marianne's suspense. 'Nick and Steve turned up in Leicester Square in a limo and offered me a lift home, that's all.'

Marianne's eyes narrowed with suspicion. 'Steve ... as in Steve Roth? Nick as in . . .'

'Nick Trent.' Unstoppable, Julia's smile spread into a grin. 'Still as gorgeous as ever, I might add.'

There was a knock at the door. Julia smiled as Marianne's recently appointed assistant announced that her meeting was about to start: young, blond, and attractive in a public schoolboy sort of way, it was quite obvious why he'd got the job.

Julia tutted disapprovingly as he closed the door behind him. 'Was he really the best candidate for the job?'

'His credentials are excellent.'

'You mean to say you actually read his CV?'

'I wasn't talking about those credentials.' Sniggering wickedly, Marianne stood up and smoothed down her short navy skirt. 'Look, I've got to go. If this presentation wasn't so important I'd cancel it. But I shall expect you at my flat at seven, on the dot.' She turned at the door. 'I'll provide the wine. You provide the juicy details.'

Marianne answered the door in a long white T-shirt and a pair of socks. Her hair was damp from the shower and she was breathless. 'Is it seven already?'

'Six thirty. I couldn't wait any longer – thought I'd take a chance and see if you were home.'

'Finished early, for once.' She turned and padded off down her hallway towards the living room. 'Bit naughty, really, but I couldn't concentrate.' She flopped on to her dark-red sofa, her hair spreading around her like streaks of sunshine.

Julia sat down beside her, shifting to remove something rigid from underneath her thigh. Raising one eyebrow, she held up the familiar black vibrator.

'I was reminiscing,' Marianne explained. 'About Nick.' Bending over, she poured red wine into the two empty glasses waiting by her feet. She passed one to Julia then, turning around so she could lean against the cushioned arm of the settee, she put her feet in Julia's lap. 'Come on then, I'm dying to know what that lecherous smile is all about.'

Julia told her everything. Every minute was included, from Sunday lunch at David's parents', to last night's adventures in the silver limo. Julia had always been able to talk details with Marianne and she left nothing to the imagination. Marianne rarely interrupted, except when she wanted more: what colour hair did the man on the train have, how much olive oil did Nick use for lubrication? She was rapt, clinging breathlessly to every word, and Julia found her own excitement intensified by that of her friend. As she shared her secret feelings, she had to squeeze her inner thighs together to quell the rising thrill in her pussy. Marianne obviously felt the same, hugging her knees to her chest and fidgeting restlessly. Julia blinked, hesitating in her storytelling as her eyes were drawn to the slit of crimson darkness between Marianne's exposed upper thighs. Beneath her T-shirt she was naked; the shocking distraction of her pouting sex making Julia lose her thread for a moment. Marianne, completely unaware, begged Julia to finish.

When she had, she sipped her wine, her innards

twisting in a dance of depraved delight. It was such fun sharing anything with Marianne, but it was incredibly gratifying to shock her into silence. For a long time both sat quietly, lost in their thoughts.

Eventually, Marianne let out a long, wistful sigh. 'Do you realise, you've had more men in the last week than you've had in the last five years?'

Julia joined her in a fit of the giggles. 'Do you realise, I've been unfaithful to David with four different men? Leon Sparrow, Richard, Steve and Nick...' It wasn't funny, but she couldn't help herself. She doubled up with inane laughter.

'What are you going to tell David?'

Julia gasped for air, trying to calm herself. 'Don't know yet. I've got till Sunday to think about it.'

Leaning forward, Marianne put her hand on Julia's arm. 'You've made the right decision where he's concerned. He wasn't right for you.'

Julia turned to her friend, making a conscious effort not to allow her eyes to flicker downward. Marianne's pretty face was a picture of sincerity, her blue eyes wide with sisterly concern. She had never been keen on David. Julia had been disappointed when her best friend had reacted with disbelief at their engagement but she had been right all along. Her own relationships may have been a succession of quick, satisfying flings, but Marianne's views on Julia's men were uncannily accurate. Julia rested her hand on top of Marianne's and smiled gratefully. Inexplicably, she had the urge to kiss her, to part her pretty lips with her tongue. Shaken by her desire, Julia took her hand away and looked down into her lap.

Marianne sat back. 'So, who's going to be the lucky man, Steve or Nick?'

'I ... I don't know,' Julia mumbled, confused by the rush of arousal she felt for her friend. Was she turning into a sex-maniac?

'Promise me I can have the loser.' Marianne let out a loud deep breath. 'God, two men fighting over you, Jules. It's the sexiest thing I've ever heard.'

Julia glanced up, looked away, then had to do a double-take. Leaning back on the armrest, Marianne was sitting with her knees flopped apart and her hand in the gap. 'What are you doing?' Julia whispered, although it was quite obvious.

Marianne half-closed her eyes and arched her upper back. 'You've made me so horny I could die.'

'Sorry.' Julia's voice was barely audible, muffled with the shock of seeing her friend desperately lost in arousal.

'Don't be sorry,' she moaned softly. 'Touch me.'

'What?'

Marianne didn't reply. She just reached out for Julia, her hand trembling slightly. Swallowing her bewilderment, Julia put her hand in Marianne's and allowed her friend to guide it downward. For an instant she hesitated: time for a million thoughts to cloud her mind. This didn't make sense. They were best friends. Then her fingertips touched the warm, silky wetness of Marianne's pussy and her mind cleared. All of a sudden, it made sense – because they were best friends. It was natural, and easy, and beautiful.

Marianne took her own hand away and opened her legs until her knees were flat. Pulling up her T-shirt, she watched as Julia discovered her sex. Julia's eyes were fixed to her fingers, her concentration so deep she almost forgot to breathe. Marianne's sex was the same as hers, and yet so different. There was pale blonde hair where hers was dark, and there were other, less obvious differences: nuances of shape and colour, subtleties of the flesh. But the reactions were the same. Stroke between the satin inner edges of her labia and she became wet, circle the tiny knob of her clitoris and it grew hard.

Julia's bright friendship with Marianne suddenly took on a deeper hue, and a dark, sticky warmth seeped within her, rich as the wine she'd drunk. It felt so simple, drawing out the pleasure from between Marianne's slender thighs. It was sex and masturbation rolled deliciously into one. It was instinctive, pure, sensuous delight.

Moving closer, Julia slid her free hand underneath Marianne's T-shirt. She gazed at her friend's delicate breasts, their gentle mounds tipped with pale-pink areolae. Fingers aching with the thrill of another woman's flesh beneath her touch, she traced the soft outlines, smoothing her palms over the slight mounds and savouring the sensation of her soft, cool skin. As she gently cupped the tiny weights in her hand, Marianne's fingers brushed over hers. Her eyelids fluttered with pleasure as Julia aroused one of her pale nipples, teasing it into stiffness with finger and thumb. Stooping, she pressed her lips to the other areola, flicking it with her tongue until the skin puckered in delight, her body quivering as Julia tentatively grazed her with her teeth.

With her breasts swollen with desire and her nipples hard, Marianne pushed Julia away. She sat up and ran her fingers down the slope of Julia's neck before unbuttoning her shirt. Sweeping the crisp cotton away from her body, Marianne reached around to unclip her friend's white bra. While Marianne pulled off her own T-shirt, Julia kicked off her shoes and wriggled out of her jeans and knickers. Copying Marianne, she knelt up on the sofa. As they faced each other and Marianne openly admired her soft curves, Julia felt a sharp pang of longing in her pussy. Her skin was pale compared to Marianne's; her pubic hair darkly lush in contrast; her body voluptuous and full next to Marianne's slim athleticism. They didn't match, and yet, as Marianne put her hands to Julia's waist and brought their bodies close together, they fitted perfectly. Their nipples pressed together – Marianne's pink and stiff, Julia's brown and soft – and both women looked down as their areolae kissed and they became one.

Marianne's fingers touched the sides of Julia's breasts, moulding around the fullness of her flesh. Their eyes met; their heads tilted and they kissed. Not a tentative kiss, but a full, reckless embrace that spoke deeply of subconscious desires. It was surprising how effortless it was, tongues, lips and fingers merging as if they belonged on each other's faces, in each other's hair. Locked in their passion they fell backward, their bodies becoming a singular entity, a writhing mass of sensuousness. Marianne's hand slid between Julia's thighs, her fingers twisting in the damp curls before she opened her pussy lips and entered her hot moistness. As Julia gasped for air, Marianne's lips pressed at her neck and throat, kissing out a rhythm that matched her pulsating hips. Julia mauled at her friend's breasts, pinching her nipples until she cried out with the deliciousness of the pain. In return, Marianne punished Julia by pressing on her clitoris until it throbbed in desperation. Shaking with need, Julia struggled to stretch her legs out beneath Marianne's, pulling at her narrow hips until they were poised above her own.

For a moment, Marianne sat astride Julia. The two women tugged playfully at each other's nipples and ground their hips together, delaying the inevitable. Then the heady scent of feminine musk hit Julia's nostrils and, like an addict, she reached out for more. Grabbing Marianne's smooth buttocks, she brought her vulva to her lips. Her breathing was rapid and hot on her friend's secret flesh as she paused, thinking how the swell of her labia was so different to her own and yet the same, a part of her own sexuality. Holding on to the backs of Marianne's lightly muscled thighs, Julia pressed her mouth between her legs.

Her instincts took control and her tongue wound a spiralling path over Marianne's sex. Straining her neck, she thrust deep inside, startled by the sensation of the pussy muscles clutching at her tongue. She kissed her labia as if they were lips, nibbling gently on the delicate flesh, sweeping over their inner surfaces. She sucked at her hard clitoris, pulling it into further, angry stiffness until Marianne gasped and shuddered above her. Marianne's inner thighs quivered as she came and, with a loud moan of relief, she collapsed beside Julia.

For a while they lay together, Marianne gently kissing away the moistness that glistened on Julia's lips. Her eyes were full of wonder. Revelling in the beauty of their gently swooping curves, they touched each other incessantly, reminding themselves of the details – pouting breast, sloping belly, silky inner thigh – that confirmed it really was another woman they were lying with.

'Steve was right,' Julia whispered eventually.

'About what?'

She looked at Marianne, her high cheekbones flushed with ecstasy. 'It feels incredible to make a woman come.' She smiled, running her fingers down Marianne's spine. 'It's like sticking your tongue into heaven. It's beautiful.'

'You'd recommend it, then?' Marianne smiled, easing her way out of Julia's arms.

'Oh, yes,' Julia murmured, losing her fingers in Marianne's soft hair as her friend's head slowly dipped. 'Oh ... oh ... yes.'

Nick

Julia paced up and down outside the tube station. She had arrived late, but Nick was even later, and every second he kept her waiting was agony. Glancing at her reflection in the window of the café across the street, she checked her appearance for the hundredth time. Her hair looked silky, its dark auburn sheen glowing in the early-autumn sunshine. Her outfit was perfect, although it had taken ages to choose it that morning, and it would take ages to clear up the discarded clothes strewn around her bedroom when she got home. She wore a pale-green V-neck jumper, a slate-grey skirt that flared to just above the knee and black, high-heeled loafers. There was a slight chill in the air, but she probably would have worn stockings for the occasion, whatever the weather. She loved the feel of the suspenders pulling against her thighs as she walked. And she would love the look on Nick's face as he took them off.

Her focus changed as someone in the café stood up and came to the door. She put her hands on her hips as she recognised him.

'I've been waiting for fifteen minutes,' she reprimanded as he approached. 'You're supposed to be making a good impression. Not a very good start, is it?'

He slid his hand through her arm and round her waist, kissing her on the cheek. 'I got here early, on purpose. I wanted to watch you.'

Her brow twitched as she looked up at him. 'You mean you've been sat in that café the whole time I've been here?'

'I thought you'd seen me. You kept looking right at me, but then I realised you were checking out your own reflection, you vain creature.' Behind her, his hand slid down to her buttock. 'I was watching your breasts bouncing as you walked. The wind caught your skirt once and I saw the tops of your stockings,' he whispered in her ear. 'Just looking at you gives me a hard-on.'

Julia caught her breath. This was unbelievable: ten seconds with Nick and she could already feel herself getting wet.

'Did you bring your costume?'

She nodded. She had had a strange phone call from Nick's secretary that morning, requesting that she bring her swimsuit and asking what size feet she had. 'What do you need to know my shoe size for?'

He tapped the side of his nose. 'All will be revealed, in good time. Now, come along. I'm dying to see you with your clothes off again.'

The pool was deliciously warm but fairly crowded. The health club was populated with all types: there were gay men, lesbians, old men and women doing slow but determined lengths, heavily made-up, nouveau-riche housewives, and young mothers enjoying the peace while their children were in the crèche. But as Julia did a slow breaststroke back to the shallow end, dodging the swimmers who had decided to do widths rather than lengths, she was aware of only one other person in the pool. The others were vague shapes, like fish glimpsed beneath the surface of a murky sea. Nick was the only clear figure, his knees bent so that everything beneath his chest was submerged in the warmth, his well-defined arms stretched out along the poolside, his eyes burning into hers like lasers.

'Stand up,' he said, as she finished her length a couple of feet in front of him. His eyes trickled over her skin like the water. Julia smiled, glad she had made the effort to get up early and buy herself a new swimming costume. This one was silky black, with a dark, slightly see-through panel starting beneath her breasts and finishing at her hips.

Nick slowly straightened one leg and hooked his foot around the back of Julia's knee. As her leg gave way and her body lowered back into the pool, he drew her nearer. He slid his hands around on to her buttocks and then downward, lifting her thighs and wrapping them round his waist. He gently pulled her closer, until Julia could feel the slight bulge in his trunks.

'I hope you don't choose me.' He smiled, his eyes twinkling. 'I don't think I could cope with having an erection twenty-four hours a day.'

Julia put her arms around his neck. 'I'm sure the novelty of me would soon wear off.'

'Never.' Beneath the water, he squeezed her cheeks. 'I'd make sure it didn't.' Holding on to her waist with one arm, he slipped his other hand between their bodies. 'I'd make sure to keep things exciting.'

'And how would you do that?' She wriggled as his hand clasped around her sex.

'By always fucking you when you least expected it.' To emphasise his point, his fingers found their way beneath the elastic at her crotch.

'Oh, Nick.' She glanced surreptitiously around her, to see if anyone was watching. 'Don't, not here.'

'Why not?' Without warning, he slid a finger inside her.

Julia bit her lip, stifling a sigh. 'Someone will notice.'

'Only if you make a noise.'

An evil leer began to twitch at the corners of his wide mouth. Julia squeezed the back of his neck, wishing his lips weren't so sexy; wishing his fingers weren't so clever. As swimmers drifted past them or came to rest by their side, another finger joined the first and his thumb pressed expertly around her clitoris. It was almost impossible to keep her face straight and her moans inside. His grip around her waist was loose enough to escape from, but his touch at her sex was irresistible.

An elderly lady swam to a stop next to them. Nick glanced at her, then back to Julia. Pursing his lips to tell her to keep quiet, he increased the torture. His thumb flickered over the raw tip of her clit, making her body jerk suddenly with the agony of it.

'Please,' she begged under her breath. 'Please stop before I scream.'

'OK.' He released her, letting her float free from his body. He smiled as he noticed her lips part with disappointment. 'Isn't that what you wanted?'

Two can play at that game, she thought. Standing beside him, looking around innocently, she slipped her hand into his trunks. Reaching beneath his growing erection, she fondled his heavy balls. Teasing her, Nick began to hum nonchalantly. Julia squeezed him harder, until he flinched. Pressing her palm hard against his penis, she unfurled it until it was straight, its head peering above the waistband of his trunks. Rubbing up and down, she felt him twitch and heard him grumble quietly.

Giggling to herself, she abandoned him and swam off. A moment later she heard him launch after her. She swam as hard as she could, gasping for air at the thought of him chasing. Any minute now he would catch up. A hand snatched at her ankle, tugging hard and pulling her down. Involuntary panic set in as her nose and mouth filled with water. They thrashed together, Julia struggling to find a way out of his strong arms. Spluttering frantically, she shook her hair as she emerged from the splashing.

'Come on.' Nick stood up and pushed his wet hair out of his face. Taking her hand, he began to wade towards the side.

'Where are we going?'

'I'd like you to meet an old friend of mine.'

It was quite obvious what sort of friend Katja had been. Tall, blonde and statuesque, she was a Scandinavian cliché. Her large breasts and wide hips were accentuated by her tight white uniform. She smiled knowingly over Nick's shoulder as he kissed her on both cheeks.

Julia waited while they caught up on what had happened since their brief affair. Katja was vacuous but sweet, giggling at Nick's jokes and half-heartedly brushing his hands away as he squeezed her round the waist. Julia suspected, by the way he kept glancing in her direction, that he was attempting to make her jealous. It was working.

'And who is this?' Katja asked, in a thick Swedish accent.

'Katja, meet Julia. An even older friend.' Nick ushered her into the small room. As the two women shook hands shyly, he beamed uncontrollably. 'My two favourite women in the same room. It's a wet dream come true.'

Katja tutted, rolling her eyes and smiling at Julia. She obviously knew Nick quite well. 'Be quiet and get on the table, Nick.'

'It's Julia who needs your magic touch today. She's very tense.'

'I am?'

Nick patted the high bed. 'Get on. Katja's fantastic with her fingers.'

'I bet she is.' Dropping her towelling robe to the floor,

Julia climbed up on to the table. Behind her, Katja laid a soft towel over her legs. In front of her, Nick settled down into the armchair. His eyes danced as Katja began to soothe her warm, oil-coated hands over Julia's back. If the feeling hadn't been so divine, Julia might have resented his leering. She hadn't expected to have to re-enact his fantasies for him, playing out a scene from a soft-core movie. But Katja did have magic fingers and Nick's appreciation of the two women's bodies was really quite arousing. Katja's nearness was exciting, too. The way she pressed deep into Julia's muscles, forcing involuntary groans from her lungs; the touch of a stranger, a woman; her businesslike movements; the rustle of her uniform. Together with Nick's expression of gratified wonder, it added up to a situation bubbling with barely hidden sensuality.

'Full body massage?' Katja asked.

'Yes, please,' Nick replied. As Katja rolled the towel down to expose Julia's behind, he sat forward expectantly.

Julia jumped with shock as Katja's fingers burrowed deep into her buttocks. The feeling was incredibly erotic, especially when unexpected fingertips brushed the silken skin around her anus. Julia shuddered, reminded of the delicious agony of Nick's long cock inside her there. The massage continued downward and, as Katja squeezed her upper thighs, Julia's sex was delicately pulled open. She closed her eyes, sliding easily into the memory of last night and Marianne.

Katja moved gradually down her thighs, calves and feet, then asked her to roll over. Making slow, deliberate progress back up her body, she pressed her thumbs into the fronts of Julia's legs, all along her arms and along the tops of her shoulders. Then, pouring more sweet-smelling oil into her palms, she stopped kneading and began to soothe her willing subject. Julia sighed as her body melted. By the time Katja's rubbing moved over her breasts, she had surrendered to a state of such deep relaxation that the woman could have brought her to orgasm with the faintest touch on her pulsing clitoris.

Julia looked down along her body. Her skin glistened provocatively with oil. The full mounds of her breasts seemed to grow beneath the masseuse's strong but gentle touch. Her nipples were stiff with excitement. Her gaze moved upward from Katja's fingers and she wondered what would happen if she reached up to unbutton her starched white dress. Did Katja feel the tension crackling beneath her fingertips? Was she as close to falling as Julia? Did she long to press her rolling curves on to another woman's, to feel her skin turn slippery with the oil coating Julia's body, to allow her fingers to continue their work in other, secret, places?

Julia was rolled over again, so that her back could be soothed as her front had been. Propping her chin on her hands, Julia smiled at the sight of Nick's discomfort. 'Enjoying yourself?'

In answer, he lifted the flap of his bathrobe. Beneath the innocent white towelling, his penis reared angrily, its head purple with frustration.

'It serves you right,' Julia whispered.

They walked down to the changing rooms together.

'You were as turned on as I was in there, weren't you?' Nick asked, his brown eyes glinting with gratification. 'It shocked you, discovering that another woman could make you feel like that.'

'Hardly,' Julia scoffed, pushing at the door to the ladies' room. 'After what happened with Marianne, that massage was tame.'

Nick grabbed her shoulder as she turned to go. 'Marianne?'

'We made love. Last night.' His amazement was thrilling. 'Close your mouth, Nick. If the wind changes, you'll stay like that.'

In the changing room, Julia's satisfaction was immediately dulled. Her clothes were gone. Looking on every peg, she searched frantically, but there was no sign of them. Standing in the middle of the tiled floor in only her bathrobe, she was wondering what the hell she was going to do, when Katja appeared.

'Nick asked me to bring you this.' She handed Julia a box. 'You're very lucky. He's quite a catch.'

'I've lost my clothes,' Julia blurted. 'They must have been stolen.'

'Oh, yes, they were stolen by your boyfriend. I think he wants you to put on what's in the box.' Katja winked. 'He always did have a thing for leather, didn't he?'

She turned and walked off, her hips swaying provocatively. Julia put the box down on the bench and opened it up. Beneath the layer of tissue paper was a neatly folded, black leather jacket. Lying beneath that was a matching pair of leather trousers and under those a pair of heavy-soled biker boots with two-inch heels. At the very bottom of the box, her stockings and suspenders lay crumpled. Julia fingered the flimsy nylons, inexplicably excited by the thought that Nick had touched them.

Clumsy with impatient anticipation of what was to come, she fumbled into her outfit. A woman sitting next to her on the bench eyed her suspiciously as she slipped on the soft trousers with only her stockings and suspenders beneath. The seam between her legs dug gently into her pussy and the feeling of the leather against her naked flesh made her juices flow again. She pulled on the boots and shrugged on the jacket. It could have been made for her, fitting snugly over her curves and meeting perfectly with the waistband of her trousers. A thick silver zipper pulled right up to the neck where there was a simple, pointed collar. Standing in front of the mirror, Julia put on a fresh coat of dark-red lipstick and surveyed her dramatic reflection. She looked like an adolescent's fantasy; she felt like a vixen. Pulling the zip open to the top of her cleavage, she flicked her hair back and smiled to herself. Nick knew what he liked. Someone less sure of themselves may have been taken aback by his openness, but she adored it. They were his ideals she was fulfilling but she was happy for him to take the lead. It made her feel like a woman.

Outside, in the reception, they smiled as they looked each other up and down. Nick was dressed in the same way as Julia, except his boots were flat and heavier, and his jacket wasn't quite as figure-hugging. His trousers weren't as tight as hers either, although the curves of his buttocks were satisfyingly obvious. He held out a black helmet for Julia.

'You look fantastic.' He gently slid the helmet on for her. 'Ever felt the throb of fifteen hundred cc's between your legs?'

'Is it anything like the throb of a vibrator?'

'Just the same.' He pushed his helmet on. 'Only a thousand times more powerful.'

The bike stood outside waiting for them, a gleaming beast of shiny black and silver. Straddling the wide seat behind Nick, Julia wrapped her arms around him. With a kick, the engine started, and before she knew it they were racing down the narrow street. Nick rode his bike how he lived his life: accelerating as much as possible between junctions. Julia felt slightly nervous at being out of control, but at the same time the feeling of abandoning herself to his care was intoxicating. She closed her eyes, relishing the freedom, the rush of air, the thrill between her legs. When she opened her eyes again the Thames was on her right. They were heading east.

Julia had to shout to be heard above the motorbike's screaming engine. 'Where are you taking me?'

'Do you care?' he shouted back.

She thought for a moment – thought of how she felt when they were together. Of how she'd felt since she'd bumped into him in the lift – excited, on edge, alive. It was like being eighteen all over again, but better. Being with Nick was dangerous and she'd craved a bit of danger for so long.

She tightened her grip around his waist. 'No, I don't care any more,' she laughed. 'You can take me anywhere.' She leant her face into his shoulder. 'I'll do anything you want.'

'I know you will.' The lunchtime traffic was thick along the Embankment and Nick had to slow down as he edged between the cars. He lowered his voice to its normal level. 'You career women are all the same.'

'Are we, now?'

'You want to have complete control of your decisions, your money and your future. But the bedroom's a different matter. What you're really after in bed is a man who'll take the control away from you. Someone who'll make you feel all helpless and sexy.'

Julia was stunned. 'Since when did you become an expert in sexual politics?'

'Since I went out with a sex therapist.' Tilting the bike, he swooped into the outside lane. 'I'll prove my theory, if you like. Unzip your jacket.'

'What?'

'Do it.' His tone of voice was harsh and arrogant. Something about it made Julia's heart pound frantically. Taking one hand away from his waist, she squeezed it between their bodies and pulled the zip open. Returning her hand, she pressed their torsos back together. The leather of his jacket was cool on her skin as she squashed her naked breasts into his back. 'You see? You'll do anything I say. It gets you wet, being told what to do.'

She couldn't deny it. The pulse deep inside her belly was turning into an ache.

'The next time we stop at the lights, I want you to let go of me. Show your breasts to whoever's next to us.'

'No way!' She laughed. 'What on earth makes you think I'd do something like that?'

'Because you've got fantastic tits and you love showing them off. And my telling you to do it is all the excuse you need.'

She squirmed in the seat, uncomfortable with his certainty. Nick was right. She loved it when she caught a man giving her the once-over – although he had to be attractive. Rather than feeling threatened by a man's attention, it empowered Julia to know that he wanted her. She would never have exposed herself as blatantly as Nick was suggesting. But, now that the thought was implanted in her mind, the idea was electrifying.

The traffic freed up a little and Nick opened up the throttle. Weaving in between the cars, he managed to get through two sets of traffic lights on amber. Julia could hardly believe it, but she found herself willing him to slow down, to get caught behind a red light. She imagined a parachutist might feel like this before a first jump: dreading the moment, but wanting it desperately, too. Inevitably, it arrived. Caught behind a car with no room to overtake, the bike came to a halt.

Nick looked over his shoulder. 'Do it.'

She hesitated, her pulse racing.

'Now, Julia!'

She looked down to her left. Beside the bike was an open-topped Escort carrying four young lads. Catching the eye of the driver, Julia let go of Nick and leant backward. Reaching around behind her, she grabbed hold of the edge of her seat and languidly arched her back. Her body parted from Nick's and her breasts pouted from the black leather, pale and shocking in contrast. Open-mouthed, the young driver nudged the passenger beside him, who whooped with unrestrained delight. The two in the rear joined in, wolf-whistling in appreciation. Power flooded Julia's pussy as their eager eyes spread all over her breasts. Turning her head slightly, she met Nick's lascivious eyes in the wing mirror. When the bike set off again she very reluctantly closed the gap between them. The rush she'd got was addictive; she wanted more, wanted to show her body to every man in London.

Nick's helmet bobbed as he nodded. 'Told you you wanted to. You enjoyed that, didn't you?' He glanced down as the Escort appeared beside them again, the four men gesturing wildly, begging Julia for a repeat performance. 'Not as much as they did, obviously.'

As they sped away from the car, Julia turned and waved at the boys. In the distance, she heard them groan with disappointment. Sliding one hand down into Nick's crotch, she smiled as she felt his hardness once again.

They drove through the City, heading towards Docklands. Julia hadn't been this far east since the opening party for a television station, in Canary Wharf. They rode past the glass landmark and carried onward, heading to the parts of the Wharf that had remained undeveloped since the commercial property boom had fizzled out. On and on they went, until civilisation was left behind and they entered a strange wasteland. Here, only minutes from London's crowded core, was something that not many city dwellers ever saw: space. But it was a desolate landscape, filled only with rubble and half-finished office blocks. The tarmac was still black, since the roads here in the capital's far east had seen little traffic. Nick swung the bike off the road and came to a stop in front of a tower of scaffolding. As the engine went silent, Julia zipped up her jacket.

Nick took off his helmet and looked up at the shell of a building in front of them. 'What do you think?'

Julia took off her helmet and shook her hair. 'Of what?'

'This.' He waved a hand towards the building site. 'It's Steve's latest acquisition.'

He'd brought her all this way to show her that? 'How interesting,' she muttered, slightly disgruntled.

'We're spending the afternoon here.'

Julia blinked the incomprehension from her eyes. 'We are?'

'Steve only let me have the day off on the condition I'd pay the site a visit.' He helped Julia off the bike. 'Don't worry. You'll enjoy yourself, I promise.'

'Somehow, I doubt it.'

He kissed her, hard. 'Just play along with me, Jules, and I swear you'll have the time of your life.'

Her eyebrows dipped. Intrigued, she asked Nick what he meant, but he was already striding off towards the site entrance.

It soon became obvious what he meant. As he inspected the site, stopping to chat with the builders, he kept his hand on her arse. He didn't introduce Julia to anyone but, as the men stole furtive glances at her, Nick acknowledged their interest, winking and sniggering with them. He was parading her around like a trophy, feeding off the lust of his staff and turning her on at the same time. As Julia basked in the heat of a hundred hungry pairs of eyes, she marvelled at his instincts. It was incredible how his extremely male fantasies fitted in with hers.

Inside the fledgling office block, Nick motioned for Julia to go ahead of him up the ladder to the first floor. Everyone working stopped at the sound of his palm slapping her buttocks as she climbed. Julia smiled at their sniggers. Enjoy the view, boys, she thought, wishing they knew that this was for her, not for them.

The first floor consisted of little more than dust. With his hand on her bottom once again, Nick guided her towards a makeshift hardboard office in the corner. He winked at Julia as he knocked at the door. Without waiting for an answer, he pushed it open.

The foreman stood up when he saw them. It was amusing to see him fawning over Nick – a man at least ten years his junior – and dressed rather incongruously all in black leather. The foreman was as taken aback by

Julia's presence as the other men had been but, unlike them, he introduced himself.

'Joe,' he said, holding out his dirty hand.

'This is Julia,' Nick butted in, before she had a chance to speak. 'Brought her along for the ride, if you know what I mean,' he sneered. 'Excuse the leathers, we came on my bike. Well, she came. All that throbbing between their legs, you know, it gets them every time.'

Joe was confused, caught between smirking at Nick's innuendo and being polite to Julia. She didn't help at all, holding on to his hand for a little too long while she took him in. He was good-looking in a rugged, grubby sort of way. His short, unkempt black hair was almost grey with dust; his stubble dark and thick across his heavy jaw. Curls of hair escaped from beneath the collar of his faded denim shirt. He was tall and muscle-bound, with thick, strong hands. Raising a flirtatious eyebrow, Julia slowly loosened her grip on his fingers.

Nick slapped Joe on the back. 'So, how's progress?'

Shouting from the doorway, Joe summoned two others to the office: a thickset black man and a lanky young redhead. Trying their best to ignore Julia, they all sat down round the table and studied the site's plans. Julia stared out of the window at the workers outside, enjoying the sound of Nick's authority as he urged for quicker progress and reduced costs. His confidence had grown supreme since she'd known him at school. He was perfect for this world, unfazed as he was by anyone or anything. Just as Julia was wondering what he had in store for her, he asked whether she was bored. There was falseness in his voice as he acted, pretending he'd just remembered she was there, but only Julia could recognise it. She suspected she was about to find out what he had in mind for her.

Play along, he'd said. She looked at him for a moment, working out what she could say that would 'play along' with his macho performance. She smiled sweetly. 'I could never be bored listening to you, darling. You know how I love to hear you talk.'

Nick's eyebrows flickered suggestively as he looked around the table. She's mine, he was saying.

'I am terribly hot, though.' She fanned her face weakly with her hand.

He got up from the table and joined her at the window. Running his fingers from her chin down to the collar of her jacket, he murmured in agreement as his touch slid in a film of sweat. 'You are hot, darling. Why don't I undo your jacket a little for you?'

'Thank you,' she smiled, struggling to contain the wicked cackle that lurked in her throat. She held Nick's gaze as he unzipped to halfway down her cleavage. She knew without looking that the upper slopes of her breasts would now be visible to the small audience.

'Shall I get you a cold drink?'

'Oh, Nick, you're so thoughtful.' She kissed him gently on the lips, the reverent kiss of an adoring woman. As Nick turned around, he winked at the other men. She's mine, he was saying. And isn't she perfect?

He left her alone for what seemed like an hour. Julia smiled vacantly at Joe and his two colleagues. Wafting air on to her flushed cheeks, she slowly walked around their table, studying the photos and maps on the office's flimsy walls. The men talked business to fill the awkward silence but Julia could tell from the direction of their voices, and the long pauses, that they were watching her. Drooling over the soft leather stretched tightly over her arse. Savouring her legs, elongated by her high boots. Hoping she'd turn round so they could enjoy her cleavage. No doubt this was part of Nick's plan. As it dawned on Julia that he'd put a lot of thought into this afternoon, she had to close her eyes for a moment, to calm herself. It was out of her control. And yet, she suspected, she really was about to have the time of her life, just as he'd promised.

Nick returned, triumphantly holding up a can. 'The Coke's not that cold, so I got you this as well.' In his other hand he brandished a dark-red ice pop. Unable to restrain his grinning, he loomed up to Julia. As she took a long drink, he unzipped her jacket further and slid his hand inside.

'You're still very hot, darling. Shall I cool you down?'

She watched as he ripped the plastic coating off with his teeth, and sucked the ice pop between his lips. Suggestively, he slid the lolly in and out of his mouth until his lips were red with its colour. Watching Julia, holding her with his eyes, he gently slid one side of her jacket away, exposing her breast. Stooping slightly, he pressed his icy lips to her soft areola.

Julia gasped. A squeak split the thick silence as Joe pushed his chair back along the floor and stood up. Slowly, the other two joined him in getting to their feet. 'I ... er ... I think we'll go for a tea break, Nick.'

Nick held up a hand, halting Joe while he finished with her nipple. He flickered over her with his tongue then grazed her lightly with his teeth. When he straightened up, the tip of her breast was engorged and stiff, and stained with the colour from his lips.

'Stay where you are, lads. You'll enjoy this.'

Joe's eyes anxiously met Julia's. The emptiness of her expression gave him no clue as to whether she wanted him to stay or go. That must have unnerved him, because he averted his eyes and looked beyond her, out of the window. 'I don't think we should –'

'Sit down,' Nick commanded. 'She won't mind you watching.' He opened up the other side of her jacket and, as her other breast was exposed, its brown areola soft and wide in contrast to the first, the three bewildered men sank back into their seats. Julia glanced at each one in turn, faking a nervous smile.

'Please,' she whispered to Nick, loud enough for them to hear. 'Please, don't.'

Nick didn't reply, his lips already full with her other breast. Opening his mouth wide, he sucked in as much of her flesh as he could. Increasing the pressure, he closed his lips until they only held the very tip of her nipple. Biting hard, he made Julia gasp with the sudden pain.

'Nick...' She looked imploringly up at him.

He poked the ice pop into her mouth, silencing her with it. Sliding it slowly in and out, he squeezed a breast in his greedy fingers. 'Be quiet, Julia. You know you want to.'

Her heart was pounding furiously. Her naked breasts were rising and falling rapidly with her shallow breathing. Wide-eyed, she looked up at Nick and shook her head.

As if he was angry with her, he snatched the lolly from her mouth. 'You don't want to? You don't want to show these nice men your body?'

'No, Nick. Don't make me.'

Moving behind her, he shoved her in the back so she stumbled closer to the table. As she stood there, acting frightened, the men couldn't resist a look at her red-tipped breasts. Inside her trousers, her pussy burnt with desire. Her mind twisted around this erotic double bluff: three men who thought she didn't want this, one man who knew she really did. It took all her strength not to unzip her trousers there and then and spread her lips for them to see. But she had to play along; the audience had to believe in the performance.

Nick pressed his palm into the small of her back, shoving her into position at the head of the small table. As she approached, Joe pushed his chair backward once again and stood up to give her room. Moving as far back as he could, he pressed himself against the door. Glancing worriedly at Nick, he looked trapped, uneasy, his body tense as if he was poised to flee this bizarre situation. And yet he didn't leave. The sight of Julia's breasts, with their staring red nipples, was holding him captive.

Nick stood at Julia's right shoulder, facing her. Breathing heavily, he slid his fingers beneath the waistband of her trousers and reached into her pubic hair. 'You're very hot down there. I think you'd better take your trousers down.'

Her mouth gaped with shock – part real, part acted. 'Nick . . . no . . . not in front of them –'

'Trousers down. Now!'

She closed her eyes at the sound of his command, as if her mind was in torment. In the darkness, Joe spoke again.

'Nick, what the hell's going on here? Leave her alone. She obviously doesn't want to.'

'You don't know my Julia.' She opened her eyes again as he touched her lips. 'She's a horny little bitch. She's dying to show you her beautiful pussy. Isn't that right, Jules?'

Joe squirmed as Julia smiled faintly at him. On either side of her the other two fidgeted in their seats. Fingers shaking, eyes lowered shyly, she undid her trousers and slowly pushed the soft leather down to her boots. All three voyeurs gasped loudly.

'Look at her,' Nick suggested, quite unnecessarily. 'She's such a slut she goes out without her panties on.' He pushed her backward until her bottom came to rest on the edge of the table. Raising her gaze to Joe's face, Julia let Nick spread her legs as much as her crumpled trousers would allow. She could feel her juices oozing as Joe's dark eyes were drawn to her pussy, shockingly naked within the frame of her black stockings and suspenders. Joe's colleagues stood and shuffled around the table to get a better view, while Nick pressed his middle finger between her open legs.

'Oh, baby, you're so hot.' He raised the ice pop to her lips as if it were an instrument of torture. Slowly, he trailed it downward, making her flinch as the cold path dripped between her breasts and over her belly. 'So hot.'

Putting her hands behind her on the dusty table, Julia braced herself. Her inner thighs twitched uncontrollably as the intense coldness touched her clitoris. She whimpered pitifully, begging Nick to stop as he rubbed the ice stick between her swollen labia. The feeling was incredible. It was a moment filled with contradictions. Her pussy was hot and cold. Her audience was desperately uncomfortable and yet completely transfixed. Julia didn't know them, didn't want them, and yet she wanted them to be aroused by her body. She wanted men to think of her as intelligent and attractive but at this moment she wanted nothing more than to be an object, an instrument for sex. It was utterly degrading and yet so exciting it made her dizzy.

Nick leered evilly as he slowly pushed the lolly inside her. Julia's spine arched dramatically, gripped in a spasm of strange pleasure. Looking down, she watched as the thin red pole disappeared inside the tight warmth of her sex. Her inner muscles pushed at the iciness, trying to expel it, but it was no use. Nick continued until only the very end of the ice pop poked teasingly from between her crimson labia.

'How does that feel?' Nick asked, arousal making his voice husky.

'It's too cold,' she replied breathlessly. 'Please, Nick ... please take it out.'

Nick grabbed the tip between his fingers and pulled. But just as her pussy began to relax he pushed again and again, sliding the lolly in and out, fucking her with it. 'Better make sure you're thoroughly cooled down, darling. Don't want you getting a temperature.' His eyes laughed at her. Her mouth was wide with shock. 'Isn't she gorgeous?' His comment was aimed at no one in particular. All three voyeurs grunted quietly. 'See, I told you she wouldn't mind you watching. She's dirty.' He curled his top lip in disgust. 'I just love dirty-minded women.'

Again, the lolly was pushed inside her to its tip. Julia could feel it melting, its juice radiating coldness into the walls of her vagina. Nick knelt at her feet. He unzipped her boots and pulled them off, then removed her trousers. His eyes hovered over her open slit as he stood up. 'Maybe Joe would take it out for you.'

She glanced at Joe. His sweat and dust-streaked face was a picture of bewildered arousal. 'I think I'd like that,' she whispered.

'Then ask him nicely.' Nick moved back into the corner, folding his arms. 'Go on,' he urged, his brown eyes sizzling.

Julia looked back at the foreman. She arched her lower back and squirmed provocatively, gripping the edges of the table and spreading her legs wider, now that they weren't constricted by her trousers. The sight must have been incredibly obscene, her red-stained nipples pointing at him from the opening of her jacket, the lolly's end like a tongue, poking rudely from between the folds of her flesh.

'Joe?' Julia watched as he pulled his eyes away from her sex. Unconsciously, he ran his tongue over his lips. 'Joe, would you mind getting the lolly out of my pussy for me? It's too cold.' She shivered to press her point, making her breasts quiver.

Joe stroked his chin and shook his head. 'Somebody wake me,' he murmured. 'This is insane.'

'I'll do it if you don't want to.' Behind Julia, to her right, the black builder's voice was deep and urgent.

'I'll do it,' Joe said quickly, looking to Nick for confirmation. Nick nodded and Joe stepped hesitantly towards her. Very slowly, as if sudden movements might scare this delightful vision away, he put his heavy hands on to her open thighs.

'Do it with your mouth,' Nick suggested. But Joe was

already falling to his knees. For a moment he hesitated, his breath hot and rapid on her silky upper legs. Then his lips pursed around the protruding tip of the ice pop and he began to suck. As the stick of ice was slowly pulled from her body, waves of coldness were washed away with ripples of deep warmth. His mouth was greedy, pulling at her tender pussy lips, guzzling at the lolly and crunching the few remaining crystals of ice between his teeth. Unfurling his tongue far inside her clutching sex, he searched for every last drop of juice. His hunger made Julia hold her breath.

She looked at Nick. Admiration burnt fiercely in his face. A knowing leer spread across his wide mouth as he looked at her naked breasts, at her flushed throat, at her pelvis thrusting gently upward to Joe's lips. Stepping towards her, he put his hand over Julia's.

'Fuck her, Joe,' he said. His voice was strained, as if he was struggling as much as she was to make sense of it all.

Joe took one last suck, then got to his feet. He wiped his mouth with the back of his hand. 'Did you say . . .?'

'I said fuck her.' Nick's fingers slid up her leather-clad arm to her shoulder. Singeing her eyes with his, he pushed her back until she lay down on the table. 'She wants you, Joe. She wants your cock. Fuck her, hard.'

Joe seemed uncertain. He looked down at Julia, then at Nick. 'But . . .'

'Don't you want to?' Nick grabbed a handful of breast and squeezed. 'Don't you want to feel her tight, wet pussy? Don't you want to hear her come?' His touch flew between her open legs, where he poked two fingers inside her welcoming wetness. 'She's horny for you, Joe. Don't you want to put your cock inside her?'

'I will, if you don't want to,' the black guy said gruffly.

Joe grunted his answer. Julia watched as he unzipped his jeans and reached inside his boxer shorts. Then her eyelids involuntarily fluttered as his thick meat was rammed unceremoniously inside her.

The back of her head pressed into the hard table and she groaned loudly. The violence of Joe's mating was just what she needed and obviously just what he needed, too. Their syncopated grunts were so noisy that she barely heard Nick's instructions. In a confused, pleasure-soaked daze, she watched as her body was manhandled. Nick and the ginger-haired lad grabbed her legs and lifted them for her, wrapping them around Joe's lunging back. Joe's thick fingers dug into her thighs as he pulled on her, levering himself further inside the hidden depths of her sex. Nick stood aside and directed the other two to her chest. As Julia looked down her body, one brown hand and one pale and freckled one enclosed her shaking breasts. More instructions from Nick followed and her head was pulled to one side. The table was cold and dusty on her cheek. The smell of musty, musky penis filled her nostrils. A second later, the taste of prick filled her mouth: a dark brown prick, as thick and meaty as its owner. She almost gagged as the yielding tip touched the back of her throat. Her jaw ached sharply as she stretched her mouth wide to accommodate his ferocious thrusting. Groaning in protest, she reached up to slow him, but her wrist was grabbed and pulled over her head. The fingers of her other hand were manoeuvred into position around the other builder's cock. She couldn't see him but she could feel that he was long and thin, and slightly curved.

It was too much. Between her legs Joe was pounding viciously, stabbing her with his prick and bruising her tender inner thighs. Another man jerked into her mouth, another into her fingers. All three were complete strangers, men turned rampant by her willingness to be used. The tiny, dusty office stank with sweat. Overwhelmed by it all, carried too far on a tide of disgusting, delicious depravity, Julia whimpered ineffectually.

'Look at her,' Nick hissed, from his position at her head. 'She's enjoying this, the filthy slut.'

'She's incredible,' Joe agreed, his words struggling to escape between thrusts. 'She's so wet. Oh, Jesus, I'm going to come . . .'

'So am I,' grunted the man whose penis was filling her mouth. 'She's so horny. I can't believe this is happening to me.'

'Gorgeous . . . tits . . . great . . . arse . . .' the other man stuttered, distracted by her rapidly jerking fingers sliding him to orgasm.

Nick leant over her. His breath was hot in her ear. 'She likes it up that gorgeous arse.' Nipping her soft lobe between his teeth, he tugged on it, punishing her for her wickedness. 'She's so tight up there, it makes her cry. But she loves it.'

'You're a lucky bastard, Nick,' Joe complained, his voice strangulated by the effort he was putting into his final, mind-numbing thrusts.

'I know,' Nick agreed. 'I never thought I'd find a woman as perverted as I am.' His tongue darted into her ear. 'A complete slut. Just like me. A gorgeous, sexy, dirty slut.' His cruel fingers closed tightly around her wrist. His voice lowered to a whisper that only she could hear. 'This is driving me insane, Julia. But it's worth it, to see you like this. Told you you'd enjoy yourself. Slut.'

One after the other, the three men who had used her shuddered and grunted in relief. The small, airless room was filled with the sounds of male satisfaction and the salty stench of sex.

Their lust may have been sated, Julia thought, as she lay there trembling. But hers was just awakening. Her body was spent, used remorselessly until she ached all over, and yet she wanted more. Nick's words echoed in her mind. The simple, frantic lovemaking of their youth had been left behind, in another lifetime. Innocence had been replaced with debauchery; childish flirting replaced with complex mind-games. She couldn't wait to find out what he had in store for her next. She was addicted to him.

What he had in store next was certainly a surprise. Pulling up outside Julia's flat, he opened the bike's pannier, handed her the clothes she'd set off in that morning, and filled the space with her helmet. He kissed her quickly on the lips then got back on the bike and turned the ignition.

'Hope you enjoyed yourself today.'

Julia blinked, peering through his visor. It was hard to make out his features through the smoky glass and the dusk. 'Aren't you coming in?'

'No.' He revved the engine decisively.

'You're joking,' she laughed, her eyebrows twitching with confusion. She found it hard to believe that such an incredible day was going to fizzle out like this. 'You're seriously going to leave, now?'

'Yes.'

'You're not coming in?'

'No.'

'Why not?'

'Because that's just what you'd expect me to do.' He zoomed to the end of the street, made a swooping U-turn and paused beside her. 'Leave 'em begging for more, that's my motto. I'll see you, Julia.'

'When?'

'When you least expect it.'

Then he was gone. Julia ran her fingers through her hair. Something was going on – this wasn't the end of their day together. He still hadn't had sex with her. And no man could watch her spread-eagled on the table, being used by three others, and then not want to have her for himself. She hugged herself, staring into the space where he'd been a minute earlier, and desperately tried to figure out what he was up to. But it was no use.

Nick had always been unpredictable. There was no way of knowing what his plan was. No way of figuring out what was going on in that warped mind of his.

She let herself into her flat. She didn't want to return to reality just yet, so she left the lights out and sat in the evening gloom until it slowly turned into night. Her pussy throbbed insistently as she closed her eyes and relived the day. Her fingers drifted over her lips, down her neck, inside her leather jacket. Her nipples were still sticky with juice from the ice lolly. Warmth prickled the back of her neck at the thought of those men: looking at her body, wanting her, taking what was offered. Her fingers slipped inside her trousers and she almost sobbed with frustration. She was wet, again, and she wanted Nick to feel it. She wanted him inside her, now.

He would be back, certainly, but when? She couldn't wait. Sighing impatiently, she stood up and stumbled through the darkness to the bathroom. The harsh light made her blink. She pulled off her clothes and studied her reflection. Her cheeks were flushed with expectation, her green eyes glittering with fire. Her breasts were heavy; her stained nipples wide and soft. Beneath curls of slick, damp pubic hair, her labia were swollen with desire. What was Nick playing at, leaving her like this?

She turned on the shower and watched her image gradually fade as the mirror clouded with steam. She stepped into the bath, pulled the shower curtain across and let the hot, strong jets of water wash away her frustration. Droplets trickled from her hair, raced down her spine and jumped from the slope of her buttocks. The spray massaged her nipples and water filled her mouth. She soaped away the evidence of her lovers: streaks of dust and sweat, sugary, red stains where the ice lolly's coldness had teased her. Her tension gradually gave way to pure, mindless pleasure. Her tight muscles stopped aching for sex and began to relax. Her head became limpid. She started to hum to herself.

She stopped abruptly, certain she had heard a noise outside in the dark living room. Straining to hear above the gush of the shower, she squinted with concentration. There it was again – a faint knock, like someone bumping into furniture, followed by a muffled curse. Despite the steam billowing in the bath, her blood ran cold. It must be David.

Her mind tripped, thoughts tangling as they wound themselves into knots. What was he doing here? He was supposed to be on location until the weekend. He must have come back early to surprise her. But why didn't he turn the light on? Why didn't he call out to her? And how was she going to explain the black leathers strewn across the floor?

The voice cursed again, louder this time, just outside the open bathroom door. It wasn't David. A wave of relief was stopped as Julia stumbled over the next thought – who was it, then? Surely a burglar wouldn't attempt to burgle while someone was in the flat. Had she left her front door open by mistake? Had someone walked in off the street?

Her racing heart jumped as a blurry black figure appeared in the doorway. She couldn't see much through the shower curtain, except that he was tall and that his black head was huge. His boots squeaked on the tiled floor as he approached. Julia put her hand to her mouth, trying in vain to stifle a cry of desperate fear. Petrified, she felt time slowing as the figure raised his hand. With a violent swoop, the curtain was torn from its hooks.

It was Nick. His wicked eyes were just discernible through the visor of his motorbike helmet. Momentary relief that it was him was immediately replaced with fury. As he stepped towards the bath, Julia reached out to push him away with both hands. He grabbed her wrists.

'You're hurting me,' she whined, trying to twist out of his grasp. 'Let me go.'

Without a word, he pushed her backward and climbed into the bath, pinning her arms up against the dripping wall. The noise of the shower was loud as it rained down on his leather jacket. The noise of his laughter was muffled by his helmet, but still it grated in Julia's head.

'What are you doing?' she gasped. 'You bastard, you nearly gave me a heart attack. How the hell did you get in?'

He ignored her question. Roughly, he turned her to face the wall. 'Shut up and close your eyes,' he hissed, grabbing her neck tightly in one hand. 'I don't want you to see me. You mustn't find out who I am.'

Julia obeyed, her pulse racing again – but not from the terror of finding an intruder in her flat. She realised now that this was another game. Another fantasy being played out for her. It was incredible the way Nick's mind worked, the way he knew just what she wanted. There was so much electricity in the air between them, it was dangerous. Behind the darkness of her eyelids, she jumped as Nick's helmet clattered loudly to the floor, and jumped again as his hand snaked around to her front and slid quickly from her tight belly up to her breast.

'Do you want me?' He squeezed her flesh in his fingers, as if forcing her answer. She could only sigh in reply and he snatched angrily at her hair with his other hand, tilting her head backward until it came to rest on his shoulder. 'Do you want me inside you, bitch?'

'No,' she breathed, aroused beyond belief.

'Liar.' His fingers continued upward, spreading over her throat, curling over her chin, filling her mouth. 'You want my cock.'

She moaned faintly. It was a feeble protest. She sucked on his fingers as if her life depended on the salt of his skin.

'You horny bitch,' he whispered, his mouth pressed firm against her ear. 'You want me, don't you? You want to feel me, inside you.' He pinched her nipple hard, and the pain made Julia flinch. 'Say it,' he urged, his voice barely audible above the roar of the water. 'Tell me you want me. Ask me to fuck you.'

'No,' she whimpered, 'don't make me.'

'Say it!' he commanded, his voice booming into her ear, his fingers increasing the cruel pressure on the engorged peak of her breast.

'Fuck me,' she concurred, her breathing shallow, her ribs expanding and contracting rapidly as he tormented her. 'Please ... please, fuck me.'

He let go of her hair and her breast and pushed her hard against the wall. Despite the heat in the bath, the tiles were cold. The shock to her skin startled Julia. Although, when she began to shiver, it wasn't from the cold. It was from the sensation of his boot hooking around her ankle and forcing her legs wide apart. The sensation of his firm palm against her shoulder blade and of his other hand delving between her legs. Her whole body shuddered as, without warning, he plunged a long finger inside her.

'Oh,' she groaned, 'fuck me, fuck me, fuck me ...'

She felt the muscles of her pussy clutch at him blindly as he thrust between her pouting sex lips. Her hard nipples rubbed against the tiles with the motion of his hand. Her inner thighs quivered as they tensed at the forcefulness of his fingers. She arched her pelvis sharply backward to meet him, feeling the delightful strain of the muscles at the base of her spine as she reached for his touch. Her body streamed with warm water and unstoppable pleasure, and her mind exploded with the joy of opening herself wantonly to this 'stranger'. A stranger who was so familiar, his roughness not frightening but exhilarating, since it was conjured like a spell from the depths of her own longing.

He grabbed her hips and turned her to face him, quickly brushing his fingertips over her flickering eyelids to remind her not to look. Julia felt him kneel in front of her, the water loud as the droplets spattered against his jacket. Her clitoris screamed in anticipation as she sensed his face moving towards her pussy. He pulled at her thighs with hot, wet palms that spoke of his urgency, and she opened her legs in reply and rested her hands on his head. For a moment his roughness dissolved and, with heart-stopping delicacy, he kissed the lips of her sex. His mouth was soft and pliable, his tongue tracing gentle, fluttering lines along the swollen edges of her labia. Julia held her breath as the moment suspended itself in time: a tentative, yearning overture to the crashing symphony that was to come. She hovered in the humid air and the whole world fell silent; they were alone in their separate, wonderful existence. Her fingers shook slightly as they tangled in his wet hair.

Then the moment was gone, and a crescendo of desperate passion crashed around her, flooding her senses with colour and light and noise. With his thumbs, he parted her pussy lips and unfolded her secret inner flesh, smooth and moist and hungry for him. He lapped at her, covering her sex with expansive strokes of his tongue, making her hands clasp at his head as a spasm of ecstasy gripped at her muscles. He poked his tongue deep inside her, tasting every inch, licking and thrusting so fervently she thought he was trying to lick her away, like a wave eroding the shoreline.

The tide suddenly changed direction, his tongue swooped upward to her clitoris, and she was thrown helplessly up on to another layer of thrashing sensuality. He swirled and sucked and nibbled with teeth that were trying to eat her alive. Pushing hard against her thrusting pelvis, his chin pressed against her gaping vulva. His desperation equalled hers and she wanted to open herself so wide that she would turn inside out; at the same time she wanted to invert and enclose him inside her, folding herself around him until he was encased within her being, trapped like a fossilised fly in amber. Her groans grew loud and frenzied above the crashing waves and, when she came, she smelt sex as her scent wafted in the steam.

Seconds later, she tasted sex. His lips were crushed against hers, his tongue twisting inside her mouth. He clutched her face and kissed her long and hard, as if with gratitude for the pleasure he had taken from her. Then he pulled away until his lips were barely touching hers and for a moment they shared the same breath. When she opened her eyes, Julia found him watching his finger as it traced a loving path around her lips. Slowly, he raised his gaze to meet hers, and for another infinite moment he forgot his rôle, lost in admiration of her. As the water ran down their faces he stared deep into her eyes.

'Julia,' he whispered, managing to inject her name with so much lust that she felt her innards jump.

Then he switched back again, back into the fantasy. Grabbing her thigh, he lifted her leg until she could put her foot on the edge of the bath. Lurching into her, he unzipped his trousers. He put his hands on the wall either side of her hips. Julia gripped his forearms, watching as his long penis reared towards her open sex. Then he was inside her, deep, deep inside, plunging, groaning, rocking his hips to the pounding rhythm of the water. Julia leant her head back against the tiles and half-closed her eyes. His ferocity made her skin crawl with pleasure. This was fucking in its purest form: his body in hers, friction, sensation. Nothing else mattered. Nothing else was relevant – just his penis in her pussy, his eyes fastened to hers, their minds empty.

With a long groan, he shuddered into her. Before Julia had time to come, his prick was zipped away, and he was stepping over the side of the bath. She watched, open-mouthed, as he retrieved his helmet from the floor and pushed it back on over his wet hair.

'Don't go,' she begged, as he walked away. The door to her flat slammed, followed by the fainter sound of the front door out in the hallway. Eyes wide with despair, her back slid down the wall until she crouched in the bath. She hugged her knees weakly, feeling small, feeling dwarfed by her lust.

She lay on her bed, dressed in some of her best underwear, and waited for him to return. Night turned into early morning and she rolled around on top of the sheets like an insomniac. But sleep wasn't her problem – she was exhausted, and could easily have drifted off. The problem was Nick, or the lack of him. She couldn't get him out of her mind. His confidence was so refreshing. She didn't have to take the lead with him, simply to allow herself to be led whichever way he chose. And she liked that. She was brimming with confidence and was used to forcing her way in a male-dominated career. It was nice to be able to abandon herself, for once.

What he'd done today astonished her. Sex with Nick had always been good, even when they had been teenagers and not known any better. It was sex for its own sake, pleasure which was pure and primitive. But now that they were adults, there was an edge to their coupling. Somehow, he knew just what she wanted. Right now, she wanted him, in her bed.

He would know that, she thought, as her hand slipped inside her silky panties. He would know she was dying for his touch, yearning for his tongue, his lips, his penis. And he would love it.

Julia jumped as the phone rang. It was a cordless one and, for a moment, she couldn't find it. Leaning over the side of the bed, she picked at the heap of discarded clothes on the floor until the ringing grew louder. Flicking out the aerial, her hand shook as she brought it to her ear.

'Nick?' she whispered hopefully.

'Are you missing me?'

She sighed with relief, then sighed again with anguish. Just hearing his rich, dirty voice was enough to start her skin prickling. 'What the hell are you trying to do to me? I'm going insane here.'

There was undisguised satisfaction in his soft laughter. 'That was the general idea. I wanted to leave you wanting more.'

'Well, you succeeded. I'm desperate for you, Nick.'

'Where are you?'

'In bed.'

'What are you wearing?'

She sat up. In the dim light from the lamp, she looked across the room at her reflection in the mirror. 'I'm wearing black stockings, suspenders, skimpy panties and a bra that's so low-cut you can see the edges of my nipples over the top of the lace.'

Nick groaned. 'I wish I could see you.'

'So do I.' Her fingers absent-mindedly traced the visible satin curve of her areola. 'Where are you?'

'On my way back to Glasgow. I've got a meeting in eight hours.'

Julia turned to look at the clock. One in the morning. She was meeting Steve in eight hours. 'Nick, I want you here.'

'Oh God, if I was there...' He took a deep breath, letting it out slowly and loudly. 'Touch yourself for me, Julia.'

Julia bent her knees up and spread her legs slightly. Her fingers stroked the tight satin covering her sex. It was damp there. She could feel the slight bulge of her clitoris. Involuntarily, her inner muscles clenched.

'Julia?' He swallowed noisily, his voice caught in suspense. 'Are your panties wet?'

'Yes.' She was hoarse and her voice was faint with desire. 'They're soaking. Tell me ... tell me what you'd be doing to me if you were here.'

He described, in incredible detail, exactly what he wanted to do. As Julia followed his instructions, one finger, then two, then three slid inside her warm pussy. Her knees flopped on to the bed. Her panties were pulled aside, and her clitoris grew hard and demanding beneath her circling, wet fingers. She was sighing so loudly, she never heard the key in her front door.

And yet, when Nick pushed open her bedroom door, she wasn't that surprised. As he put his mobile phone away in his jeans pocket, a wide smile spread across her lips. Underneath her fingertips, a warm glow spread across her sex.

'I knew you'd be back,' she said.

Sitting beside her on the bed, he took the phone out of her hand. His fingers brushed hers away, and he took over stroking at her eager sex. 'I can't stay long,' he said, his voice thick with regret. 'I really do have to get back to Scotland.'

'So why are you still here?'

'I had to see you, one last time. No games, no one else in the room, just you and me. If you don't choose me Julia, this is our last time together.'

She arched an eyebrow. 'And what if I do choose you?'

'I promise you that every day will be like today.'

She doubted it. And for a split second she doubted that she would want her life to be like this. After all, they'd barely spoken to each other all day. He hadn't bothered to ask her anything about her life, her job, her lovers – that didn't matter to Nick. All that mattered was the present. And, for now, she was happy to live for the moment. To bathe in the warm lust of his eyes, to cut herself adrift, and to throw her body to the mercy of a stormy sea of pleasure. Lying down, she pulled him down beside her.

'Nothing's changed,' he hissed, burying his face in her neck. 'We're older and kinkier, and you're more gorgeous than ever.' He sucked hungrily on her skin. 'But, apart from that, it's just like when we were teenagers. We still drive each other wild.'

And we still don't talk, Julia added silently, closing her eyes. Then he banged his lips down on to hers, thrust his tongue inside her mouth, and she forgot all about talking.

Steve

Steve was already there, pacing nervously, when she arrived. Standing outside the National Portrait Gallery, he looked out of place amongst a congregation of foreign students in their bright clothes. On the other side of the street, Julia waited for the traffic to slow at the zebra crossing, and she watched him. He looked quite stunning, his tall frame rising head and shoulders above the small crowd, his beautifully proportioned body a picture of casual sexiness – a sexiness he probably didn't even realise he had. In honour of the overcast day, he had a trendy mac draped over his arm. He was wearing heavy, oxblood-coloured shoes, dark jeans, a pale-grey T-shirt and a soft brown V-neck jumper which matched his chestnut hair and made the paleness of his eyes all the more intense. As he paced, marking out a square metre of territory for himself, his eyes flickered anxiously around, searching for a sign of Julia. As she crossed the road he noticed her, and he blinked with relief.

'I was getting worried,' he said, struggling to smile. His hands faltered at her shoulders, undecided whether to hug her or not.

Julia glanced at her watch. 'I'm only three minutes late.'

'I know, I know.' He looked down at his feet. 'I just thought you might have changed your mind about all this.'

She put her hand on his waist and he looked up. 'Why on earth would you think that?'

'I thought you might have already made your decision. I know how well you and Nick get on together.'

She flinched, taking her hand away. Suddenly, inexplicably, she felt guilty knowing Nick had only left her bed hours earlier. It was ridiculous that she should feel like that – after all, they'd made a deal, the three of them, cold and simple. Yet now, in the grey light of the overcast day and the grey hurt of Steve's eyes, the 'deal' seemed bizarre, dangerous even. Someone was going to get hurt.

'Let's not talk about Nick,' she said, trying to muster a nonchalant smile. 'Today's about you and me.'

He seemed unsure. His head bowed. Julia kissed him on the cheek, which roused him. He looked her up and down, taking in her calf-length brown boots, her short brown skirt and the dark camel polo neck which clung to her curves. With her brown moleskin jacket flung over her arm, their outfits couldn't have matched better if they'd tried.

'You look gorgeous,' he said, and smiled. Taking her hand, he linked her arm in his. 'Come on. There's something in here I want to show you.'

The atmosphere inside the gallery, once they'd escaped the gaggle of students, was like a perfect Sunday afternoon – despite the fact that it was Friday morning. It was warm and quiet, and full of people enjoying the simple pleasures of beautiful paintings and gentle conversation. Julia could easily have dozed off in there if she had been alone. Lulled by the hushed voices and studious calm, she could have happily curled up on one of the padded bench seats.

But with Steve by her side, sleep was the last thing on her mind. She felt proud to be seen with him and, as always, she felt totally at home in his company. There was no pretence between them at all as they talked easily about the relative merits of each artist's work. It was as if they shared parts of each other's minds. Julia would set off on a train of thought and, before she'd even finished it in her own mind, Steve was continuing it for her. She looked up at him as he talked and a warm glow of happiness swept over her.

'What?' he asked, noticing her staring.

'I was just thinking. Nothing much has changed between us, in all these years.'

'You're wrong, Julia. Everything's changed.'

'It has?'

'Of course.' He blinked hesitantly. 'You never knew how much I liked you, when we were younger. You do now.'

She looked away from him, turning back to the painting they were standing in front of. She smiled coyly. 'I always knew that you liked me.'

'You did? How?'

Returning to his gaze, the warm glow began to spread down her spine. 'It was pretty obvious, Steve. The way you used to look at me. The way you never bothered talking to any of the other girls.' She paused, remembering the moment she'd really been sure that Steve had fancied her. 'I'll never forget the look on your face, the day Nick asked me out.'

He winced. 'I'll never forget that, either. That was one of the worst days of my life.'

She reached for his hand, gently stroking his fingers. 'You know, if you'd asked me out instead, I would have said yes.'

He huffed with disbelief. 'No you wouldn't. You were

one of the most fancied girls in the school. You had to go out with someone popular, someone cool, like Nick.' His fingers laced with hers and he squeezed. 'Admit it, Jules. You'd never have been seen with someone as quiet and nerdy as I was.'

That thought was uncomfortable. He was probably right. At the age of eighteen, appearances had mattered more than anything. 'You're not quiet and nerdy now,' she said, fudging the issue.

'In other words, what I said was right.'

She gave him a wry half-smile. 'You never asked me out. So we'll never know.'

There was a long, potent silence. Julia was reminded of another thing she used to love about spending time with Steve. When the conversation tailed off, there was no need to talk – their silences said just as much.

'What was it you wanted to show me?' she asked, at last.

'It's over here.' He cupped her shoulder, guiding her through an archway into the next room. 'This is it.'

They came to rest in front of a wide portrait. Sitting down on the bench in front of it, they both stared at the beautiful woman stretched out on the bed. She had dark hair, straggling over her shoulders and tousled messily around her face as if she'd just woken up. She was lying on her side, propping her head up on one hand, her languid curves draped on the rumpled white sheet. She was naked, the shadow of her pubic hair a contrast to her pale skin, one breast hidden by the book she was holding. She wasn't reading, though; she was looking over the edge of the paperback, straight out at her audience. Her eyes were incredible, pale green and wide, and glinting with a challenge. She was obviously looking at her lover.

'She's beautiful,' Steve said, his voice soft with awe. 'I found her, years ago. Every time I'm in London, I have to come and look at her.'

Julia could understand why. She was mesmerising.

'I like to imagine that she's looking at me, telling me with her eyes to come back to bed. I can't think why I'm not in bed – I'd have to have a good reason not to be with her. Perhaps I'm on the phone, or something. But I'm looking at her, wanting her desperately, not concentrating on my phone call because I need her so badly. The second I've finished, I'll kneel down in front of her, pull that book out of her hands, and kiss her.' His hand slid across the seat on to Julia's knee. 'Does she remind you of anyone?'

She looked hard, but she couldn't see a resemblance to anyone she knew. 'Not really.' She shrugged, turning down the corners of her mouth.

'It's you, Julia. You've got the same eyes.'

Slowly, she turned to face him. Flattered that he compared her to such a vision, she opened her mouth to say so. But his face was moving towards hers and instead she waited for his kiss. When it came it was soft and tender, and quickly followed by another, and another.

'I've always imagined that woman was you, Julia, and that you were lying in my bed, waiting for me.'

Another kiss. Julia closed her eyes as she began to spin out of control. His lips were so gentle, so full of yearning. She slipped her hand around his neck.

She opened her eyes to find him slowly pulling out of her hold. He got to his feet, looking down at her with the same rapt attention he'd lavished on the painting.

'Where are you going?' she asked.

'I have to arrange something. It'll only take a minute.'

'The last time you said that, you left me alone for two hours.'

He cupped his cool hand to her cheek. 'I promise I won't be long.'

She watched him walking out, his long strides echoing faintly around the quiet room, and the glow she'd felt before began to twist into an ache. She turned back to the canvas. There was a deeper meaning to its subject now, after what Steve had told her. She loved the thought of him visiting the painting, worshipping at the shrine of that beautiful woman and imagining it was her. Closing her eyes, she bowed her head, as she always did when she wanted to hide in her thoughts. Her hair swished forward to cover up her blushing and she dipped into Steve's fantasy. She was in the painting now, waiting for Steve to finish his call, and urging him back to bed. In a second he would finish talking, kneel down in front of her, pull the book out of her hands, and kiss her. Then he would roll back into bed; back into her.

Someone sat down beside her. Gentle fingers pulled her hair back from her face and tucked it behind her ear. Julia felt herself flushing with desire.

'You did that to me on the last day of school,' she said.

Steve's dark eyebrows twitched. 'Did what?'

'That.' She put her fingers over his as they smoothed her hair away.

'Christ.' His hand slipped underneath her bob and touched her neck. 'You remember that?'

'Yes.'

'So do I.'

She shifted excitedly in her seat, wondering whether his recollection of that moment was the same as hers. 'What do you remember, exactly?'

He didn't hesitate. 'You looked stunning. You were wearing a green dress that matched your eyes perfectly. The sun was shining on your hair, making it look redder than it is. We were filling in those lists and you didn't want to do it. I said you looked gorgeous. You were embarrassed and dropped your head forward so you could hide behind your hair. I was desperate to look at you, so I pushed your hair back from your face.' His fingers trailed wistfully down her forearm. 'Nick was playing football with the others. You told me to do something impulsive.' He glanced at the painting. 'You looked at me just like she does, challenging me. I pulled you down on to the rug. I was about to kiss you when Nick came along and took you off into the woods.' Steve's eyes hardened. 'I remember it so clearly.'

Incredibly clearly. Julia hadn't realised that men stored moments like those, just like women did. It made her tingle inside. 'That's amazing. You left a bit out, though. You were about to tell me something when Nick came back. I wrote to you, asking what it was you wanted to say. You never replied.'

'I know.' He looked down at his hand as it came to rest in hers. 'When Nick came back, the moment was gone.' Lost in his thoughts, he stared at their entwined fingers for a while. 'It's the same thing I wanted to tell you at the castle. I didn't get the chance then, either.' Hanging his head to avoid her questioning eyes, he rubbed his forehead. It was as if he was trying to rub away a stubborn pain. 'It's the same thing I wrote on that bloody plan that's ruled my life. Imagine if I'd told you, that day at school.'

He shook his head slightly, and Julia got the feeling he was now talking to himself. He was different: on edge, agitated, his body tense.

'At least I wouldn't have had to spend the last seven years in hell, wondering what you would have said. I would have known, either way . . .'

Julia lifted his chin, bringing his line of sight back up to hers. 'Why don't you tell me now?' she whispered, touching his cheek ever so gently, as if he were a sleepwalker she had to carefully ease back into consciousness.

He took a long deep breath and made a concerted effort to calm himself. 'I'll tell you, when the time's right.' He blinked and, like the sleepwalker waking up, it was as if nothing had ever happened. He smiled and got to his feet. 'Come on,' he said brusquely. 'Places to go, people to see.'

On their way out of the gallery, they moved through a small photography exhibition. There were grainy, black and white portraits of prominent politicians. both living and dead. Of royalty and statesmen, dictators and revolutionaries. It was a fascinating display. Each photographer had managed to take a portrait that said so much about the subject. As they slowly travelled round the quiet room, the strength of the pictures made Julia squirm.

'What's the matter?' Steve asked.

'Nothing,' she replied brightly, attempting a smile to cover up what she was feeling.

'There is something.' He stopped her with a strong hand on her arm. 'I can see it in your eyes. What is it?'

She glanced at the wall. A huge portrait of Lenin seemed to be bearing down on her. Next to him, Adolf Hitler stooped to pet a deer in an image so incongruous it chilled Julia to the core.

'Hold me,' she whispered, moving into Steve's arms. He hesitated but he did it, enfolding her in his warm, strong grasp. She leant her face into his shoulder, a dark place that smelled comfortingly of him, and she struggled not to sob out loud.

A jumble of thoughts scrabbled for escape from inside her head. Julia made them line up in an orderly fashion, so she could work out why she suddenly felt so weak and silly. It was what she always did, when she was about to cry: analyse what was going on in her mind, try and dull her emotions by making sense of it all.

She'd had very little sleep. That was making her feel dizzy. The bizarre events of the day before had left her on a high. A high which had come crashing down with guilt when she'd seen Steve. That was confusing. Then she'd discovered that the moment that had infiltrated her dreams for the last seven years was remembered just as vividly by Steve – that had struck her deeply. There was the anticipation of whatever it was he had to tell her. Her suspicion of what that might be was making her tremble. To make things worse, these photographs were so brilliant they reminded her of her own career, and that reminded her of David. A wave of shame washed through her as she imagined the look on his face when she told him it was over between them, the engagement was off, she'd made a mistake...

Steve gently grabbed her shoulders and pulled her out of her thoughts. 'Julia?'

'I... I need some fresh air,' she stammered.

They sat in Trafalgar Square. The air wasn't exactly fresh, but it was cool. Julia absent-mindedly watched the tourists while Steve went to get her a drink. The smiling young couples, hand in hand, seemed to mock her with their simple affection. What the hell was she doing, getting involved in this ridiculous game? Playing with lust and love was more risky than playing with fire. Someone was bound to get burnt and she had a strong premonition that it was going to be her.

Steve handed her a can and sat down beside her. For a long time, they sat in silence. When he spoke, his voice was tight with resignation.

'You're having second thoughts about all this, aren't you?' When Julia didn't reply, he shook his head angrily. 'I knew it. I knew this whole thing was a mistake. I shouldn't have let Nick talk me into it. I was drunk, and desperate to see you again.' He snatched at her arm, making her jump. 'I'm so sorry, Julia. We shouldn't have put you in this position. What must you think of me?'

She turned to meet his panicked eyes. 'This situation *is* bizarre, but I agreed to it, remember? It isn't your fault.' It's my fault, she thought to herself. She'd gone to Scotland to see *Steve* – why couldn't she have left Nick alone?

It was greed. Greed had made her tease Leon Sparrow in the middle of a shoot. Greed had made her screw that man on the train. Greed had made her accept the challenge to choose between Nick and Steve. She craved Nick's passion, but she also longed for Steve's intensity, his adoration, the easiness of being with him. She wanted everything. All of a sudden she realised that that was impossible – but it was too late now.

'Let's just get on with our date,' she said, her smile twitching nervously.

'Are you sure? If you're not happy with all this, I'd rather you just said –'

'Steve.' Her fingers silenced his lips. 'I'm happy just being with you. Let's not think about this too much. Let's just enjoy each other's company.'

The sun came out as they walked through Hyde Park. Julia felt important, knowing that Steve's chauffeur was waiting at the gate to drive them the short distance to Piccadilly. They had lunch at the Ritz, and the wine took the edge off Julia's unease. An hour passed to the genteel music of a string quartet and the clinking of crystal glasses. She began to relax, giggling as she spotted a minor celebrity with a young woman who was obviously not his wife. If she'd had her camera with her, she explained, one shot would have got her back into George's good books. She discussed her career with Steve, amazed when he guessed that the photos in the exhibition had unnerved her. Without being patronising, he encouraged her to follow her dream, at any cost. Julia felt her whole being turning warm as she basked in his serious attention.

'Life's too short to be unhappy,' he said, reaching across the table for her hand. 'You've got the talent, Julia. Don't waste it doing work that bores you. If you want something badly enough, you've got to pursue it to the very end. If you don't, you'll never forgive yourself.' His eyes dropped for a second, as the waiter surreptitiously eased the bill on to the table. In that instant, Julia realised that he wasn't just talking about her job.

'You're the only person that understands,' she sighed. 'Everyone else thinks I'm mad to want to leave the *Chronicle*. It is a wonderful job,' she added. 'Most people would sell their souls for my job. Going to film premières and opening parties, mingling with the stars ... but it's just not enough for me.'

He leant over to touch her cheek. 'I'd sell my soul, too. For you.'

The other diners in the restaurant faded away into silence. There were only the two of them, alone in the world, suspended in time. He wasn't joking. She knew that if the devil appeared at their side at that instant, Steve would happily hand over his soul for her.

Her head felt heavy. Her doubts and worries dissolved in her wine-soaked mind, and the greed took over again. 'Steve, where can we go?'

His sensuous lips parted. 'You mean . . .?'

'Yes.' Her voice was wobbly, her breathing shallow, but her mind was steadfast. She wanted those lips now, on her face, on her throat, kissing away the ache between her legs. Beneath the shield of the white tablecloth, she touched his ankle with the toe of her boot. 'Let's get out of here.'

'And go where?' He whipped some notes from his wallet and folded the bill around them. Getting up, he looked around anxiously as he helped Julia into her jacket.

'Where's the car?' she asked, although she didn't really want to give the chauffeur another free peepshow.

'I gave the driver the afternoon off. He's not picking us up until five.'

'So, what were we going to do all afternoon?'

He slipped his arm round her waist, guiding her quickly out of the restaurant. 'I was going to take you to

New Bond Street. I wanted to buy you a dress ... something special for you to wear this evening.'

A spark of wicked excitement swirled in Julia's lungs, making her breath shudder. 'Perfect,' she whispered.

'What do you mean?' He smiled sheepishly at the doorman as they hurried out. 'I thought you wanted to —'

'I do. But we can shop as well.'

Outside, the sky had clouded over and it was beginning to drizzle. As they crossed Piccadilly and made their way up Old Bond Street, the drizzle increased into a downpour. Steve grabbed Julia's hand and they ran, giggling like teenagers, as they tried to dodge the rain. As Old Bond Street became New he pulled her under the awning of the Chanel shop, throwing her off-balance so that she tripped, panting, into his arms.

He smoothed her damp hair, his breath hot and rapid on her face. Julia looked again at his mouth and she almost crumpled with longing. 'You're so sexy,' she sighed.

'I am?' he laughed, unconvinced.

'You know you are. Now, bring those sexy lips down here.' She reached for his neck, pulling his mouth on to hers. She had launched this situation, taking control, but Steve had only needed a little push. His kissing was urgent, matching hers, drifting all over her mouth and then down, across her cheek, under her jaw, on to her neck. One of his hands clutched at her shoulder, squeezing, the other slid beneath her jacket and spread over her breast. Oblivious of the passers-by, Julia moaned softly.

Steve froze as something caught his eye over her shoulder. 'Jesus, look at that.'

She turned to share his view. In the window, a stunning, blood-red evening dress hung from a perfectly proportioned mannequin. There wasn't much of it, but what there was was beautiful. It was an asymmetric design, with only one wide shoulder strap. The neckline swooped in a diagonal line, cutting low across the cleavage. The waist was clingy, the skirt long and straight and, again, cut asymmetrically so that the hemline came to a narrow point at one side. On the other side, the sloping hem rose dramatically, revealing the dummy's leg up to mid-thigh.

'You'd look stunning in that,' Steve said.

Julia had to admit that it would suit her. The rich colour would look shocking against her pale skin and dark, auburn-tinged hair. 'I was going to get married in that colour,' she said, without the faintest twinge of remorse.

'I'd like to buy you that dress.'

'Have you any idea how much a Chanel number costs?'

'I don't care.' He held the shop door open for her. 'I want to see you in it.'

Julia's heart was pounding as she stepped inside the glossy world of designer shopping. She'd been in the boutique before, with Marianne. But, if she was honest, she didn't particularly like the shop, with its too-perfect, snooty staff. She swore they had X-ray vision, and could see precisely how empty her purse was. She'd bought some nail varnish in there once, when Marianne had bought a suit for work, and they had made her feel like a fifteen-year-old who had come up to town to spend her pocket money. She had sworn then never again to set foot in a shop where the assistants looked like supermodels. And now here she was, about to try on what was probably the most expensive item in the collection, and about to use the changing rooms for more than just changing.

Steve was masterful, oozing the scent of money. He was obviously used to being fawned over, and had no qualms about commandeering three assistants to fawn over Julia. With deferential voices – drawing the line at actual bowing and scraping – the immaculate staff ushered them up to the top floor where they joined a select group of customers. By the time they arrived, the dress was waiting for Julia inside a small, mirrored room. At least, it was small for a room but, in terms of fitting rooms, it was palatial. One of the assistants helped her on with the red creation, murmuring appreciatively as the smooth material slipped over her curves. She called out to one of her colleagues and, a minute later, a pair of spindly black stilettos appeared.

'These will give you a better idea than your boots, madam.'

Julia agreed. She put them on, stepping up on to the four-inch heels. Without stopping to admire her reflection, she walked back out to where Steve was waiting.

The small clique of customers and assistants all went quiet as she appeared. Julia could tell from their envious glances that she made quite an impression. Steve got up from the sofa and drank her in slowly, from the tips of her shoes to her shining, expectant eyes.

'Well?' she asked, turning her back on him. In the long mirror, she watched him approach behind her. 'What do you think?'

His long fingers slid tentatively around her waist. Looking over her shoulder at her reflection, he answered her question with his eyes. 'You look incredible.'

Her eyes pierced the glass, and in an instant she could see that he was on her wavelength. He knew now exactly what she'd meant when she'd suggested combining her two favourite pastimes: shopping and sex.

'Help me take it off.' She took his hand and set off for the changing room. One of the assistants followed them, hovering anxiously.

'Is everything all right, madam?'

'Yes, thank you.' Julia flashed her a saccharine smile and closed the door on her perfectly painted, flapping mouth.

Inside the spacious cubicle, Julia stood with her back

to the wall. 'Do you think it's a good fit?' she teased. Seeing the emotions change on Steve's face, from astonishment to desire, made her flutter rapidly inside.

Steve took a step towards her. Half a smile lifted one corner of his wide mouth. At the same time, in slow motion, he lifted his hand. With his eyes fixed on Julia's, his touch trickled over the side of her breast, down her waist and on to her hip. 'I'd say it was a perfect fit.'

'It's cut very high over my leg.'

'Yes, it is,' he agreed, his palm continuing downward to her thigh.

'I'm worried you might be able to see my suspenders.'

'Oh. I'd better have a look, then.' He dropped slowly to his knees, curling his fingers round her ankle. His other hand stroked upward, moving with tortuous slowness up the inside of her exposed leg. 'No. I can't see them.' He looked up, wide-eyed with disappointment.

Julia's fingers twitched with anticipation as she pulled the skirt aside. Looking down, she saw Steve's lips form a silent O, and her pussy tensed in reply.

Delicately, his fingertips followed the path of one black satin suspender. Moving upward, with a finger either side of the narrow strip of elastic, he lightly caressed her naked upper leg. He hesitated at the top, savouring the marble smoothness of her secret skin. He moved back down to the top of her stocking and traced its edge round towards her inner thigh. Unsteady in her heels, Julia parted her legs. Unsteady in his lust, overwhelmed by his closeness to her sex, his hand visibly shook as it rose to her mound. Julia heard his breathing deepen as he brushed the lips of her pussy through her tiny, satin knickers. Inside the covering of her soft pubic curls, Julia's bud began to stiffen and throb, demanding attention.

'God, that feels so good,' she said, her voice barely louder than a breath. Reaching down, she rested her fingers on top of his. The way they moved, gently exploring the hidden folds of her flesh, made her rage inside. 'Oh God ... Steve ...'

She left her sentence hanging in the air, telling him what she wanted with actions. While she held her skirt aside with one hand, the other pulled at the skimpy veil of her panties. She moved her legs wider apart and waited, displaying her sex for him, watching his head roll slightly with intoxication.

She didn't have to wait long. First with his thumb, and then his mouth, he rediscovered the pleasures of her pussy. He brushed over the curled edges of her labia, teasing them apart. He felt the sacred smoothness of their inner surfaces, delved inside the secret they held. Julia's buttocks tensed as his thumb pushed slowly inside her, and then his tongue was flickering all over her pouting sex. His fingers spread across her groin and he pulled her urgently into his face. Mumbling appreciatively like a ravenous man at a feast, he devoured her aching until it was all gone. Ripples of pleasure undulated fluently over her body, interrupted with a faint jerk as his nose banged against her clitoris.

'You like that, don't you?' he said, pausing to look up at her. 'You like it when I touch you there.' The pad of his thumb brushed fleetingly over the raw tip of her bud.

'I love it,' she gasped, dropping her skirt so she could touch the juices smearing his lips. I love you, she nearly said. But her words were swallowed up.

Steve grabbed at the fallen skirt, rumpling it in fingers which didn't care that it was Chanel. His lips dived to her pulsating clitoris and, with wicked flickers of his tongue, he rapidly brought her to the brink of orgasm. Julia sighed and shuddered, ecstasy radiating throughout her body. She could have climaxed just thinking about his need, his urgency for her flesh. But she didn't need to think at all. His lips, his tongue and teeth demolished all thought and left her nothing but sensation. He emptied her soul and then refilled her with a satisfaction so pure and mindless it was addictive. She wanted more, and more, a never-ending cycle of build-up and release. When her first orgasm spilt over her she held his swinging head close, urging him to continue to give. He did, tirelessly kissing and sucking on her moistness, trying in vain to suck her dry.

A knock at the door stopped it all. 'Sir? Madam? Is everything all right in there?'

Julia closed her eyes. Unable to speak, she could only offer a groan in reply.

'Everything's fine,' Steve added. 'We're just having some difficulty getting this dress off.'

'Oh.' There was an uncertain pause. Julia could almost hear the poor woman's mind working. She had a dilemma – two customers fooling about with a two-thousand-pound couture creation. Two customers she couldn't afford to offend. 'Would you like some help, sir?'

'No, thank you.' Julia looked down to find Steve's hand snaking up to her breast. He smiled naughtily. 'I'm sure we'll manage.'

Julia could see that something was wrong the minute they got into the car. No sooner had they settled into the plush leather seats than Steve's brittle aura of confidence cracked. The playfulness she'd seen in the shop had been pushed aside. He was edgy, shifting in his seat and staring determinedly out of the window as if he was trying to avoid her.

Julia watched as his eyes glazed over and he retreated into his private world. She'd seen this expression before, and she recognised the way his features were set and his body was coiled. He was thinking about something that was worrying him. A surge of love swirled inside her and set butterflies flitting in her stomach. She put her hand on his thigh.

'What's wrong, Steve?'

He was so deeply engrossed in his thoughts, it took a slow moment for his eyes to clear. 'Nothing,' he lied, trying to muster a smile and failing.

'Oh, come on. You can't fool me, you never could. There's something on your mind.'

His gaze briefly met hers before dropping again. Watching his fingers clasp and unclasp in his lap, he winced. Hurt was straining in his face. 'Did you have a good time yesterday, with Nick?' The name sounded sharp on his tongue, like a sliver of broken glass.

Incredulous, she shook her head. 'I thought we agreed we weren't going to talk about this?'

He turned away from her questioning gaze. Immediately, Julia understood: tonight they would make love, for the first time. Knowing Steve, knowing how seriously he took everything, he had probably envisaged every last detail. He would be carrying a lot of heavy baggage in his mind – mostly, she suspected, to do with Nick. There would be the memory of her crying as Nick had taken her from behind; the moment Steve had discovered them, at the office; the thought of them losing their virginity together, years ago; and the idea that he was competing with whatever Nick had given her yesterday. Steve should have been looking forward to their first night together with excited anticipation, as she was. Instead, he was turning it into an ordeal. Thank God he didn't know just how good Nick had made her feel.

She watched the anguish wrinkling his face and she wanted to comfort him. She felt like an older woman about to deflower a beautiful youth, wanting to hold him to her breast and slowly ease him into shared pleasure. His anxiety was deeply moving, but she couldn't think of anything to say that would help.

Steve frowned bitterly. 'I bet you had a fantastic time with him, didn't you?'

Julia couldn't deny it. She opened her mouth to speak, but nothing came out.

'I knew it,' he huffed, shaking his head. 'Why have I let myself in for this? How can I ever compete with that arrogant sod? What can I possibly do that's going to impress you?' Narrowing his eyes, he closed his fingers over the edge of the seat, making the leather squeak in protest. 'How many times did he make you come, Julia. Four? Five? Did he fuck you hard? Did he make you cry?'

His vicious tone of voice made her mouth gape. 'Steve!'

He slammed his fist down into the seat, punishing the leather for his jealousy.

Julia flinched, taken aback by his anger. This was a side of Steve she'd never seen. 'You don't have to do anything to impress me,' she said softly, attempting to calm him. She rested her hand on his taut fist and tried to soften its pent-up fury. 'You don't have to compete with Nick. Just be yourself.'

Steve's fingers gripped into an even tighter ball of tension beneath hers. His eyes glittered icily. 'I can't bear the thought of you and ... and him.'

'Steve,' she said, struggling to keep the growing annoyance out of her voice. 'Today's about you and me. That's it – you, and me.' She spoke deliberately, as if she was carefully explaining something to a difficult child. 'I want you, and you want me. Tonight ... just show me how you feel. Show me how much you want me.'

'Oh, I'll show you,' he promised, menace in his voice.

Julia's hand jumped away from his. The determination in his expression was shocking. Again, the feeling that this game was spinning out of control washed over her: a feeling laced heavily with fear. 'Steve –'

'Stop the car.' As the limo pulled smoothly into a parking space, he scrambled out, slamming the door behind him. He stooped at the driver's window to mumble instructions, then, as Julia watched openmouthed, he stormed off down the street without a backward glance.

'What the hell was that all about?' she gasped, leaning forward in her seat.

The driver concentrated on the traffic while he pulled back out into its flow. Then his eyes met hers in his rearview mirror. 'I'm to take you home, wait for you to get changed, then take you to meet Steven.'

'Why?' Her eyes searched eagerly amongst the crowds on the pavement, desperately hoping for a glimpse of him, a clue to what was going on. 'Where's he gone?'

'I don't know, miss. He said he had something to prepare for tonight.' His dark eyebrows flickered salaciously. In his eyes, Julia could see the treasured memory of the other night in the limo, when Steve and Nick had spread her legs in full view of the chauffeur. She looked away from his lecherous grin, furious that Steve had left her in this situation.

She made the driver a coffee and settled him in front of the television while she went for a bath. She felt uncomfortable with him in the flat but, despite her urging, he wouldn't leave. He had his orders, it seemed, and he was sticking to them. Trying to forget that he was sitting in her living room, on the other side of a bathroom door with a broken lock, she filled the tub with heat and bubbles. Sinking gratefully into its comfort, she waited hopefully for her tension to be soothed away.

But like the faint bruises on the soft tops of her inner thighs – tangible reminders of yesterday – her tension was not dissolved by the water. In fact, the longer she lay there, the tighter her nerves bunched up. Her apprehension sharpened itself into a spear, twisting painfully into her guts.

Steve was worrying her. His behaviour was becoming obsessive. The pressure of tonight was obviously weighing heavily on his broad shoulders. She had hoped and imagined, over the years, that sex with Steve would be as wonderfully intense as their conversations. But now she was beginning to doubt the possibility of a night of fluid passion. He would be so wound up with expectation, so concerned with what she and Nick had done together, that he wouldn't be able to allow the evening to unfold itself naturally. If only Steve's mind wasn't governed by this ridiculous rivalry. It was unbelievable that he was still competing with Nick, after all these years.

Nick, in contrast, hadn't mentioned Steve at all during his day with Julia. That was the difference between the two of them. Nick was supremely confident in himself. Despite the fact that Steve was his boss, and that he was more wealthy, more intelligent, and perhaps even better looking than he was, Nick had no qualms about his prowess when it came to women. It was quite apparent that he knew what women wanted. At least, he knew what Julia wanted. She rubbed her thighs together under the perfumed water, twitching excitedly as she thought back over the previous twenty-four hours.

Admittedly, she and Nick hadn't spoken much during their date. But then, they hadn't needed to. They'd communicated on an altogether more primitive level. Julia's heart jumped with the realisation of what she'd done, in front of those builders, and her eyelids drooped with satisfaction at her fragmented memories of their highly charged time together. What Nick lacked in conversation, he more than made up for in passion. He never had to be prompted, second-guessing her every sexual need. In many ways, he was just what she wanted in a man: forceful, masterful, happy and able to take control. And he had a mind as filthy as hers.

If Steve's mind was filthy, he was doing a good job in keeping his sordid thoughts well hidden. He was confused, angry, and as serious as ever – but he wasn't masterful. He wasn't in control, at all. It was Julia who had forced the afternoon to a climax, in both senses of the word. Without her initiation, she suspected he would have done nothing more than kiss her so far. His hesitancy was touching, in a way, but it wasn't what she wanted. They weren't teenagers any more, tiptoeing shyly around their emotions. She felt sorry for him; after all, it wasn't his fault. His adolescent crush on her was making it difficult for him to let go.

She slid down in the bath, sinking under the weight of regret until her head floated on the bubbles. With her ears beneath the water her hearing was muffled. There was only the sound of her breathing, the steady thump of her heartbeat, and the gradual untangling of her thoughts. She realised now that accepting this challenge was a big mistake. Comparing the two men was unfair, and making a choice was going to be impossible. They were so different, with different things to offer her. How could she decide between them without hurting the one who was rejected?

It would have been better to put a stop to it now, before Steve wound himself up any further. But that was impossible, too. He would be waiting for her, counting the minutes until he finally got to fulfil his fantasy. And anyway, she was curious. It was selfish and greedy, but she couldn't walk away until this night was over. She wanted to know how Steve's years of wanting her were going to feel.

And so, when she got out of the bath, she prepared herself for sex. Rubbing faintly perfumed body lotion into her limbs, she made her skin feel soft and smooth. She couldn't wear a bra underneath that dress, and decided to give Steve a treat and go without panties as well. Hopefully it would be a pleasant surprise for him when he took off her dress, to find only her sheer stockings and suspenders, dark against her pale skin. Eyeliner and mascara widened her eyes and intensified their drama. She didn't need blusher – her cheeks were already flushed. A bloody scarlet lipstick matched her dress perfectly. Standing on her black stiletto heels, she admired herself in the mirror. She looked fantastic, the slopes of her breasts and buttocks startlingly obvious in the slender sheath of fabric, one stockinged leg stretching tantalisingly from the high slit down to the sexy pointiness of her shoes. She was ready and willing, for whatever Steve had to offer.

Julia could see that something was wrong when the driver showed her into the flat. She had been delighted when the limo had swooped slowly into St Katharine's Dock. Overlooking a small crowd of expensive-looking yachts, the penthouse had a stunning view of the marina. Rising in the background, the floodlit splendour of Tower Bridge loomed dramatically. But the flat itself was eerily bare. There was no furniture and, as she discovered when she flicked unsuccessfully at the light switch, there was no electricity either. Outside, the tall lamps surrounding the miniature harbour twinkled merrily on the navy-blue water; inside, it was cold and dark, and rapidly getting darker.

'What are we doing here?' she asked, turning her back on the window.

'This is Steven's new place. He's just bought it. He hasn't moved in yet – as you can see,' he laughed, motioning to the empty space. 'Well, have a pleasant evening, miss.' He waved nonchalantly as he sidled to the door.

'Are you going?' Julia took a nervous step towards him. 'When will Steve be here?'

The driver shrugged. 'I don't know, miss. I was only told to bring you here.'

She tried to swallow her unease. 'Can't you stay for a while . . . until Steve comes?'

'Well . . .' He twirled his cap in his fingers, smiling

like someone about to break bad news. 'Not really, miss. It's my night off, you see. I'm going to meet my girlfriend.' He took tiny, shuffling steps backward as he spoke, trying to make his escape before she noticed.

'You'd better go, then.' Julia winced as he shut the door loudly behind him. 'Goodbye,' she whispered to the back of the door.

Hugging her coat closer around her, she looked around the room. Squinting through the darkness, she could see nothing. But then there was nothing to see. On one side of the room, a long corridor stretched out of sight into impenetrable blackness. She would have liked to explore, but she was wary of the unknown. At home, the night was her friend. She often sat in with the lights off and only the flickering of a candle or the television for company. But, in unfamiliar territory, the gloom held a host of invisible terrors waiting to pounce: cobwebs, spiders, mice, rats, men.

As if to confirm her fears, a creak echoed down the corridor. Julia stood, frozen to the spot, waiting for another. When nothing happened she assured herself that it was only the noise of an empty building. Wood expanding and contracting in the changing temperature. She forced herself to move and went and stood by the window. There, at least, she could see signs of life. Couples were strolling alongside the marina, looking at the boats on their way out for the evening. There was the distant hum of laughter and music coming from the pub, which was out of sight, and the faint chug of taxis as they pulled up to the Tower Hotel. Julia clung to those sounds, wrapping them round her like a comfort blanket.

She'd forgotten to put her watch on, but she seemed to have stood there for an hour. How long was Steve going to keep her waiting? If this was his idea of a joke, she wasn't laughing. This was a waste of their time together. What the hell was he up to?

She strained her neck to look down below the window as she heard footsteps approaching outside. It wasn't Steve though, and she sighed heavily and began to shiver. It was getting cold in the flat, and she was becoming distinctly uneasy. Unwilling to disturb the silence with the click of her heels, she tiptoed towards the door. Steve was obviously held up for some reason – business, probably. She'd go to the pub for a while and sit in the warmth. She'd leave a note for Steve, telling him to meet her there.

She jolted as she realised she had left her bag in the car. Not only was her pen and paper in there, but also her money, her mobile phone and her house keys. Pausing, she tried to quell the worrying thought that she was stranded, miles away from home, without a penny. What if Steve didn't turn up? She'd have to go to the pub, make a reverse-charge call to Marianne, and ask her friend to come and collect her. But it was Friday night. Marianne would be out. Who else had keys to her flat? David, but he was still on location. There was the set Nick had pinched the other day and forgotten to give her back – but he was in Scotland. Besides, she didn't know his number. Think, she urged herself. Think, think.

Thought was futile. She couldn't get out. Twisting frantically at the latch, she pulled and pulled, refusing to believe that she was locked in. But that was the truth. She couldn't see how, and couldn't work out why, but the door was stuck. Panic oozed in a cold sweat from her pores as she realised she was stuck here, in the dark, without a hope of escaping.

The sound of another loud creak startled her. She spun around, backing up against the door. Her shivering turned into shaking, her elbows rattled against the door as she jerked with fear. Another creak, and she held her breath. There was someone else in the flat. Someone had been lurking in the darkness the whole time she'd been there. The noise she'd heard before wasn't the sound of an empty home but the sound of a stranger, shifting his weight as he watched her in the gloom, waiting.

Biting her lip, she fought the urge to cry out. Straining every sinew to peer into the black beyond, she could just make out a tall figure. She couldn't see him getting closer but she could feel him. She could sense his presence edging nearer. She could hear his breathing getting louder.

Fright creased her forehead as she closed her eyes. There was no way out of here. Down the corridor, a stranger was looming towards her. Behind her back, the door was immovable. It was a long way down, out of the window. All she could do was pray quietly, to whoever might be listening.

'Please,' she whispered, terror quaking in her voice. 'Please, leave me alone.'

There was no reply but the sound of the dark figure's breathing, growing steadily nearer. His footsteps were deliberate, and terrifyingly slow on the bare floor.

'Oh God, please . . . please –'

He grabbed her as she tried to get away from him, pushing blindly past him into the corridor. He was strong and twisted both arms behind her back before she knew it. 'Don't hurt me,' she whimpered.

'What makes you think I want to hurt you?' His lips pressed against her neck, and Julia recognised his subtle aftershave.

'You bastard!' she screamed, struggling in his grasp. He held her too tightly for escape. Her mind flicked desperately through snippets of self-defence information she'd read. Using the only weapon she could think of, she lifted one foot and scraped the wicked tip of her heel down his shin. He flinched, loosening his grip just enough. Seizing the opportunity, she whipped out of his clutches and flung herself round to face him. Using all the nervous energy bubbling inside her tortured guts, she flailed at him. She hit and punched him everywhere:

arms, chest, stomach. He didn't retaliate, but caught at her hands and shoved her back against the wall. Pinning her arms down, he loomed over her. His breath was rapid on her face.

'Calm down,' he said, his voice scarily emotionless. 'It's me.'

'Calm down!' she screeched, her voice hysterical. 'I've been locked in here for hours in the pitch black, thinking I was alone. Then you appear out of nowhere like a bad dream. What the fuck are you playing at, Steve?'

He lifted her hands above her head. Crossing them at the wrists so he could hold her in one of his hands, he opened her coat with the other. 'You've only been alone for forty-five minutes, Julia, that's all.'

She writhed, vainly attempting to squirm away from the threat of his body. 'I was petrified, Steve.'

'Were you?' he whispered, sounding satisfied. 'Did you feel alone and helpless? Did you feel like there was no way out, like you were being suffocated with fear?'

'Steve,' she begged, 'please let me go. You're frightening me.'

In reply, he squeezed her wrists even tighter, while his other hand eased round her neck. 'You wanted me to show you how I felt. Well, now you know. You've endured three quarters of an hour, Julia. I've felt like this for the last seven years. Alone. Helpless. Suffocating.' He pressed his body into hers, pushing his erection against the softness of her pussy. 'I fucked other women, Julia, but it did no good. I still felt the same way afterwards. Alone, helpless, suffocating, wanting you.' He sighed heavily under the weight of a lifetime of longing. 'I'd be attracted to women simply because they reminded me of you. They had your smile, or the same colour hair, or they wore the same sort of clothes. But they weren't you, Julia. They left me feeling empty and bitter, and wondering how much better it would feel to be with you. Inside you.'

She gasped. She'd never heard this tone in Steve's voice before: the sound of desolate, raging determination. She was scared of the change that had come over him, but behind her fear was a bud of excitement, slowly growing.

'If you wanted me so badly, why didn't you keep in contact?'

Bitter laughter echoed down the narrow passageway. 'You wouldn't have wanted me, Julia. I had to change, to prove myself before I saw you again. I knew that I had to make something of my life, otherwise you wouldn't give me a second glance.'

'That's not true,' she insisted, shaking her head. 'I always liked you.'

'But you liked Nick better.'

'For God's sake,' she pleaded, exasperated. 'I went out with Nick for a couple of years, at school. That was a long time ago.'

'But you still like him now. You still want him, don't you?'

A nervous sigh shuddered in her windpipe. How could she tell Steve what he meant to her without offending him? 'I do like Nick. But I like you in a different way. I always did.'

'I know, I know,' he spat, grinding his pelvis against her. 'You liked me because I could give you all the things that Nick couldn't. You could talk to me. I was serious, and quiet, and sensitive, and romantic.' His hand flew from her neck, slamming loudly against the wall just by her ear. 'But I'm a man, Julia. I adored you. But I also wanted to have sex with you.'

Her pussy twitched inside, flames of desire searing her as she felt the length of his prick straining at her yearning flesh. 'You're right,' she sighed. 'I liked you for all those reasons. I enjoyed the fact that I could talk to you about anything. I loved the sweet, romantic notion of you and me, lying on the school lawn, wanting to kiss each other. But that night, at your castle, I wanted you in another way.' She paused, gasping as his swollen cock rubbed against her clitoris beneath her dress. 'I wanted you to fuck me, Steve.'

She could see nothing, but in the dark she felt his breath move closer. His face dipped to hers, his lips hovering over her open mouth. 'I'm going to fuck you now, Julia. Now.'

Tugging at her wrists, he dragged her roughly down the passageway. Stumbling behind him on her high heels, Julia struggled to catch her breath. His urgency was shockingly erotic, and more suited to Nick than Steve. Never in her wildest dreams had she imagined him taking control like this. It was thrilling to feel his desperation reverberating up her arm as he pulled at her body. She was angry with him for scaring her, but her anger was overtaken by fierce desire as he twisted her round through an open doorway. Manhandling her, he tore her coat off and threw her down on to the floor. In the slow-motion moment of falling she abandoned herself, waiting for the pain of the hard floor meeting her soft limbs. But she landed on something yielding; a mattress had cushioned her fall. Gasping for air to replace the lungful that had been knocked out of her, she watched as Steve lit a candle by the makeshift bed. The flickering light caught the ferocious glint in his eyes and made her wriggle with anticipation.

Crouching by her side, he looked down at her for a moment. His fingers were gentle as he stroked her cheek. Moving down her throat and over the sloping neckline of her dress, he rested his hand on her breast. Julia put her fingers on top of his, pressing them into her until she could feel the rhythm of her pounding heart echoing in his palm. At that, he flipped, losing any trace of gentleness. He flung her hand away and climbed on to the mattress, kneeling astride her hips. As he leant forward Julia felt the hardness beneath his trousers once again.

She gasped at the feel of him, so rigid in his lust, and gasped again as he pulled one arm out to the side and buckled her wrist into a leather cuff dangling from the wall above her head. She strained her neck to watch the other hand being tied, her pelvis squirming beneath his weight. It was exhilarating to be crushed by him, to feel him bearing down on her and to know that he couldn't be stopped. He wanted her so much his breath was rasping in his throat.

'How long have you had all this planned?' she whispered.

'Since this afternoon.' He sat back on his heels and admired her pinioned body. 'I was going to take you to the theatre, and then to dinner, and then to a room at the Savoy. I was going to be romantic, and sensitive, and caring. Just what you'd expect from me.'

'What happened? What made you change your mind?'

His eyes burnt into hers. 'It was when you told me to show you how I felt.' Grabbing the material at her hips, he rumpled the skirt of her dress, pulling it up over her legs. 'This is how I feel about you, Julia. This is how I feel when I see you in that dress.' Looking down, he grunted quietly, gratified by the sight of her naked pussy. 'This is how I feel when I imagine you with Nick.'

He knelt up and unzipped his trousers. The palm of one hand slid smoothly up the inside of her stockinged thigh and pushed her legs apart. Julia bent her knees, bracing herself as he lowered his body over hers. With a deft stroke of his businesslike fingers, he spread her pussy lips ready for him. Then his penis poked its head between her labia. He planted his hands either side of her face and hovered for infinity. Their eyes locked as they waited, poised on the brink of insanity, breathless with the thought of what was coming.

Then he rammed his full length deep inside her. Julia cried out at his brutality, arching her throat as her spine was gripped with tight, cruel ecstasy. He was remorseless, selfish, pumping his hips so hard into hers that he bruised the already tender skin of her upper thighs. Lifting her legs, she wrapped them around his back, trying to clasp him tightly. But nothing could slow his pace; he was frantic, out of control. Helpless underneath his onslaught, Julia had no choice but to abandon herself to the rampant pleasure overtaking her senses.

This wasn't for her, she thought, as she lay prone beneath him. This was for him: a desperate release, a frenzied outpouring of need, a violent outburst of lust. It was all the tensions and frustrations of the last seven years boiling over – and it was wonderful. The jerking friction of his cock burnt her; his turgid, throbbing length filled her; his relentless, mindless thrusting scarred her, deep in the hidden core of her. Her mind numb with delight, she moaned and ground her pussy against his sliding, trying to extinguish the flames licking at her clitoris. But he didn't pay any attention to her twisting body. Her faint, pleading cries had no effect on him. He probably didn't hear them. He was coming, shuddering violently inside her clasping vagina. His torso collapsed on top of hers, crushing her beneath his heaving chest. A long, tangled sigh of anguish and relief escaped from his mouth and curled around her neck. Julia shivered, shocked to the roots of her soul by the force of his feelings.

After a while, he began to make love to her. This time was different. Without a word, he stood and shed his clothes. Kneeling at her side, he gently unbuckled her wrists and helped her to sit up. Slowly, he peeled her dress away from her trembling limbs before laying her down again. His fingers preceded his lips all over her body, exploring her moistness, her tenderness, stroking every undulating dip and swell. He unclipped her suspenders and reverently rolled her stockings down her legs. He slipped her suspender belt down over her hips, his fingertips discovering the slight indentations left in her skin by the harness. He kissed her toes, her inner thighs, her belly. His tongue darted into her navel, the hollow of her throat, her warm mouth. He eased her over on to her front and softly planted kisses down the satin curve of her spine. Nuzzling at her buttocks, he spread her cheeks with kind but eager fingers. His lips sucked avidly at the puckered rim of her anus before flickering over its sensitive skin with his tongue. Julia sighed with unashamed delight and arched her pelvis up towards his mouth. Answering her need, Steve gently poked his tongue inside her secret hole. He held her hips to prevent her from squirming away from him and then thrust further inside her. Tiny, almost infinitesimal sparks of pleasure radiated through her, starting at the nerve endings embedded inside her hidden passage and filtering gradually throughout her spent body.

Together, they were fluid, their bodies moving like thick, viscous oil. Flowing through the dream of their emotions, Steve eased her limbs towards his. He knelt on his heels behind her, pulling her up into his lap. With her back to him, Julia raised her sex above his looming penis and slowly lowered herself. This wasn't violent, or frantic; this was slow, like licking their way through syrup. His body moulded to hers as she gently slid up and down on his long, thick rod. Turning her head, she rested in his shoulder. His warm hands reached around her rippling body to cup her swollen breasts and, as he squeezed she arched her back, raised her arms behind her and rested her fingers in his hair. His lips caressed her neck. One hand dropped between her legs and found the deep ache of her clitoris. Her bud grew heavy and hard beneath his circling fingers and she whimpered quietly, feeling just as helpless as if she'd been pinned down.

Her head rolled in the crook of his shoulder. She was lost in the gentle communion of their two bodies, the thick atmosphere making her sleepy. She wasn't cold any more; encased in the heat from Steve's body, her skin glowed with shared warmth. Basking in the aftermath of his explosive lovemaking, she felt her body melting into his. A deep, rumbling climax started at his fingers and trembled down her thighs. Steve held her tight, absorbing her shaking.

Before the gentle quake of her orgasm subsided, he was moving her again. He eased her body off his cock and pushed her forward on to her hands and knees. Julia had a vague sense of fumbling behind her, then something warm and oily was rubbed into her cleft. Wrapping one arm around her waist, Steve tentatively nudged at her anus with the tip of his penis. Slowly, carefully, he inched inside the incredible tightness of her arse, stretching her into utter speechlessness. Eyes tightly shut, mouth wide with shock, she teetered on the edge. Below her, over the precipice, was a long, dark fall. With every deliberate stroke Steve pushed her nearer to the edge. Then he was buried inside her to the hilt, his fingers twitching over her raw clitoris again, and she went over that edge. She spun into free fall, crying and shaking. This time, there was nothing to cushion her landing: just a complete, mind-blowing, terrifying rush of ecstasy, roaring through her veins and bubbling in her blood. She gave up the fight and succumbed to the unstoppable power of his cock, his fingers and her orgasm.

Steve and her; her and Steve – that was all that existed. They crumpled together on to the mattress. Lying on her side with Steve behind her, his thick penis still embedded between her cheeks, tears rolled down her face. Convulsions racked her exhausted limbs.

Steve touched her tear-streaked face. 'You're crying,' he whispered into her hair. 'Was I too rough? Did I hurt you?'

Julia shuddered in his arms. 'I'm crying with pleasure,' she breathed. 'Too much . . . pleasure.'

'Oh God,' he sighed gratefully. 'That was amazing.'

'Yes,' she agreed.

She had made her choice.

Julia woke up confused. Disorientated, she blinked several times. Stuck in the limbo between sleep and consciousness, it took her a while to work out where she was. When she had established that, it took another long moment to work out where the voice was coming from. Eventually, she pulled herself awake enough to realise that it was not a part of her dream. The muffled sound was coming from down the corridor.

Rolling out from under the blankets, she crept to the door. Peeking out into the gloom, she saw a faint light dancing in time with soft, padding footsteps. It was the display of Steve's mobile phone, glowing in the dark like a strange insect. Steve's voice was hushed.

'Face it,' he whispered. 'You've lost.' There was silence while he paced around. 'I'm telling you, Nick, she's mine.' A dirty laugh hacked dryly in his throat. Unable to keep it quiet, he allowed it out and it echoed around the empty flat. 'Yes, she did.' Another pause. Now, his voice was conspiratorial. Julia could tell he was smiling. 'Yeah, she did that too. It was fantastic.' There was a humph of disdain. 'No, she hasn't said so, not yet. But she will. I know she will.' Another pause, another wicked cackle. 'For once in your life, Nick, you're just going to have to admit defeat.' His pacing stopped. His tone of voice changed: he sounded deadly serious, determined, as he had done earlier with Julia. 'No, I haven't. But I will do, I promise you ... Oh, come on, Nick. Don't be such a bad loser.' There was a faint beep as he turned the phone off. 'Same to you,' he muttered into the darkness.

Julia scrambled soundlessly back to the mattress. She stubbed her toe on the way but stifled her yell. Huddling beneath the covers, she concentrated on her breathing, slowing it down to make it seem like she was still asleep. After what she had heard – the unmistakable sound of locker-room gloating – she didn't want to have to speak to Steve.

He came back into the room and climbed back in beside her. Lying with her back to him, Julia flinched inside as his fingertips brushed down her neck. Resisting the urge to push him away, she clenched every muscle and squeezed her eyes shut. His touch had been warm before, and she had welcomed his desire as it had seeped beneath her skin; now his touch was so cold it chilled her blood. She could hardly bear to be near him.

Then he began to mumble to himself. 'Jules,' he whispered. 'Please God, you've got to choose me now. I've already told Nick that he's lost.' His fingers swooped into the dip of her waist. 'I can't let him beat me again,' he sighed, his palm spreading over her hip. 'I won't let you go this time, Julia. I've got too much riding on this. I've got to win. I've got to complete my list.' Shuffling closer, he curled his body around hers. His knees fitted into the angle made by her legs. His cock, hard again, nudged at her cleft. 'I *will* complete my list, if it's the last thing I do.' His words danced on the back of her neck. 'It's all I care about, now. Nothing else matters any more.'

It was a battle with herself to hold still, repulsed as she was. She swallowed hard, itching to roll over and use the full force of her anger to slap him. Wincing with disgust, she resisted. A single tear squeezed its bitter way from beneath her eyelashes. She had been so close to telling him that she wanted him, that he had won her hand in this ridiculous challenge. Hit in the guts by his violent lust and then lulled by his tender passion, she might even have admitted that she was in love with him.

He did like her, possibly more than any man had ever liked her before. But scratch beneath the surface of his desire and there was his real motivation, for all to see. He wanted her body, yes; he possibly even wanted her mind, too; but, above all else, he wanted to finish off the list that had ruled the last seven years of his life. And it was quite obvious now what his ultimate goal was: to finally beat his childhood rival, Nick. Steve had already won where their careers were concerned, and now he wanted to come out top in the sexual stakes. It was pathetic that a grown man should be so preoccupied with another man, judging himself not on his own achievements but on how they compared to Nick's.

When Steve and Nick had urged Julia to choose between them, she had been flattered and wildly excited by their macho game. Now, she just felt sad. She had allowed herself to fall for Steve, only to be slapped in the face by his childish obsession with winning something – winning her – from Nick. Her premonition was coming true. It was Julia who was going to be the loser in their vicious battle.

She almost wished she hadn't woken up. If she had stayed buried in the cushion of sleep, she would never have heard him talking about her as if she were a prize. It would have been so easy. She would have come to in the morning, in his arms, and told him that he was the one. She would have said a fond farewell to Nick and David, and not given them another thought. What a mistake that would have been.

She cursed herself. How could she make such an error of judgement? How could she allow herself to be drawn into this game in the first place, let alone to fall for Steve – a man who worried more about what was written on a piece of paper than about her feelings. She despised herself for being so greedy. Why couldn't she have been happy with the man she had? David; sweet, kind, trusting David. Gorgeous, sincere, intelligent David. His name pounded inside her head, taunting her.

She lay awake, her shoulder aching painfully, but she

dared not move until she had a plan fixed in her head. There was only one thing on her mind now – getting back to her old life, before it was too late. As she waited for Steve to fall asleep, she wondered what on earth had been going through her mind during the last week. Her thoughts had been tangled ever since that bloody reunion. There had been some half-formed, half-baked idea that waiting around the corner was a new life. A better life, filled with incredible sex and meaningful conversations and a wonderfully fulfilling career. She must have been mad.

It took ages for Steve to fall asleep. Every time she thought he'd gone past the point of no return, she would shift on the mattress ever so slightly and he would mumble and wrap his body tighter around hers. Then the process would begin all over again: waiting for his breathing to deepen, gradually easing her limbs out of his. Julia felt like a prisoner trying to outwit her kidnapper, her pulse racing as she anticipated him waking up at any minute. But he was exhausted and eventually he slept. She managed to get one wrist cuffed tightly before he fully realised what she was doing.

'Julia?' he mumbled, his words slurred with confusion. 'What are you doing to me?'

She pulled his other hand over his head. Strapping his wrist into the leather handcuff, she buckled it tightly. She gave a tug on the chains attaching the cuffs to the wall. They were firm. He would have no chance of escape.

'Julia?' He raised his head from the mattress as she stood up. 'Jules?' He sounded anxious now.

She crouched down and relit the candle. Moving calmly through the flickering light and ignoring Steve's bleating, she got dressed. He smiled while she rolled her stockings over her thighs and clipped them back into her suspender belt, thinking this was a game. But when her dress was slipped over her head, and her shoes and coat were retrieved, the realisation hit him. His smile disintegrated.

'Is something wrong? Are you going somewhere?'

Bending down, she fumbled in his jacket pockets. She picked out a set of keys and a twenty-pound note from his wallet. 'I'm going home, Steven. My bag's in your car, so I'm going to borrow this money for a taxi. I'll send you a cheque.'

'Wh–why? Why are you leaving?'

'I've got things to do,' she said coldly. 'My fiancé's coming home tomorrow.'

He tried to sit up, but the chains prevented him. 'Julia!' he shouted, stopping her at the doorway. 'What ... why ...?'

She turned and glowered at him with eyes that wanted to do him some damage. 'I heard you, before. When you were on the phone.'

Steve's mouth opened and closed. As he struggled to emerge from sleep, Julia could see that it was hard for him to remember exactly what had been said.

She reminded him. 'You'd barely finished fucking me, and you were calling Nick to boast about it.'

'Huh?' He blinked himself awake. 'It wasn't like that, I just –'

'Just what? I heard every word, Steve. You told him you'd won.'

He shook his head with tiny, frantic motions. 'Julia, I'm sorry. I didn't mean ... you don't understand.'

'Oh, I think I do. I heard you when you got back into bed, too. You thought I was asleep, but I heard every word.' Her throat grew tight with anger. 'You're obsessed, Steve. Obsessed with that bloody list of yours. It's all you care about – that's what you said.'

'Please, let me explain. The list –'

'No.' Slowly, she shook her head and her eyes narrowed with resolve. 'Let me explain. I am not a piece of property for you and Nick to squabble over. I'm not a prize to be won and then ticked off your pathetic list.' Fury flooded her mind. She picked up one of Steve's shoes and flung it at the wall behind his head, making him jump. Her voice wobbled with emotion. 'I cared about you, Steve. I was under the impression you cared about me. But, let's be honest, whatever's on that stupid list is more important to you than I am.' Her eyes narrowed. 'Beating Nick. That's your final goal, isn't it? Getting one over on him, after all these years.' Her chest was heaving with rage. 'I'd expect that sort of immature behaviour from him, but not you.' She sneered with disgust. 'You and Nick are perfect for each other. You should cut out the middle man and get together, the pair of you. Fuck each other, instead of fucking with me.' Her voice was like a dagger, its threat making him squirm with fright as she had done, before. 'What's the matter? Don't you like that idea? I thought it would appeal to a cold, heartless businessman like you.' She turned to go. She needed to leave before he saw the tears brimming in her eyes. 'Goodbye, Steven. So sorry you didn't get to complete your sodding list.'

'Don't go. Don't go. Please, don't go. Don't leave me, not now, let me explain...'

His words followed her down the corridor, the pleading in his voice trying to pull her back. But she resisted. She fiddled clumsily in the darkness with the keys.

'Julia!' he screamed. 'It's not what you think! Please, if you care about me, let me explain...'

She slammed the door on the noise, but not before the heart-rending cry reached into her soul and gripped her. 'Goodbye,' she whispered.

'Julia? Pick up the phone, if you're in.'

Julia closed her eyes. Slumped on the sofa, she hugged her knees into her chest.

'Julia? Julia!' David's anxious voice sounded tinny on

the answerphone. 'It's very late for you to still be out. I hope Marianne's not leading you astray. I'll try again in a little while, darling.'

Her head dropped on to her knees, heavy with the weight of her guilt. There was David, ringing in the early hours of Saturday morning, his voice full of innocent concern. And there she was, huddled on the sofa, trying to calm the turmoil in her mind. Silent tears poured down her face at the thought of how she had betrayed her fiancé. This was the sixth time he had rung and she hadn't yet found the courage to pick up the phone. How could she? How could she speak to him, pretending that nothing was wrong?

Half an hour later, the phone went again, its shrill ringing like an alarm going off inside her head. Pressing her hands over her ears, she winced, urging the answering machine to intercept.

'Julia? It's David, are you there?' He paused, waiting hopefully for her to pick up the phone. 'It's three in the morning, where the hell are you?' Another pause, while he thought. 'I need to speak to you. I'm going to call your mobile.'

Her mobile was still in Steve's car; the driver might answer it. Julia lunged for the phone. 'Hello, David.'

'Thank God,' he sighed. 'Where've you been? I've been trying you for hours.'

She bowed her head. 'I've been out with Marianne.'

'Until this time? Where did you go?'

'To a nightclub. It was . . . sort of a hen-night thing.'

'Ah hah! I might have known you'd be up to no good. Enjoy yourself?'

'Not really,' she said, trying her best to sound as if it had been a boring evening.

'Oh, there's no need to pretend, darling. I know what goes on at hen nights. I bet you and Marianne had a wild time. Dressed to kill and flirting with anything in trousers if I know you two.' His gentle laughter made Julia squirm. 'Did you?' he asked quietly.

'Did I what?'

'Flirt with someone?' His voice was low and eager. 'I don't mind if you did, you know.'

Julia was confused. 'You make it sound like you would have *liked* me to flirt with another man.'

'Well, it might make me feel a little better if you had.'

'David? What are you going on about?'

He laughed nervously. 'Have you seen the papers yet, darling?'

'David?' she urged, wishing he would get on with it, whatever it was he had to say.

She heard him take a deep breath. Then his words came out in an unstoppable rush, as if he had rehearsed his lines over and over again, and was determined to get them right first time. 'Look, Jay-jay, there may be a little piccie of me in some of the tabloids this morning. Most of the cast weren't needed today, so we had our end-of-series wrap party last night. For some unknown reason, some complete idiot thought it would be good publicity for the show to invite some bloody tabloid photographers, and said photographers may – just may – have caught me ... er ... kissing Verity. But it's nothing, darling. We were drunk and fooling about. You become quite close, you know, when you work together so much –'

'Verity,' Julia said, completely calm now that she had something else to think about other than her own infidelity. 'Verity, as in the actress who plays your wife?'

'Er, 'fraid so, darling. But it didn't mean anything, honestly. Julia, you've got to believe me. We were blind drunk and it was a goodbye kiss and if that sodding photographer hadn't been there I wouldn't even need to mention it. It was nothing. Less than nothing.'

Julia smiled bitterly to herself. What a twist: David ringing to diffuse the fall-out of a kiss with his on-screen wife, while Julia had slept with four different men while he had been away. And fallen in love with one of them.

'So that's why you were so keen to get in contact,' she said. 'You weren't worried about me at all, were you? You just wanted to smooth things over before I saw you in the papers.'

'Darling,' he simpered, his voice sugary sweet. 'I just didn't want this blown out of all proportion. The papers know I'm engaged, so there's bound to be some nonsense about my being caught cheating on my fiancée, with my "wife". You know what the tabloids are like,' he sneered disparagingly.

'I should do. I work for one of them,' Julia bristled, suddenly defensive about her job.

'Exactly, so you know how most of what they put in is utter rubbish. Anyway, I thought the photo might cause you some embarrassment. And I wanted you to know that it was only a kiss. Nothing else.' He coughed uneasily, as he often did when he was trying to be emotional. 'Julia, I don't want to lose you over something as silly as this.'

Julia closed her eyes. Verity was beautiful: tall, blonde, statuesque. Imagining David kissing her put a pin of jealousy in Julia's heart. A kiss, that was all it was, and yet she wanted to tell him to forget the wedding. She wanted to break down, to make him feel the devastation she felt and to blame it all on that innocuous kiss. But David wasn't stupid. He would know that something else was wrong and she would have to tell him.

Keeping her mouth tightly shut in case anything stupid came bursting out, she waited for the ripple of envy to subside. 'Thanks for ringing,' she said softly.

'What ... Does that mean ... Are you all right about this, Julia?'

'I'm fine. It was only a kiss, like you said. We'd be stupid to let something like this spoil our relationship.'

'Oh, you're so wonderful.' He sighed with relief. 'Do you realise, it's only a week until we tie the knot?'

'Yeah. I can't wait.' She wrinkled up her eyes as the tears began to burn again. 'Tell me you love me,' she whispered.

'What?'

'I want to hear you say it.'

'Of course I love you,' he said.

That was it: matter of fact, no passion or desperation. Just 'of course', as if she had asked him whether they were going to his mother's for lunch on Sunday. 'I need some sleep. I'll speak to you tomorrow,' she said, trying to control the quavering in her voice.

'I'll *see* you tomorrow. I'll set off early and meet you at Mum's at around one. You are still on for lunch with the parents?'

'Of course,' she said, through gritted teeth.

Julia was just drifting into sleep when the buzzer went. She let Marianne into the building, opened the front door to her flat and slouched back to the sofa. She smiled wanly as her friend appeared.

'I've been trying to ring you since eight o'clock this morning,' Marianne said, stalking in grumpily. 'Your phone was dead. What's wrong with it?'

Too tired to explain, Julia wafted her hand towards the telephone socket. It was empty, the wire coiled uselessly on the floor beside it.

'What the hell did you do that for?' Marianne tutted, squatting on her heels to plug the phone back in again. 'Incredibly mean, I call it.' She grinned, wagging a nail-varnished finger. 'I've been dying to know what happened with Naughty Nick and Serious Steven. Well?' She waited expectantly. 'Wow,' she added, her smile fading slightly with envy. 'What a dress.'

Julia looked down her body at the long red sheath. The bodice was stained where her tears had dripped from her face, but she didn't care. She wasn't going to wear the dress again, ever. 'It's Chanel,' she whispered feebly.

'I know,' Marianne cooed in awe. 'I've seen it in the window. It's gorgeous. It really suits you.'

'Steve bought it for me.' Julia's ribs jerked as another wave of sorrow began to build inside her.

'Did you have a good time with him?'

'I had a wonderful time,' she sobbed. 'It was the best night of my life.'

'So why are you about to burst into tears?'

Julia broke down. Marianne sat beside her on the sofa and held her, rubbing her soft hands over Julia's shoulders as they shook uncontrollably. Choked with anguish, Julia was unable to get a single word out that made any sense. Marianne waited patiently, comforting her until her trembling died down.

She poured Julia a strong drink and fetched the duvet from the bedroom. Tucking it around her shivering body as if she were an invalid, she perched on the arm of the settee and smoothed Julia's hair. 'Christ, you look terrible.'

'Thanks,' Julia muttered.

'Are you going to tell me what you're so upset about?'

Julia told her. Self-pity overtook her voice once or twice and she had to stop to have another cry. But eventually all the details were divulged: Nick's kinkiness, Steve's passion, the realisation that she had made her choice followed by the kick in the teeth. 'He's only concerned with that bloody list of his,' she spat. 'That's all he cares about. And I thought . . .' She shook her head, disgusted with herself for making such a mistake. 'I thought he cared about me,' she whispered.

'What a bastard,' Marianne hissed in agreement. 'I always said he was a bit of a weirdo. He's got a crazed look in his eyes, like he's in a world of his own.'

'That's where he belongs,' said Julia. 'In a world of his own, on his own.'

Marianne got up and went to the window. She opened the curtains on a beautiful sunny morning. 'Of course, you're presuming that this mysterious final goal of his is all to do with him and Nick, and their infantile rivalry over you.' She gently pulled at the net curtain, poking her nose between the greying muslin drapes. 'It could be something quite different he has in mind.'

'Like what?' Julia snapped.

'Like . . . marrying you?'

'I doubt it,' she huffed, but nonetheless the thought struck her cold. 'Let me explain,' he had shouted after her. 'It's not what you think . . .'

Marianne turned round slowly with a silly smile on her glossed lips. 'He's sitting outside in a huge silver car, with some gorgeous stud who looks suspiciously like Nick.'

Flinging the duvet to the floor, Julia sprung from the sofa. Hiding behind Marianne, she peeked out. The two men were sitting in the back of the limo, their heads bobbing as they talked earnestly.

Steve looked up just as Marianne waved. Jumping out of the car, he hesitated for a moment like a runner confused by a false start. Then he stumbled up the path to the front door, while Nick eased himself languidly from his seat. Leaning over the roof of the car, he smiled at Marianne. Aghast, Julia watched a hint of a leer begin to form as he caught Marianne's eye.

'Oh Christ. Get rid of them,' Julia hissed, as the intercom buzzed.

'Don't you want to talk to them?'

'No.'

Marianne raised an eyebrow. 'I think they'll want to talk to you.'

'No! Why d'you think I unplugged my phone? I'm not

talking to either of them.' She flounced off towards the bedroom. 'You waved at them. You deal with them.'

She cowered behind her half-closed bedroom door, straining to make sense of the muffled voices in her hallway. She heard Marianne saying no several times and then cackling with laughter, but couldn't make out much more.

A moment later, Marianne was back. 'They won't go away,' she said. 'They said you've got to make a decision.'

'Well, I'm not going to.' She shooed Marianne away. 'Go on! Tell them that.'

She sat down on the bed. No sooner had Marianne's footsteps clicked away towards the hall than they were returning again.

'They said you had a deal and you can't back out of it.'

Julia seethed. 'Well that's exactly what I am doing. Tell them I don't want either of them.'

Marianne rolled her eyes. 'They're not going to give up that easily, Jules. Can't you come out and tell them yourself?'

'No.' Julia folded her arms sulkily. 'I don't want to see either of them, ever again.'

'Poor old Nick,' Marianne said. 'He didn't do anything wrong.'

'But I don't want Nick,' she hissed. 'I've already explained all that to you.'

Marianne's eyes sparkled wickedly. 'Forget Steve, I'd have Nick, if I were you.'

'I don't believe you,' Julia snapped. 'I'm in turmoil here, and you're flirting with Nick, aren't you?'

Marianne sat on the corner of the bed, grinning stupidly. 'He is rather lovely, Jules. I can see why Steve's out of the picture, but why not give Nick another try?'

'Another try?' She shook her head. 'I told you I have nothing in common with Nick except sex. You may be happy with that sort of relationship, but I'm not. There has to be more.'

'Does there?' Marianne looked wistfully out of the bedroom door in the direction of the hallway.

Julia pushed her friend's shoulders, urging her to her feet. 'Marianne, I don't care how you do it, just get them out of here.'

There was a longer interval this time before Marianne returned. Ignoring Julia, she made straight for the dressing table and began working her way through her friend's small collection of lipsticks. Finding one she liked, she put a thick coating of deep red on her lips.

'Well?' Julia asked. 'Have they gone?'

'Steve said he's not leaving until you come out and speak to him.' Marianne fluffed her golden hair. 'He said you've got it all wrong and he wants to explain.'

'Well, you explain this to him: I'm fed up with his childish games. I've decided to go through with my wedding after all.'

Marianne stopped preening. Open-mouthed, she stared at Julia as if she had two heads. 'You're not serious?'

'Close your mouth and go and tell him.'

Marianne looked worriedly, deep into Julia's eyes. 'Don't settle for David just because Steve let you down.'

Julia lowered her eyes.

'Jules. Jules, look at me. What happened to the woman who said she'd fight for love and truth? Don't you think you owe it to Steve to let him explain?' She moved closer and gently lifted Julia's chin. 'Don't you think you owe it to yourself? You are in love with him, aren't you?'

Julia closed her eyes and gritted her teeth. 'Please, Marianne, I've made my decision. I can't see him now.'

Sighing, Marianne went off to deliver her message. She sighed again when she came back to deliver the reply. 'He says you can't get married without hearing what he has to say. And he's leaving on a business trip this afternoon. He'll be away for a week, so you have to see him now.' She flung Julia's handbag on to the bed. 'Apparently, you left this in his car.'

Julia retrieved her purse and got out a twenty-pound note. 'Give him this,' she said. 'It's what I owe him. And tell him to go.' There must have been a note of uncertainty in her voice, because Marianne didn't move. 'I'm not going to speak to him,' she insisted, more firmly this time. 'I don't want to hear whatever it is he has to say. Tell him my fiancé's due back any minute and I want him out of here, now.'

As Julia waited for her go-between to relay her final word, a strange mixture of thoughts whizzed in her head. There were sharp slivers of anger, bitter slices of disappointment and, above it all, like an aftertaste of chilli bursting on the tongue, there was excitement. Hearing footsteps approach, she held her breath. Part of her was disappointed when Marianne burst back in alone.

'He's gone,' she said triumphantly.

'Oh.'

Marianne rolled her eyes. 'For God's sake, Jules, you told me to send him away. Do you want me to call him back now?'

'No.' She looked nervously at her friend, searching her blue eyes for clues. 'What did he have to say for himself, then?'

'Nothing.'

'Nothing?'

Marianne rapped on Julia's head with her knuckles. 'Hello, anyone in there? You didn't want to hear what he had to say, remember?' Marianne paused on her way to the door to check her reflection once again. 'Now, will you be all right on your own?'

'Where are you going?'

'I'm going for a coffee with Nick.' She grinned. 'You don't mind, do you?'

Tossing her long blonde hair, Marianne breezed out of the flat. As the doors slammed behind her, Julia felt the sound echoing in her mind. Alone and empty, she drifted to the window. Nick and Marianne were walking off down the street, already laughing and flirting. Steve was leaning against his car, his hands thrust deep into his trouser pockets, his shoulders slumped as if he, too, felt empty inside.

From behind the veil of the net curtain, Julia watched him staring at the window. His eyes were vacant and desolate. She ached for him. Perhaps there wouldn't be any harm in hearing what he had to say. Seeing him standing there, his body deflated as if he had been punched in the guts, Julia realised that Marianne could have been right. Maybe Steve's final goal wasn't anything to do with her and Nick.

Before she could pull the curtain aside, the driver emerged from the car. Opening the passenger door for Steve, he glanced meaningfully at his watch. Turning away, Steve nodded slowly and climbed into the front seat. His head was bowed as the limo smoothly pulled away. Julia watched them go, struggling for breath like a lottery winner whose ticket had just blown out of her fingers.

The Final Reunion

The following week was the strangest week of Julia's life. She felt as if she was heavily sedated and watching through a thick haze as events unfolded, despite her. The days rolled by, one hour merging meaninglessly with the next. as if this wasn't her existence but someone else's – someone she had no control over. She could only watch from afar as her wedding grew inexorably nearer.

David had never been more lovely. Since the photo of him with Verity had appeared in several of the tabloids, he had lavished so much attention on Julia that, if she had been her usual self, she would have felt completely smothered. As it was, she accepted the flowers, the chocolates, the kisses, and the slow, tender sex without being affected in the least. His love piled on like an avalanche, but she was lying perfectly still beneath it. She could hear the snow rushing over her, could see the powder filling the sky until it disappeared from view, but she couldn't feel a thing. Beneath the roaring torrent it was still and quiet. So she smiled, and kissed, and moaned appreciatively beneath the sheets. But inside she was painfully empty.

She got on with her job with the quiet obedience of someone who had been brainwashed and broken. George even asked her what was wrong – why she wasn't complaining any more – but she just smiled wanly. Nobody knew. Neither David, George, nor Marianne had any idea of what was really going on inside her head.

One thought kept her going through Sunday lunch with David's parents. The same thought that comforted her when David's sister came round to finalise the catering arrangements for the tiny wedding reception. It was the same thought that dulled the torture of endless photo shoots and pre-nuptial, celebratory nights out with her work colleagues, and evenings in with David. That same thought that made David's body feel like someone else's when he was inside her.

But by Friday, Steve had still not rung. Julia finished work early – a wedding present from George – and paced around her flat. She had things to do, things to get ready for tomorrow, but she couldn't be bothered with them. The only thing on her mind was whether or not she should phone Steve. Part of her was still angry with him; another part was astounded that he hadn't contacted her. But another part just wanted to hear his voice and give him a chance to explain.

She knew she was making a mistake before she had even finished dialling. When the receptionist answered in a cold, polished voice, Julia hesitated.

'Hello?' the voice said, bristling with impatience. 'Hello? Hello?'

'Hi,' Julia said quietly. 'I was wondering ... Would it be possible to speak to Steve?'

'Mr Roth?' the receptionist corrected, as if it was blasphemy to use his first name. 'Who may I say is calling?'

'Miss Sargent,' Julia snapped sarcastically. 'I'm a friend of his.'

'Oh, I see. Please hold.'

Julia held, her fingers drumming rapidly in time with her heart.

'Ms Sargent?' the voice chirped. 'Mr Roth is in a meeting.'

'This is important,' Julia pleaded. 'It will only take a minute.'

'Well, if it *is* important, he may take the call,' she said, in a sing-song tone that made it quite clear that nothing could be that important. The line went dead for a moment. 'I'm so sorry,' she said insincerely, 'Mr Roth really cannot be disturbed. He asked me to take a message. Hello? Are you still there?'

Julia put the phone down. It hit her, then. If he had had anything to say to her, he would have been in contact before now. Quite possibly he didn't have her number, but he would have found it out somehow. The truth was that he didn't have an alternative explanation; what she had suspected was true. Steve was obsessed with winning her from Nick, but he didn't care about her.

Well that's that, she thought, going back into her bedroom and flopping on to the bed. Her wedding dress was hanging expectantly from the wardrobe door. As she looked at it, the last escape hatch slammed down violently inside her head. 'That's that,' she whispered to herself. 'I'm getting married tomorrow, to the nicest man in the world.' She rolled over on to her front, her body shaking as she cried into her pillow.

'Call it off.'

Julia rolled her eyes and slammed her hairbrush down on to the dressing table. 'Piss off, Marianne.'

Marianne looked hurt. 'That's not very nice.'

'Well, you're supposed to be here to help me get ready, not to talk me out of it.'

Marianne stood behind Julia. Picking up the brush,

she began to gently move it through Julia's silky hair. 'I know, I'm sorry. But I'm your best friend, and I just can't believe you're going to go through with it.'

Julia's eyes glazed. She couldn't quite believe it herself. 'David's good for me,' she said, but she felt as if she was reading the lines in a play, not talking about real life. 'I need someone like him to keep my feet on the ground. You know me, I do things without thinking of the consequences.'

'Yes, like marrying the wrong bloke.' Marianne stopped brushing and squeezed Julia's shoulder. 'You don't love him.'

'I do.'

'Not in the way you love Steve.'

Julia got up from the table and walked away from Marianne and away from the truth. Leaning over the bed, she fiddled with the lingerie laid out there. It should be white for weddings, she thought to herself. But this was not a normal wedding. The bride would be dressed in red, with black stockings and suspenders, a G-string, and a satin Wonderbra. Julia never did what was expected of her.

'Steve,' Marianne repeated. 'You're thinking about him now, aren't you?'

'No,' she lied. 'I haven't given him a thought all week, and he obviously hasn't thought about me. If he wanted me, he would have called.'

'How would he get your number? You're ex-directory.'

Julia swallowed. 'He would have found a way.'

'There isn't a way.' Marianne sat down on the bed, poking her head forward into Julia's line of sight until she was forced to look at her. 'There's no way of finding out an ex-directory number.'

'Then he should have come to see me.'

'He was going to be in Spain on business until yesterday.'

Julia shrugged. 'He could have written.'

'Have you checked with the other flats? Perhaps someone else picked up your mail by mistake. That has happened before.'

Julia shook her head. 'Look, I'm going to be late if you don't stop whingeing on. Now, help me.'

Half an hour later, she looked a lot better than she felt. Her short, dark-red dress was perfect. It was imitation Prada, with a wide collar, buttons down to the hem and a narrow belt slung low round her waist. Julia had bought some new boots to go with the dress; these were soft black suede, calf-length with fashionably spindly heels. A short black coat, reminiscent of Audrey Hepburn and the sixties, completed the outfit. Marianne had smoothed something on to Julia's hair to give it an almost impossible, lustrous sheen, and her make-up was subtle apart from her lips and nails, which matched her dress. The curves of her cleavage were sexily visible, pushed up by her bra, and her other curves were just obvious enough beneath the short skirt of her dress.

'Does David know what you're wearing?' Marianne asked, as she pinned a white rosebud to the lapel of Julia's coat. 'I can't wait to see his face,' she laughed. 'I hope he's not expecting you to turn up in a demure little off-white number.'

'If he knows me at all, he'll know not to expect anything.' Julia jumped as a hooter blared outside. 'That'll be the taxi.'

Marianne hesitated, gazing earnestly into Julia's face for a sign of surrender. Then she hugged her. 'Be sure,' she whispered.

'I'll be late,' Julia said, avoiding Marianne's eyes as she pulled out of her embrace. 'I'll see you there.'

Marianne nodded. 'I'll just tidy up all your mess and then I'll hop on the tube. I'll be there before you.'

* * *

Marianne opened the front door to find Steve standing there, his finger raised to the buzzer.

'We're in London on business,' he blustered, as if he needed an excuse to be there. 'Nick and I...' He motioned towards the car. Nick was sat in the back, and he waved as he saw Marianne. 'Is Julia in?'

'You've just missed her. She's on her way to the registry office.'

Steve's wide mouth fell open. He blinked slowly, scratching his head. 'I see,' he said quietly, and he turned to go.

'Wait a minute. What's that?' Marianne gestured towards the wide flat package under his arm.

'It's a present. For Julia,' he added, as if Marianne might be disappointed that it wasn't for her.

Marianne tugged at his sleeve. 'Come in,' she said, opening the door to Julia's flat. 'You can leave it in here for her.'

Steve followed her inside. He wandered around Julia's living room, staring dreamily at the photos that lined the walls. He seemed to be in shock. Marianne eased the package out from under his arm and propped it up on the sofa.

'What is it?'

Moving slowly, as if it was a tremendous and painful effort, Steve pulled the protective layer of bubble wrap from the present. It was a framed print. Marianne recognised it from Julia's description.

'That's the painting from the gallery.' She looked at the small white card perched in one corner of the frame. She read out loud: 'Every time you look at this picture, think of me. I'll be thinking of you, wishing I could be with you, and wondering why you didn't let me explain.'

'Oh, that's so romantic,' Marianne sighed. When she looked up at him, she recognised the anguish in his face. 'You're in love with her, aren't you?'

Steve gave an almost imperceptible nod, as if he loved her so much he had lost the strength to move.

'The final goal on your list – it's nothing to do with Nick, is it?'

'No.'

'Come on,' she said, taking his hand. 'We've got to get to that wedding.'

Steve gently pushed her away. 'It's too late now. If she didn't respond to my letter, she's not going to now. Once Julia makes her mind up about something, that's it. And she's obviously made her mind up that I'm more concerned about beating Nick than being with her.' He sighed forlornly. 'She's got it so wrong.'

'Letter?' Marianne's eyes narrowed. 'You sent her a letter?'

'I posted it before I left for Spain. It explained everything.'

Marianne whisked out into the hall. Flinging envelopes from pigeon holes, she checked the mail for each flat. Amongst the bundle for the second-floor flat was the envelope for Julia. Before she thought about what she was doing, Marianne had torn it open. Her eyes flicked desperately through the words, her fingers shaking as Steve's emotions jumped off the paper and into her heart.

'Oh God,' she whispered hoarsely. 'Oh Jesus.'

Julia stood at the front of the small room. All eyes were on her as she looked around nervously at the handful of guests. David softly squeezed her elbow. 'We can't wait for ever, darling.'

'We can't start without Marianne,' she snapped, under her breath. 'She's got your ring.'

David tutted quietly. 'I knew we shouldn't have relied on her.'

Julia seethed inside. Where the hell had Marianne got to? Going by tube, she should have easily beaten Julia to the registry office. Julia had spent at least a quarter of an hour putting flowers on her parents' grave on the way, and had been fully expecting to see Marianne waiting for her on the steps when she arrived. Every second's wait felt like an hour: a long, embarrassing, nerve-wracking hour.

'Thank God for that,' she whispered, as she heard Marianne's voice outside. She turned to the door, smiling expectantly.

She could immediately see that something was going on. Marianne's eyes were wide with a mixture of excitement and worry. She walked in and stepped aside for the two men following her. Nick was first; he grinned sheepishly and waved at Julia. Steve was last. He strode without hesitation up the aisle.

Julia gulped. 'What the hell are you doing here?'

'Who is this?' David asked.

'This is Steve,' Julia replied shakily, although introductions seemed slightly out of place as she stood there, on the verge of marriage. 'Steve's an old schoolfriend of mine.'

'I'm more than a friend,' Steve said calmly, aiming his words at David but looking steadfastly at Julia.

Julia attempted a smile, but her facial muscles wouldn't respond. 'Did you want something, Steve?'

'I wanted to give you this.' He produced a crumpled envelope from inside his jacket and handed it to her.

'What is it?'

'It's the letter he sent you,' Marianne called out from the back of the room. 'It was in the pigeon hole for flat two. Read it,' she urged.

Julia took a deep breath and pulled the letter from the envelope. She could feel everyone's attention burning into her as she read. The sudden heat in the room made her cheeks flush violently. 'Is this true?' she whispered, looking up at Steve.

In reply, he brought out another envelope. He pulled

out a folded sheet of paper and handed it to Julia. She recognised it immediately.

'The Aims and Aspirations of Steven Roth,' she read to herself. 'One, get a first at uni.' She knew that bit. She skipped to the end. 'Seven...' She drew in her breath. 'Why didn't you tell me this before?'

He shook his head sadly. 'I tried to. I wanted to tell you at school, the day we wrote these blasted lists. I wanted to tell you at the reunion, but then I found out about him.' He jerked his thumb dismissively towards David. 'I wanted to tell you when you came up to Glasgow but Nick got in the way.' He smiled ruefully. 'I wanted to tell you the other night, after we made love, but I got scared.'

'Made love?' David spluttered.

'Scared?' Julia whispered.

He raised a hand and stroked her burning cheek with his cool fingertips. 'You're the only woman I've ever really wanted. I was terrified that you would choose Nick, again. I thought it would be best not to tell you until you'd made your decision, just in case. I didn't want to make a fool of myself.'

'Decision?' David snapped, looking from Julia to Steve. 'What decision?'

Julia ignored him. 'I was going to tell you ... that I'd chosen you ...'

'But you heard me boasting to Nick. And then I started ranting on about my list, and you put two and two together.'

'And made five,' she agreed. 'I'm so sorry. I should have let you explain.'

Steve's delicate touch flowed down on to her neck. 'I can't blame you. I'm the one who should be apologising. I've made a total mess of all this. I should never have gone along with this contest.' He threw an angry glance at Nick. 'It was never going to work.'

'It's my fault. I shouldn't have agreed to it.' Julia

reached up and slipped her fingers around the back of his neck. Her thumb caressed the edge of his jaw. 'There was no need for you and Nick to compete for me. I knew all along which one of you I'd choose.' Julia looked up at the sound of Nick clearing his throat in protest. 'I'm sorry, Nick. I enjoy being with you, I always did. But Steve . . .' She looked adoringly up at him. She practically wept with relief as Steve's lips descended to hers. He kissed her long and hard, pressing his body into hers as if he had finally found the missing piece in his life; as if, without her breasts flattening against his chest, without her hips pushed up against his, he was incomplete, only half a being. His hands moved all over her, clasping her neck and then moving over her shoulders, her waist and then her hips. Sliding round behind her, his hungry palms pulled her further into him.

'Would someone like to tell me what the fuck is going on?'

Julia opened her eyes. Lost in the depth of Steve's kiss, she had forgotten that there were twenty people in the room who had come to watch her marry someone else. Easing herself reluctantly out of Steve's arms, she turned to face David. 'I'm so sorry. I never meant to hurt you.'

His eyes glittered fiercely. 'Are you saying you don't want to marry me?'

She answered with a silent, guilty shake of her head. As David's expression turned from anger to incomprehension to hurt, she waited for him to plead with her. Any moment now, she thought, he'll tell me he loves me desperately, he can't bear to be without me, he'll fight for me and won't give in until he's won my love back.

But he didn't. When he opened his mouth it wasn't to beg but to spit venom. 'How dare you do this to me? You've made me look like an idiot.' He raised his hand and it hovered there like the threat of thunder in the air.

'Don't,' Julia urged, wanting to keep the inevitable scene as low-key as possible.

'Don't you dare touch her,' Steve added quietly.

David slowly lowered his hand. 'My parents were right about you,' he said, his handsome face distorted with fury. 'I should have listened to them. You weren't my type.'

Julia put her hand to David's shoulder. 'I didn't mean for any of this to happen.'

'Get off me,' he shouted, flinging her hand away. As his eyes bored into hers, a tall blonde vision appeared at his side. She cooed and fussed, soothing him with quiet words and a pat of her manicured hand. It was Verity, David's on-screen wife, the woman from the tabloid photo.

Julia was shocked. 'You invited *her*?'

Verity bared her teeth. 'We're sleeping together, dear.' David spun round to silence her, but it was too late. 'Well, the bitch might as well know now,' Verity hissed.

It was Julia's turn to look wide-eyed from one to the other. Stunned, she probably would have stayed there all day if Steve hadn't pulled her away. 'Come on,' he urged. 'Let's get out of here.'

Julia smiled up at him. All around her, guests were murmuring busily to themselves. The low sound of intrigue filled the small room. 'Where shall we go?' she asked him.

He didn't answer. Proudly parading her back down the aisle to the door, he jerked his head to Nick and Marianne and they followed him out. And Julia realised that, wherever he wanted to take her, she would willingly go.

The school gates were locked as it was Saturday. All four giggled manically as they helped each other over the crumbling wall into the grounds. Nick's hand slid up Julia's skirt as he gave her a leg-up, but she barely noticed, and she didn't bother telling him off. It was Steve who was waiting at the other side for her, his arms outstretched to catch her. It was Steve who was ready with a kiss as he gently lowered her to the ground. It was Steve who held her so tightly she could barely breathe, and who stood so close that she could feel his penis thickening against the softness of her pussy.

Drunk with the childish exhilaration of breaking into the place they once couldn't wait to break out of, they carried on laughing as they lay on the lawn and ate the picnic they had bought on the way. Being in that place again stirred up so many memories, and Nick, Marianne and Julia talked nonstop. Steve was quiet though, and Julia's insides clenched every time she glanced in his direction and caught him staring at her. Now that she finally knew what was on his list, he had no need to flinch and look away. Instead he smiled, gazing back at her with pure, undeniable devotion. There was rapture in his pale grey eyes, and it made her as wet as if he had been touching her.

The conversation lulled as she too went quiet. Nick and Marianne sensed their need to be alone – although it wasn't difficult. The fact that they were sitting silently staring at each other made it fairly obvious. Steve smiled as they left them on the picnic rug, his eyes leaving Julia's for the first time while he watched them walk away. Julia turned at the sound of their laughter, and she smiled as well.

They had found a football. Marianne had kicked off her high heels and hitched up her skirt, and was playing roughly with Nick. 'It's just like the last time we were here,' Julia said, sitting back and leaning on her hands.

Steve lay down on his side, his head propped up on one wrist. 'We were sitting here watching them, and you were telling me that you didn't believe in planning ahead. You were right all along.'

'Was I?' Julia dropped her head back. Through her sunglasses the sky was the colour of thin gravy. 'Your plans didn't work out so badly. You've achieved every one of your goals.'

'I nearly didn't,' he said quietly. 'It could have so easily gone wrong. Just think, if I'd arrived at your flat ten minutes later and Marianne had already left...'

'But you didn't, and she hadn't.' The late-afternoon sun bathed Julia's skin. She wallowed in its warmth, and in the perfection of the afternoon.

'I wish I'd told you, seven years ago.' His sigh was heavy, loaded with the regret of so much wasted time. 'I wonder what you would have said.'

Julia smiled to herself. She knew exactly what she would have said; it was the same now as it would have been back then. 'Try me,' she invited. 'Let's pretend we're eighteen again, and this is the last day of school. We've finished our exams, and you and I are sitting here, alone, while all the others are playing football.'

Excitement sped inside Julia's limbs, building from a faint wisp into a whirlwind. Down by her side, Steve fidgeted with the same sense of anticipation. She could tell from the way he hesitated that replaying this memory, this treasured souvenir from their past, was as thrilling for him as it was for her.

He reached out for her wrist. He held her for a moment, his thumb pressed gently over her pulse. Then he pulled. Julia allowed herself to be eased backwards until she lay on the rug. Rolling on to her side, she propped her head up on one hand. Her heartbeat began to quicken as Steve carefully took her sunglasses off.

She blinked once, trying to steady herself. A kiss was brewing inside her, forcing its way up from the tight tension of her belly and into her brain. Her mind cleared of everything except Steve. Memories of the last seven years – of joys and disappointments, and men who had given her both – dissolved into insignificance. Birdsong faded into silence, along with the sound of Nick and Marianne's raucous laughter. All thought crystallised into a single, startlingly lucid idea. She had never felt so completely happy in her life.

'Julia, there's something I want to tell you.'

'Yes?' she whispered, already knowing what it was.

He hesitated, glancing from her left eye to her right, left to right, as if he were searching for inconsistencies. Her lips parted. Steve's did, too, as his eyes dropped from hers, to her mouth, and back up again. Imperceptibly, inevitably, their faces moved closer together.

'Julia,' he breathed.

'Yes?'

'I'm in love with you.' His eyes radiated desire. 'I fell in love with you the minute I saw you, way before I knew what falling in love was supposed to feel like. I've loved you ever since.' He smoothed back a lock of hair where it had fallen over her face. 'I'll always love you, Julia.'

'I know.' She smiled, her head suddenly lighter than air. 'I love you, too.'

She gasped into his mouth as he fell on her. They rolled together, marooned on the rug, safe in each other's arms. He smothered her with love and then his tenderness gave way to lust. He crushed his lips to hers, kissing her so ferociously it was hard for her to breathe. His tongue was hot as it thrashed wildly inside her mouth. His mouth was wet with their saliva, his body hard and urgent. Pulling away, he leant over her, breathing fast. He supported himself on one arm and, with the other hand, began to unfasten the buttons of her dress.

Julia looked down at his fingers, then up at him. 'They'll see,' she said, rolling her eyes towards the lawn where Nick and Marianne were playing.

'I don't care,' Steve mumbled. His hand slid inside her dress. It was open to her waist, and he pushed the two halves of material aside to expose her pale skin and black bra. Moaning quietly in appreciation, he traced the edges of her cleavage where her breasts were forced upward dramatically. He bent his head and reverently kissed the upper curve of one breast. His hand spread over the satin-covered mound, squeezing greedily. Then his fingers delved inside the satin cup and scooped her flesh out of the soft black cradle of her bra. His fingertips soft with awe, he delicately stroked the incredible tenderness of her nipple. Circling the dusky-pink disc of her areola, he watched intently as her skin quickly stiffened in response to his touch. Diving on to her, he sucked at the engorged peak of her breast. When he had finished he began again on her other breast, his fingers cruelly pinching one nipple as his mouth pulled on the other.

Julia held his head to her body, arching her throat with pleasure. The tingling sensations of pain and delight at her breasts started her pussy throbbing and, feeling his penis nudging at her hip, she groaned with the pressure of the longing between her legs. Sensing what she wanted, Steve dropped his hand to her leg. Sliding up underneath the soft material of her dress, he caressed her naked inner thighs before stroking her mound. Moving backward and forward over the silky dampness covering her pussy, he teased the sensitive edges of her labia. Julia sucked in air as he touched the tender, aching bud of her clitoris, searching for the oxygen that had been robbed from her by the sharp pang of ecstasy. Bending her knees up, she forgot about Nick and Marianne and urged Steve inside her panties, guiding him with eager, trembling fingers.

'You're so wet,' he murmured, his words warm against her neck. 'You're so beautiful.'

Julia shuddered as his finger found its way beneath the edge of her skimpy G-string. Impaled on his touch, she threw her arms back over her head and opened her knees wider. Lubricated on the heavy dew of her arousal, he slid effortlessly in and out of her clasping pussy.

Another finger pushed inside her, then another, gently stretching her inner muscles. A deep, pulsating rhythm echoed in her belly and she began to thrust her hips with tiny, yearning movements, reaching for more of his hand with every plunge of his fingers inside her.

Then his fingers were inside her mouth, the taste of her musk coating her tongue. Julia strained her neck to suck every droplet of pleasure from his skin. Steve cradled the back of her head and bent to kiss her, sharing the sweet taste of her sex. Pulling away, he paused, gazing down at her with eyes that shone.

'Kiss me,' Julia whispered urgently.

He knew exactly what she meant. Shifting his position on the rug, he lay down beside Julia. He pulled on her hand, and she knelt astride him, her sex above his face. His eyes lowered down her body and feasted on the sight beneath her dress, between her open legs. He put his hands on her buttocks, and slowly pulled her down.

He kissed her through her knickers. His tongue lapped the damp, silky strip covering her pussy, making it even wetter. His teeth nipped at the material, stimulating her labia beneath and making Julia softly cry out. His hands reached under her skirt, one clasping her hip, the other moving behind, between her buttocks. Discovering that there was only a narrow string of fabric in her cleft, Steve grabbed at the thong and pulled and let go, pulled and let go. With every tug, Julia's panties were stretched taut over her mound, the string slicing between her pussy lips and rubbing over her anus. Julia sighed loudly and squirmed with confusion. The pleasure was so close to the edge of pain, the two so inextricably linked together that it was hard to distinguish which was which. It all blurred into one writhing mêlée of agony and ecstasy, love and lust, wanting and needing.

The blur stopped for a moment as Steve's grappling fingertips tore at the silk. Holding the tiny triangle aside, he began to torture her with his mouth, one moment licking her with warm pleasure, the next making her shiver with the cold cruelty of his teeth. Again and again he nibbled at her succulent labia, making her hold her breath with the gentleness of his torment. Then he would poke his tongue deep inside her open flesh and her breath would rush out in relief. Then he would softly bite her clitoris, and every muscle in her body would seize up with the intensity of the feeling. It was incredible and wonderful, but almost too much to bear, like fireworks exploding inside her mind.

She came as he sucked voraciously on her bud. Pausing only long enough to allow her sharp climax to dissolve into seeping warmth, she turned her back to him and unzipped his trousers. Grabbing inside his shorts, she brought out his long, thick penis and she leant over him. She watched as his prick bobbed in anticipation, like a shy animal emerging tentatively into the daylight, its tiny blind eye weeping. Licking her lips, she took him into the dark, warm sanctuary of her mouth. Opening her jaw as wide as it would go, she sucked on as much of him as she could. She flickered frantically with her eager tongue, caressing the purple head of his cock with her lips, wanting to give him the pleasure he had given her. She breathed deeply, inhaling his musty, salty smell and trying to absorb him completely with each of her senses.

Inside his shorts, she cradled his warm balls in one hand. Julia felt his legs jerk slightly as she fondled and sucked him, and a moment later her thighs quivered in reply. His palms were spread over her buttocks and his mouth was between her cheeks. With his lips pursed to the infinitely sensitive rim of her anus, his tongue pushed beneath the tight string separating her arse cheeks and poked inside her. Forgetting what she was doing, Julia hung suspended in pure, forbidden pleasure while Steve's penis throbbed inside her mouth. Then she began her rhythm again, pulling him to orgasm with strong lips and rapid tongue. Behind her, another type of pleasure stung her already overloaded senses.

When his coming had slowly shuddered to a halt, Steve sat up. As he shifted backward on the rug, his sticky penis was pulled from her mouth. Julia sat up too, feeling slightly dizzy, and turned round to face Steve again. He was leaning back against the tree shading their rug, and holding his hands out for Julia. Moving closer, she straddled his hips. Already, she could feel his prick beginning to twitch back into life.

She leant into his kiss. His hands slipped beneath the suspenders stretched over her buttocks and they stayed there, as if he was trapped. Julia wanted to trap him, to fix his hands to her flesh, his tongue to hers, and to sheath his prick inside her for ever. 'I love you,' she whispered, as he kissed her throat.

His hands flew to her face. Catching her, he held her still. His eyes overflowed with gratitude, adoration and passion, and seeing the strength of his love made Julia crave him inside her again. She raised her hips over his and reached down for his stiffening rod. She poised above him, savouring the moment his hardness nudged between her pussy lips, and clinging to the unspoken words humming in the air between them.

Nick coughed loudly. Julia ignored him, thinking it was the same sound of protest she had heard in the registry office. But he coughed again, more insistently: a stage cough, as if he was trying to get her attention.

Julia and Steve both looked up at the same time. Round the corner of the school, a horde of huge young men in rugby kits were stomping in their direction. Julia looked back at Steve, and they both shared the same realisation: the school teams often played matches on Saturdays, and the pitch was on the other side of the lawn. In a matter of seconds they would be discovered, both in a state of undress and about to make love.

Laughing nervously, Steve and Julia scrambled to their

feet. Holding on to their clothes and each other, they ran for the cover of the woods.

'Look at them,' Marianne sighed.

Nick tutted. 'They're a bit young for you, Marianne.'

'I don't mean *them*,' Marianne giggled, glancing at the rugby players as they trooped past. 'Although I always did like men in shorts,' she added wistfully. She seemed to remember she had particularly liked Nick in shorts. She fluttered her eyelashes at him, flirting playfully. 'I was talking about Steve and Julia. They're so sweet together.'

Nick curled his lip. 'Sickly sweet. It's disgusting if you ask me, all that kissing and gazing into each other's eyes. Not to mention fornicating in public – which is all for my benefit, by the way.'

'Ooh, you're such a cynic,' Marianne teased. 'Haven't you ever been in love?'

'Nah,' he said dismissively. 'Nearly, once.' He gazed off towards the woods. 'Or maybe that was lust . . .'

'Don't you know the difference?'

'I'm not sure I want to.' He put his arm around Marianne's waist and guided her towards the sports master, who was looking suspiciously at them. 'I mean, look at Steve. He's been obsessed with that list of his ever since we were teenagers, and what was his ultimate goal? To pluck up the courage to tell Julia that he loved her. It nearly destroyed him. I hope it's worth it, after all this time.'

'Of course it is.' She stopped him with a serious hand on his shoulder. 'One day, if you're lucky, you'll find a woman who makes you understand what it means to love someone completely, like those two do.'

'Maybe.' He nodded slowly as a grin broke out across his face. 'But, until I find her, I reckon I'll have some fun looking.'

He kissed her. As his hand clasped over her breast,

thirty adolescents wolf-whistled appreciatively. Warmth flooded Marianne's body, but not from embarrassment. She had often imagined this moment over the last seven years, wondering what would have happened on the last day of school if Julia hadn't been around.

9 780352 346667

Printed by Libri Plureos GmbH in Hamburg, Germany